"I hate it when I cry in front of other people," Jessamy said . . .

"Tante Ellen says I'll be a woman soon, and that sometimes I'll cry before my monthly courses." She swallowed with an audible gulp. "I hope that doesn't happen soon, because they—they'll marry me off at once."

"Well—but you'll be a woman then," Stevana said reasonably.

"No, you don't understand," Jessamy whispered. "It's because of what Papa did—and I don't even know what it was. But they're afraid of him. And they're afraid of what I might become. That's why they want me married quickly. My future husband is already chosen."

Stevana's eyes had gotten wide as the words tumbled from the older girl's lips.

"Who are *they*?" she breathed.

Jessamy shook her dark curls. "I'm not supposed to talk about it," she said. She sounded so forlorn that Stevana hugged her again and changed the subject as they turned to leave the Grotto of the Hours, for the hints she had gleaned from her own kin also suggested something so terrible as to be beyond discussion.

—from "The Green Tower" by Katherine Kurtz

"Kurtz's love of history lets her do things with her characters and their world that no nonhistorian could hope to do." —*Chicago Sun-Times*

DERYNI TALES

An Anthology Edited by

KATHERINE KURTZ

ACE BOOKS, NEW YORK

DERYNI TALES

An Ace Book / published by arrangement with
the editor

PRINTING HISTORY
Ace edition / June 2002

Visit our website at
www.penguinputnam.com
Check out the Ace Science Fiction & Fantasy newsletter!

ISBN: 0-441-00944-1

For
Carolyn Shilts, Melissa Houle, and Susan Werner,
and the good Dr. St. Mark (Shilts),
who keep the website running at www.deryni.com

and for
all the contributors to *Deryni Archives: The Magazine*.
Without you (and all my loyal readers),
this anthology would not have been possible.

CONTENTS

�

INTRODUCTION

✤

I DID NOT write these stories, other than the last one, though some of them sound a great deal like me. They are exceedingly faithful to what has become the Deryni canon, and in some cases, the authors have told the story as well as I could have done—perhaps better. These are talented folk, who all do other things to earn their daily bread—and a diverse lot they are, from a fascinating variety of occupations and professions. What they have in common, besides talent and imagination, is that all of them have fallen under the spell of the universe of the Deryni, and have felt obliged to write about it.

In this respect, literature is unusual within the realm of what we regard as the arts. Though the author's skill in manipulating the language will be of varying importance to any given reader, the story itself can and often does reach beyond mere aesthetic considerations to have a more direct and profound effect on the author's audience than the fruit of any other artistic endeavor.

I know of no other art form that can change lives the way writing can and often does. It could be argued that music comes closest, in its ability to influence the listener's mood and even to trigger spurts of new creativity; many artists of various kinds listen to music while they pursue their own art. But listening is akin to reading; it is interpretive, though perhaps in a more abstract sense. The composer's act of pure creation, like that of the author, is a mostly solitary occupation, and involves a similar process of forming a concept and putting down black marks on paper to anchor it in a form accessible to others outside the creator's mind; words and musical notations are not too dissimilar. But between the composer and the listener comes interpretation and the performance aspect of music.

The latter is itself an art form, and one that, as an aside, always fills me with a degree of awe, especially in its symphonic and choral aspects. Perhaps this comes of growing up with musicians in my family—a flutist, a clarinetist, a trumpeter, and a choral soloist among us. It still seems to me a very human wonder that dozens and even scores of people should gather together to read little black squiggles off a page and then, at the direction of a conductor, employ their instruments, whether fleshly voice or an external instrument of wood or metal or some combination, to produce sounds that evoke wondrous moods and emotions in the mind of the listener.

The performance of theatrical works also requires interpretation—and artistry—on the part of the performers, and similarly combines the diverse talents of many people, coordinated by a director, to produce an artistic illusion that is then witnessed by an audience. The theatre experience is similar to what happens at a musical concert, but the language of music is both more and less precise than verbal language. Theatre is verbal, but it is also visual and aural and also sometimes musical, and again involves interim steps between the playwright's craft and the theatregoer's experience of the play.

Which brings us, in a somewhat roundabout manner, back to writing—and especially the writing of fiction. Granted, there are interim steps between the author's manuscript and the printed page that the reader reads (or listens to when read aloud), but none of these is really interpretive. An editor can cure or kill a story, of course, but the storyteller's art begins with the timeless introduction of "Once upon a time" and suffers very little in the translation to the printed page. In that sense, writing is probably one of the purer of the artistic forms available to humankind, despite the fact that artistic terminology tends to stress what we would regard as the "fine" arts of painting and sculpture and other disciplines that involve a literal hands-on participation to create the final product.

But all creation begins with a vision or a dream, the inspiration to craft something out of nothing more than an idea. This is certainly how authors approach the creative process. We want to tell such a good story that readers will become totally caught up in the fate and predicaments of the characters in the story, at least for the time they're reading it. We want them to identify with those characters, to find themselves wondering how they themselves would cope in similar circumstances, to rejoice in the characters' successes and mourn with them in their tribulations—and maybe even to learn from what the characters have experienced.

Successful authors learn to do this very well. Especially in fantasy fiction, readers do tend to get caught up in the stories. They become involved with the characters, they care very much about what happens to them, they want to know more—and the creative urge is definitely infectious!

Just how infectious, I had no idea, when I first began weaving the verbal tapestry that became the Eleven Kingdoms, more than thirty years ago. I had no inkling how the vision would grow—or how profoundly it would affect so many readers. I set out to tell a story—based, quite literally, on a dream—but it soon became clear that other people wanted to explore this dream; that it wasn't just my dream but, on some level, a very real world that spoke to many readers far beyond what one normally expects of even the best-written works of fiction.

Nor does such a profound connection end when the reader closes the cover of the book. Especially in the area of fantasy fiction, I suspect that there are an inordinate number of readers who have writing aspirations of their own. I can think of no other field of fiction that encompasses so many would-be writers, many of whom, upon finishing a book that particularly speaks to them, at least consider adopting the world and characters of that book to continue the adventure. They've come to care about the characters and the adversities they must overcome. They want the story to go on—and if the author does not or cannot continue the story fast enough to suit them, they write their own.

Now, many authors resent this intrusion into the world they've created, and forbid readers to dabble there— which is about as useful as forbidding the tide to advance and recede. If an author has done his or her job well, readers *will* speculate about what happens next, or what might have happened, or what was happening behind the scenes. They'll find others who share their fascination, they'll talk about it, and some of them will want to write it down and possibly share it with other like-minded folk.

Some authors regard this as some kind of threat, but I tend to view it as flattery. I would be the first to agree that, if there's money to be made as a result of such writing, I certainly deserve a share in it; after all, I created the concept, and my writing is my living, as well as my art and my joy. But I've also always felt that part of the fun of creating something that's admired by others is sharing it—and if possible, not only sharing the finished product, but also some of the excitement of the creative process. It's necessary, I think, to set well-defined boundaries—one does have to protect one's intellectual properties, after all. Fortunately, my readers have always respected the boundaries I've set, and the resulting association has been pleasant, I think, for all concerned.

It hadn't much been done before, when I came on the fantasy scene. In the realm of science fiction, Marion Zimmer Bradley had begun letting readers write and publish fan fiction in her Darkover universe, and had used this as a vehicle for encouraging and boosting new talent, but no one had done anything similar in the fantasy field. Indeed, there *was* no fantasy field in the sense we think of today. When I sold the first Deryni trilogy in 1969, I was lucky enough to be in the right place at the right time with the "right stuff" to be part of the foundation of the modern fantasy genre, thanks to the pioneering work done by Betty and Ian Ballantine. Before then, encouraged by the commercial success of J. R. R. Tolkien's *Lord of the Rings Trilogy,* the Ballantines had begun cautiously reprinting "classic" fantasy authors such as William Morris, E. R. Eddison, James Branch Cabell, and C. S. Lewis . . . until 1970, when they published *Deryni Rising* and Joy Chant's *Red Moon, Black Mountain,* the first new novels in their Ballantine Adult Fantasy series.

The seeds sown on such fertile ground flourished in the years to come. Less than a decade later, with the first two Deryni trilogies selling well and readers clamoring for more, reader feedback had made it clear to me that more was happening here than merely telling good stories that were fun to read. Readers wanted to become more involved with the Deryni universe; many of them were already more involved with the Deryni universe: talking endlessly among themselves, collaring me at science fiction conventions to pump *me* for information, writing stories, doing research into the real-world medieval history from which I had drawn much of my own inspiration.

When this happens, an author has several choices. You can ignore it. You can get grumpy that other folk are playing with your toys without permission. Or you can recognize this reader reaction as the sincere form of flattery that it is and embrace it; and by gently and constructively directing it, you can make it a vehicle of growth that might even make a real contribution to the betterment of the reader's mind-set and maybe even his or her life. Believe me, this does happen. I've always said that the first job of an author is to entertain, to tell a danged good story; but if I can also catalyze an eagerness to learn things that will help a person grow as an individual, that's even better; it's icing on the cake. When all is said and done, if I could be remembered for one thing, it would be that I made my readers think, and enjoy doing it, and that I left their lives richer than they would have been if they'd not read my work. I don't aim to change people's minds, but I do try to open them.

The stories in this anthology definitely opened the minds of their authors, and probably many readers' minds as well. All save my own were privately published in one of the sixteen issues to date of *Deryni Archives: The Magazine,* which I began in 1978 as a showcase for some of my readers' literary efforts. Not only have many of the stories been of professional quality, raising the level of *DA* far above most amateur publications, but some of the stories are so true to the Deryni Canon that I wish I had written them myself—which is, perhaps, the highest praise that one author can render to another.

This present collaboration gives me the opportunity to share some of this talent with a wider readership than was possible in a private publication. And by giving these authors professional publication, some of them perhaps will find themselves properly launched into their own literary careers. I sincerely hope so; because after more than thirty years in print myself, it gives me a great deal of pleasure to be able to help along the next generation of new writers. I have no doubt that you'll be seeing more of the work of some of these authors in print in the future.

—Katherine Kurtz
Co. Wicklow, Ireland
March 2001

A MIDSUMMER'S QUESTING
898

Our first story is the only one in this collection set at a time when Deryni were still free to use their powers mostly openly. By internal dating, since we know it has to be the summer before Camber's son Joram was ordained (which occurred in May 899), we can place it in June of the previous year, before the beginning of *Camber of Culdi* and before Evaine and Rhys were married.

The story deals with all three of these events, but it's basically Joram's story: home to Caerrorie for a visit from seminary and wrestling with certain aspects of his spirituality, not in terms of his priestly vocation with the Michaelines, but in terms of his personal relationship with God. His task is made no easier by his awareness of the chemistry between his sister and her beloved Rhys, by the weather change from soggy springtime to the first flushes of summer, and by nature's celebration of the season, as the sap rises and the observances of Midsummer mark the return of life to the land.

A MIDSUMMER'S QUESTING

✦

Laura Jefferson

"FATHER, I THINK you are being completely unreasonable!"

Joram flinched as his sister began the latest scene in an act that was making all the residents of Caerrorie increasingly uncomfortable. It had been raining for twelve days—no, fourteen—he was leaving out the two days' travel that had brought him home from his studies for the diaconate, soaking wet. The crops were behind—the ploughing and planting had been late, for that matter—and though their winter stores held out well enough to ensure that no one would starve anytime soon, the cold wet spell had everyone worried. The castle smelled of damp clothes, damp bedding, damp kindling, and garderobes in need of draining.

And Rhys was visiting. Joram was never sure whether that made things easier or not. The wedding certainly would, but these days Evaine pined for her betrothed when he was away and both of them pined for each other when he was there.

Cathan, thank Saint Michael and Saint Genevieve, was

at Court. He had tempered his feelings about Rhys, and no longer suggested that their sister could make a better match. Joram loved his sister. Unlike Cathan, who believed all that stuff about women, Joram knew her nature was as passionate as that of any of her brothers. How any Deryni, or any marginally sensitive human, or hound even, could fail to understand that. . . .

He sighed and checked his shields again, gently. Rhys felt the ripple and glanced over to him; he was trying to read something, choosing between chill nearer to the window and indifferent light nearer the fire, which was smoking. Some Deryni were good at fire; Joram reminded himself to ask Father Emrys when he was back at the school. . . .

If he went back. Evaine's desire, Rhys's steadier, calmer anticipation, springtime—even this wet and cloudy one—nagged at Joram, made him wonder about a decision he had believed fully resolved.

Alister had warned him: celibacy was a decision he would make every day, no matter how many days he had behind him. Whoever desired to offer God that gift would not offer it once and for all, but daily or weekly.

Over the last several months, all the peace Joram had usually felt with his decision to lead a chaste life had crumbled away. That was part of his returning home for the Easter season, to consider the binding vows he would make at Pentecost. He was tired of considering them. At the moment, Joram wanted to be in a particular tavern near the seminary, well known for the wide choice of wine and the wide smiles of the table maids.

He was a nobleman's son; his life offered him plenty of choices and mates, within holy wedlock and outside it. His father had enough land. . . . Joram knew his abilities as a courtier were far subtler than Cathan's, and potentially more useful to the Crown. He could be a credit to the family, to the realm, and to God without being a soldier-monk.

If he were going to be a Michaeline, he wanted to be

one of the good ones, like the men (and the few he had encountered of the secretive, somewhat frightening women in the Second Order of Saint Michael) whom he admired. Their honor made their vows worth more than form or circumspection or things left unsaid.

Joram avoided chances to risk falling in love—a concept that, for his class, was neither well developed nor practical. He had deliberately kept himself too busy. He had friends outside his family, but none to whom he would consider permanently, exclusively attaching himself. He knew from watching Rhys and Evaine that a fullhearted union of gifted individuals took time and effort. The taint around marriages founded on less than mutual respect, at Court or among his age mates, was familiar and unwelcome. Joram liked to consider himself too good for that, and as a working Deryni and devout Christian, he doubted that he could endure less than love.

He knew enough of the clerics of the less scrupulous kind to doubt that a celibate life actually strengthened magical potential; but it certainly did leave more time to hone one's skills, to meditate, and to try new spells. Joram knew he was ambitious enough for that to matter to him. He hoped God sympathized with his pride in his abilities, that by Divine Grace Joram would remember his powers were for service. But was ambition—holy ambition, and the sort of pride in himself based on what he knew of his abilities—were these enough?

He felt lonely here, though there were people all around him: his sister, working full-time at running the castle and her spare thoughts, as well as some that ought not have been spare, fixed on Rhys; his father, Camber, working on lines of research he had no intention of sharing with a Michaeline, even his son—although Joram knew that Camber shared them with Evaine—and unwilling to distress Joram and argue about his choice of Order yet again; Rhys, trying to keep out of everyone's way, feeling like a poor relation and also busy as a Healer with the local illnesses and what material he could dig out of Camber's library relating to Healing and still trying to be close to Evaine. The castle chaplain was some kind of cousin, "a dear man, not confusing about God, like some," according to Cook, without enough Latin to enjoy Augustine, and no Greek or Hebrew at all.

I am too educated to live here; Father is right about the Michaelines ruining simple piety. I can't stand it, Joram thought despairingly, even while his body, responding to the season, suggested a few things he could still learn about.

The chapel bells rang *Terce*. Camber put his set of parchments aside. He had appointments coming, rents to arrange, taxes to adjust. Joram could tell Camber was as tired of the weather and his daughter's arguing as his son was.

"My dear," he said, and Joram caught the edge of his impatience, "I know you want to go a-Maying, and I do not think it unusual for you to want to ride out with Rhys, and I know very well that you can look after yourself; I am very proud of your abilities and I have every confidence in your discretion. . . ."

More than I do, thought Joram, surprised at himself.

"But I don't want the two of you out alone. Take your maids. . . ."

"Who aren't even Deryni, who can't ride as well as we can, who get frightened every time they think they see an adder. . . ." Evaine said mutinously. "Honestly, Father, we can take care of ourselves better than we can take care of them."

"I don't want two Deryni to have to 'take care of themselves,' as you put it," Camber said firmly. "I don't want our people to know how much you're capable of."

"You don't mind if they know what Rhys is capable of," said Evaine. "Healers can be as Deryni as they like, and carry swords, and no one says, 'Oh, be careful, you'll scandalize the tenants.' "

"The tenants understand swords," said Camber. "They don't understand Healing, but they are willing to accept it. If Deryni are to live in peace, we would do well to be mindful of being stumbling blocks for those who fear that our difference from them is as ill intentioned as theirs would be in our place. Take some of the men; they'll enjoy looking after your maids. If it ever stops raining."

Evaine did not look mollified. Joram understood. She was tired of being surrounded by convention, as well as other people—damp, irritable people who smelled like cabbage and smoke. Although her father's men-at-arms were respectful of her, they were not the companions Joram would have chosen for a contemplative ride in the woods, or whatever Evaine had in mind. A trained magician needed more privacy than most people, more often. Joram found his in the chapel with the Sacrament. Evaine had always loved the outdoors.

"I'll go with them, Father," he said suddenly. "I carry a sword as well, and no one would think Rhys and my sister easy pickings if they have a Michaeline Knight—even one still in training—riding with them." He could feel Camber's consideration resting upon him. "And I think even an older brother will do to preserve her reputation."

"And the reputation of Rhys as well," Camber agreed after a moment, with one raised eyebrow. "Thank you, Joram. Does this suit you, Evaine? Rhys?"

"Whatever pleases my lady, and you, my lord," said Rhys, bowing. He hated to be near his betrothed and her father during their generally rare disagreements.

"I hate it when you talk like that," said Evaine. "Thank you, Joram, and you, Father. I'm going to see if it's stopped raining. And if it hasn't, could we go out tomorrow, whether it stops or not? I'm running low on herbs, the garden is late coming on, and the Saint John's wort might be out. . . ." She rushed from the room, her lighter mood changing its atmosphere even as she left it.

The men looked at one another, relieved.

"Perhaps she'll find herself some valerian as well," said Camber with a faint grimace. "I'm sorry, Rhys, I just

didn't think it was wise. These are not entirely comfortable times, and although I dislike keeping her away from
Rhemuth"—they all knew he meant "and the lecherous
Imre"—"I know she gets very bored. She'll do better in
a home of her own, though I will miss her sorely. It's
good having all of you here, even at close quarters. How
are matters with you, Joram? We've not had much time
to talk. I haven't even heard whatever Michaeline gossip
you can pass on."

"Just the usual Godless international intrigue," Joram
said, echoing the opinion of many of Gwynedd's nobility.
He hesitated to say the words he had been carrying around
for the past few weeks. "It's just. . . . It's hard, I suppose,
with perpetual vows coming up."

"That's not what you usually say," said Rhys. "Doesn't
sound very promising."

Camber's face showed similar concern. "Has something
happened to change your understanding of your vocation,
son?" He was being as gentle as he could, Joram knew.
Camber's opinion of the Michaelines was both better informed than many of his contemporaries and less patient.
Camber said bluntly that he found both their tactics and
their spirituality too political to be entirely holy. (The Michaelines preferred to think of it as "engagement in the
world.")

"If you mean, do I still want to be a priest? Yes, I think
so—very much," said Joram. "But it doesn't feel as simple as it did when I was twelve or fourteen. I don't think
it's just about celibacy. But that's where I keep getting
stuck." Now that it was out, he felt a little better.

"I'm glad you're noticing you're only mortal," said
Camber. "I hope you'll mention this again. For the moment, I'll just say that everything looked simpler when I
was sixteen, and by the time I was thirty, I noticed it had
been simpler when I was twenty. I am hoping things will
clear up in my seventies."

"At least Evaine will be older then, too," said Rhys
wistfully.

*   *   *

As THOUGH THE skies had taken their orders from Evaine, the next day was sunny. By midmorning, the smells had begun to change: things drying, bread baking, plants beginning to warm in the sun and flowers to release their scent. Their horses were restive, and the prospect of following his sister on one of her terrifying gallops lifted Joram's heart. Rhys looked happier, too. He was no slouch: a fair rider, an excellent scholar, a patient and thorough ritualist, but:

"Being cooped up with your family, Joram, is too much," said Rhys, checking the girth on his saddle one last time before mounting. "I love Camber, and of course I love Evaine, but . . ." He hesitated. "It's too much like being under a burning lens, when they both get into one of those moods." He did not need to add that Joram, brooding, only made matters more intense.

"They've grown closer since Mother died," said Joram. "And Evaine thinks for herself more than our mother ever did—which is Father's doing, of course. You don't provoke her the same way he does, so she won't be so exasperated with you. Look, Rhys, I don't know what you and she have done to make Father so . . ." Rhys mutely hoped Joram would not ask, so Joram continued, "And it's not my business to ask, but would you both mind, ummm, behaving well enough—not that I don't think you haven't been—so that I don't have to spend too much time looking the other way and humming loudly?"

"Better ask me," said Evaine, riding up to them.

"Evaine," warned Rhys.

"Well, Joram, will you spend *some* of the time looking the other way?"

Evaine was genuinely pleading. Joram felt the quick touch of her presence. He loved her, and he had longings of his own, and the church said betrothal was legally binding.

"I may have to go for a walk while we rest the horses," he said. "A short walk."

THEY TROTTED ALONG the outskirts of the village fields, careful not to tread inside the edges where the seed was coming up thickly. Once away from the houses, Joram felt the tightness in his chest relax as the sun warmed his back. His sister's and Rhys's laughter carried on the breeze back to him; separate horses were very efficient at maintaining a discreet distance.

But they were all happy in the early summer air. He allowed his shields to drop, allowed the world's energy to appear to him, all but visible, the corona of love and life and joy from Rhys and Evaine surely obvious even to an observer without Joram's gifts.

Evaine really intended to gather herbs, and they stopped several times to cut leaves and stems and fill the sacks she had tied behind her saddle.

"Look, here's my Saint John's wort," she said. "This is early, isn't it, Jo? It's not Saint John's feast yet." She blessed herself and the plants before cutting them, the knee-high stalks crowned with yellow flowers.

"Near enough," Joram said. "I saw a Maypole back there."

"What do Michaelines think of Maypoles?" asked Rhys.

Joram shrugged. "I've heard it said that they are the Tree that lifted up Our Lord, and the bright colors are His blood renewing the face of the earth."

Rhys was barely too polite to snort. "You know perfectly well it's the Old Religion."

"It's been a long time since the Old Religion condemned any Deryni for being who we are. I wish Christ could say as much for His followers."

"Joram!" said Evaine. "I've never heard you talk like this."

"You know what Father says about Michaelines. We're

too clever to save our souls." *We,* he thought. "Look, I don't give a fig for the Old Religion, but it doesn't give one for me, either. I imagine all these people were properly christened. I know Christ died for them whether they were or not."

"True enough," Rhys admitted. "But I can't see it going down very well with old Archbishop Anscom."

"Neither do the Michaelines," said Joram. "If the Lord showed up in His Grace's chancery, a lot of tables would be getting tipped. The Old Religion isn't worth bothering over. I'd rather try to get people to do what they say they believe."

Evaine tied up the latest bundle of stems and they rode on. They drew closer to the edge of the forest, the trails where Camber's court hunted its deer.

"The Old Religion is more than that," Rhys said finally. "I've worked with people who saw—well, someone. And it wasn't Saint Hubert, or at least there was no crucifix between its antlers." He allowed his big horse to lag behind, closer to Joram's, and added under his breath, "And when Evaine is in this mood, she's not like *any* of the saints."

"Does the Old Religion have any better descriptions?"

"At least three," said Rhys. Joram raised an eyebrow at him. Rhys laughed, causing Evaine to look back at them. She wore an expression so identical to Joram's that both the men laughed.

"What are you two on about?"

"Rhys is having trouble keeping up with MacRories, as far as I can tell."

"Eyebrow magic," suggested Rhys. "Have pity on a poor Healer. . . ."

Evaine laughed with them, told her horse to trot, and gave the other two a MacRorie to keep up with. She was the best natural rider of the three, though Joram and Rhys had more practice and the Michaeline-trained horse had his pride to maintain. It was a wonderful gallop.

They ended up not far inside the forest, trotting down

a wide trail. They stopped where it came to a small, clear lake; the sweet water was surrounded by pollarded willows. Evaine opened the loaf and a bottle, and brought out the wrinkled apples and chicken and raisins she had taken from the kitchen. They lay back in the still-damp grass and ate with the sun welcome in their faces. It felt to Joram as if it had been years since he had been so warm and contented. He basked like the turtles in the lake.

The sun was still high when he rose to his feet and stretched. "I think I'll walk off some of that bread," he said casually. "I'm as stuffed as a goose." Evaine and Rhys looked at him with entirely innocent faces. "I'll be back around the time the shadow reaches there," and he pointed at a branch.

"Don't go off too far," said Evaine. "God forbid you should have to take care of yourself like a Deryni." Even here, she pitched her voice low.

"I don't intend that anyone notice me in the first place," said Joram, "and if you continue to stay in the open, you might want to consider doing the same. And please, keep your clothes on."

"I think I'm supposed to challenge you for besmirching her honor," said Rhys, through a mouthful of apple.

"Since I'm supposed to challenge you for the same thing, I think we'll call it a draw."

Joram drew a shield close around himself, as much to protect their privacy as his own, and walked off. The willows were cut often enough to provide a meadow for deer. He walked around one edge to a trail narrower than the one they had ridden down, and went into the forest.

Little sun penetrated the thick branches of ancient trees and newer ones, fighting for a place in the canopy. But the wood was marvelously alive to his senses. Joram could hear the cries of birds defining territory and frightening would-be predators, nestlings wheezing as their parents returned to feed them with beaks stuffed full of worms and caterpillars, things that munched or flew among the fresh green leaves. Joram was seen by squir-

rels, who for the most part avoided his gaze, although he
felt their observation. A mouse crossed his path, suddenly
noticed him, and froze in panic, as a weasel came silently
out of the brush behind it.

"Be off," suggested Joram. "I am to be a knight, sworn
to protect the weak." He reached down and placed the
mouse carefully off the path behind him. The weasel, almost as dainty, vanished into the brush again.

"And what of my weasel?" came a voice that startled
Joram as much as he had the mouse. "Shall she not eat
and be satisfied? Her little ones cry out for her milk."

Joram reached out with his senses, brushing against little lives in the forest around him, but no one his own size.
Another Deryni? He could sense no other's shield, either.
He called out, "Will you not show yourself, that we may
discuss the matter of your weasel further?"

But no one answered. He cast out with his senses again.
Only the wood answered. Perhaps he had been indoors,
behind monastery walls, too long.

He set the moment aside and continued down the trail.
He knew it from not too many years past, riding with his
brother and sometimes his father or sister, helping hunt
the deer for the castle's table, learning some of the craft
that not only trained his Deryni senses but also made him
a useful member of his father's household.

Before long, he came to a clearing, a gap along the
path really, running up to a huge old stone. It was unlike
any others in the area. Joram had always believed it had
arrived in the Flood, though he could not recall who had
told him so. He had spent hours of his boyhood atop it,
commanding a view of the trail, particularly hiding from
his tutors when he was twelve. It had been his rock "for
all generations," he thought. It was here he had first realized the call to priesthood. He wondered if his coming
again today would give him some kind of resolution.

He sat down, intending to pray—*How manifold are all
thy works!*—but the psalm died on his lips. Nothing belonged to him here. The very concentration of *being*

around Joram struck him to the heart. The intense green-
ness of the trees served to underline his loneliness, his
isolation from his kin and his own hearth. Whether he
caught a trace of Evaine's laughter in the air or merely
thought he had, the emptiness within him, beside him,
seemed overwhelming, a void that felt like pain.

This is not myself, he thought. "Lord my God, deliver
me," he whispered aloud. "I can see the beauty of the
world You made for us to meet You in. It should fill my
heart, not leave it so empty. What do You want of me?"

No answer came, unless it was a deeper pain yet. Joram
choked back a sob. He had known moments and days of
sorrow, boredom, anger, desolation; this made them seem
like straws in a torrent. Nor did it resemble any psychic
attack. This was enough to make him believe in more
distinct demons than the most superstitious peasant. He
longed to feel his life pour out over the rock where he
sat, if only death would bring him peace.

"Son, why are you crying? What are you looking for?"
It sounded like his mother's voice, he realized later. Those
may not have been the words, exactly, but they were what
he felt breaking in on his loneliness like a distant light.

"I don't know," Joram answered, though he could hardly speak. His throat closed with pain. "I don't know who
I am."

Gentle arms, irresistibly strong, enfolded him, surrounded him. "Joram," she said. He opened his eyes and
looked into a face not quite the same as his mother's. The
woman who held him was older and infinitely stronger,
marked by years and sadness and deeper peace. She
seemed huge, big enough to hold him like a child of three
years. Her hair was streaked with white. Her eyes were
deep. . . .

"Ancient of days," Joram whispered. She smiled.

"I am, that. No need for you to feel the best of your
life is gone already." She held him close as Joram's breath
caught in a sob again. He drew in courage and looked at
her again, but his mother was gone. She who held him

now was young and lithe—if as old as Joram, then surely
no older. Her eyes were green or gray, like stones under
clear water. She had long hair. Although he could never
put a name to its color, it was as soft as the new-sprouted
grass they had passed in the field.

"Lady or—or damsel—who are you? Why are you
here?" he heard himself say.

"I am the beauty of the world," she said.

A light wind swept through the leaves, scattering sunlight across her face like melting shards of glass. Joram's
senses, Deryni and human, were engulfed. The wildness,
the liveliness, the beauty of the summer and the forest and
the woman were their own praise. There was nothing he
could add, not even consciousness of his delight or his
awe.

He could not tell how long the intoxicated moment
lasted. He came back to himself—or thought he did—as
the vision folded into a point, a question, a kiss. He had
been lost in the green world, formless; now he was lost
in someone's arms, in her breasts, in the scent of her hair,
in her warmth. No longer cradled like a child, Joram felt
her within his own arms, alive like water flowing beneath
their skin, as strong as trees waving in a storm, tossing
and bending.

The high winds ceased, dying to billows, puffs of
breeze. The pain in Joram's heart, driven like clouds before the wind, had gone. She kissed his lips once more
and stroked the side of his face.

"Do you know me, Joram?"

"You are the beauty of the world," he said, fascinated
by the light upon the planes of her face, her brow, her
eyes. He plunged into those depths like swimming in centuries.

"Joram," she said, amused. "And no wonder you would
meet me like this, on this day of the year, in this place,
despite your lack of courtesy. Don't look so—but there
is more to the Mother than just Her Son, just as there is
more to my way than righteous deeds."

Despite his light-headedness, Joram tried to frown; it was too hard.

"I don't know what you're talking about, I'm afraid." He smiled at her seriousness and touched her hand to his lips. Her eyes met his gravely across the kiss and watched him with compassion as he felt the wound in the wrist he held.

Horrified, Joram reached for her other hand and found a matching gash, sticky with blood. Her face began to change as Joram met her eyes; no longer so young or so finely boned, taller than Joram, dark eyes, dark hair.

A moment before he had possessed and been possessed in shattering ecstasy. Joram's body was still shaken with longing as he looked into a face more mortal than anyone he knew.

He had no form or majesty that we should look at Him, nothing in His appearance that we should desire Him, ran the line through Joram's mind. That had not mattered to the Prophet either.

"Now that you know Me," said the latest stranger, "did you think I would leave you so alone?"

"I was afraid you would," Joram whispered. "But not now."

"And now . . . ?"

Joram felt his mother's love again, seemed to smell the flower-scent the maiden had carried with her. He looked once more at the man in front of him, whose broken hands he still held.

"I think I know you best this way, Lord."

"Then come and follow Me."

Joram looked down at the wounded hands. They felt real and strong. He needed none of Rhys's talents to catch an echo of their pain, which was real, too. Gently, he held them to his heart and lost himself in the dark eyes. . . .

. . . and slowly Joram awoke to normal sight again; alone but no longer empty in spirit. He took his time to start breathing again, familiar with trance but not with ecstasy. He tried out the memory like words in a very

foreign language, hoping it would not grow threadbare
with too much handling. It was too soon even to give
thanks. He was still absorbed in wonder when he heard
Rhys come up the path.

"Your shadow's crossed the branch and gone, Joram,"
the Healer called. He looked up and saw Joram. "You
said *we* had to keep our clothes on. . . . I think your shirt
is down here." He tossed it up to Joram.

"Thanks," said Joram. "Ummm. The sun felt very
good." He pulled his clothes back on as quickly as he
could.

"We were worried about you," Rhys told him as he
clambered back down to the forest floor. "It's been
strange. . . ."

"Is Evaine all right?"

"Yes, certainly. Have you ever seen a unicorn?"

This drew even Joram's attention. "Not outside of a
book or someone's crest, no. Have you?"

"It came and put its head in Evaine's lap. It was kind
of surprising." Rhys hesitated, gnawing his lower lip for
a moment. "The more since. . . ."

"Please don't confess. I'm not ordained yet," Joram
said unkindly. "But it ought to reassure my father."

"We are *not* going to tell Camber we saw a unicorn,"
said Rhys. "There are whole topics I just don't want him
to go near."

They missed seeing Evaine sitting next to the lake, until
she saw them and dropped the veil of her magic.

"You say you saw a unicorn?" Joram asked. Evaine
nodded vigorously.

"I'm so glad Rhys was here, too. It licked my face."

"And nibbled at my fingers," Rhys said.

"What was it like? Goaty or horsey?"

"More like a deer, except for the mane and tail," Evaine
said. She reached over and picked something up: a long,
silvery hair. It wasn't one of hers. She wound it carefully
around a finger and put it in the sack of herbs. "More like

a unicorn than anything else, I guess. I never knew this was an enchanted wood."

"I think they all are at Midsummer," said Rhys. "Or where you are." They blew each other kisses. Joram's patience surprised himself.

"Shall we be getting back?" he asked. They mounted their horses, who apparently had not noticed the unicorn.

"I'm sorry you didn't get to see it," Evaine said. "It's too bad you missed the adventure."

Joram wondered if he should tell them about his own encounter. He wanted time to savor it, to consider, maybe even risk praying about it.

"I was well refreshed," he said finally.

❈

AUTHOR'S NOTE: Although Father Joram MacRorie, OSM, is most widely known for his political activity in the Haldane Restoration and its bloody aftermath, his Order maintains a different view of him. He is remembered in the Michaeline Ordo for his love of God, expressed often in counseling and conversation. Several intense and passionate sermons concerning "the wideness of Christ's embrace" are attributed to his pen.

ARILAN THE TALMUD STUDENT
1105

When the concept of the Deryni universe first began to take shape, with a gifted people persecuted because they are different, I found myself drawing conscious parallels with the discrimination and persecution historically experienced by the Jews of our own world—also a persecuted people set apart by factors not readily apparent, many of them forced to live secret lives. Though I am a Christian with a great affinity for the kind of spirituality I've sometimes explored through the vehicle of the Deryni and some of their religious interactions, I suppose I was more aware of the Jews' predicament than most, because of growing up in Miami, Florida, where a large proportion of my classmates all through public school and university were Jewish; so Jews didn't seem all that different to me, because I regularly hung out with them, visited in their homes, and attended the occasional Seder or other Jewish observance. Some of the things some of them did seemed somewhat exotic—but I found that *interesting*, not threatening.

But I was well aware that this had not always been the case in other places and times. Sometimes people do feel threatened by things or people that are strange or different. I was brought up to judge people for who they were as individuals, not by their religion or the color of their skin or other superficial characteristics over which they had no control, but I was also aware that blanket discrimination was still very much with us. (If discrimination based on sexual preference existed when I was growing up, I was not aware of it, but it had become so by the time I was laying out the background of the Deryni; and thus, the Deryni also became a vehicle for talking about homosexual issues, as well as religious and racial ones.)

Not all my readers recognized this parallel between the Deryni and the Jews, because some of them asked about the apparent absence of Jews in Gwynedd—though when I told them what my intention had been—that, in a sense, the Deryni were the Jews of Gwynedd—they saw it. I also told them that there were, indeed, Jews; but because the Deryni were taking the heat that would have been reserved for the Jews in our own world, the Jews in Gwynedd mostly got left alone. (This was before I wrote the section in *The Bishop's Heir*, where Denis Arilan cites Talmudic tradition as the basis for regarding the real Presence of God in the Reserved Sacrament as a valid witness, paralleling that role taken by the Torah in Jewish tradition.)

By then, I had revealed portions of the *Adsum Domine,* the Healer's song, which also spoke to many of my readers of the gifts of a special people, chosen by God, and the responsible use of one's gifts. It was because of the *Adsum Domine* that I first met the authors of our next story, Jay Azneer and Dan Kohanski, who were working on a new translation of the Sabbath liturgy for their local temple, and wrote to ask if they might use parts of the *Adsum* in it. Both have a scholarly familiarity with the Talmud, as many Jewish men do, whatever other work they may do, and Jay is a rabbi's son; so I was hardly surprised when, a few years later—and after I had met both of them in person at a science fiction convention— I received the following story from them, which I immediately decided to publish in the next issue of *Deryni*

Archives. Clearly an attempt to account for Arilan's knowledge of Talmud, in that section of *The Bishop's Heir,* it is definitely one of those stories that I couldn't have written nearly as well myself.

ARILAN THE TALMUD STUDENT

❊

Daniel Kohanski and Jay Barry Azneer

SWEET JESU, THE man *even* looks *monotone!*

Denis Arilan was the most diligent of students; he was determined early on to come to the attention of those who, making priests, think of them as future bishops. But Father Joset *droned*, and Denis doubted that even the use of Deryni techniques to banish fatigue could get him through the next hour. In a faded cassock the color of his graying hair, the priest went on and on about the most obscure twists and turns of the Apocrypha. Here was the man to make the Last Judgement dull.

"Now the sixteenth chapter of Sirach is an exposition on punishments for sin, and how sin can be forgiven. While this might appear on first reading to contradict the Gospel of Luke, in the fifth chapter, verse twenty-one, when the scribes and the rabbis are about to begin a discussion on the details of the laws of forgiveness (which we know that they were wont to do because we have similar examples in the Talmud), we see, however, that Jesus argues with their point of view. . . ."

Talmud? What in the name of Saint Michael was the Talmud?

When the lecture was over, Denis waited until the rest of his classmates had left the room, then squared his shoulders and took a deep breath before approaching the aging priest. Joset, after all, was a scholar of formidable proportions, known to have little patience with students' questions—or with anything else that might interfere with his private devotions, as narrow and unyielding as his scholarship was wide.

The old man had indeed already begun to turn to walk out the door when Denis began, "Father. . . ."

The priest did not even turn around. Barely breaking stride, he said, "Yes, young Arilan?"

Denis realized how tentative he must have sounded. He could have bitten his tongue for letting it betray him, but having spoken out, he must continue.

"You spoke of something called the Talmud. Forgive me, Father, but I've never heard of it."

"Talmud, Talmud. . . . Oh, yes, the Talmud, the Jewish books of law."

"Jewish books?" The idea took Denis by surprise. He had known, of course, that the Jews were called the "People of the Book," but that Book was the Bible—the Old Testament, really. It had never occurred to him that the Jews had written other holy books.

"Yes, yes, Jewish books. As I remember, it is actually a collection of many books, a record of the arguments of Jewish scholars, as they picked over every conceivable point of law. Let me see. . . . They would have started about a hundred years after the Alexandrian conquests, which would be about two hundred years before the birth of Our Lord and Savior, and gone on up to, oh, about two or three hundred years ago, I believe—"

Denis already had ambitions as a student of dialectic, and could barely contain himself. A thousand years of arguments!

"Forgive me, Reverend Sir, but is there a copy of this Talmud here? Would it be possible for me to study it?"

The old scholar was not used to being interrupted. He

glared at the fourteen-year-old for a moment.

"Young Arilan, *if* you please. I am old, I am tired. I have more than earned a respite from your earnestness. You have not even studied Hebrew yet, or Old Testament, and for the Talmud you would need Aramaic as well, which no one studies here. Go pester Brother Mearad, if you must; the library has a few volumes. But I warn you, he cannot help you much, though he *may* be more inclined to overlook your impetuosity!"

With that, Father Joset headed once more for the door, finality in his every movement. No one would dare to interrupt him now.

Denis watched the old priest walk off into the darkness of the hall.

Earnest! Impetuous! Must he hide even his joy of learning under the same cloak of secrecy that warded his Deryni gifts? And if he did, at what cost to his soul? Every warding had its price. He had long known what the cost would be in secrecy, in discipline, if he wanted to become a forbidden Deryni priest, but must he sacrifice his curiosity as well? Suppose a too-knowing question, or knowledge he ought not to have, should slip past his lips? But if he stopped asking questions, would this change in behavior be itself noticed by the ever-suspicious seminarians? Did Father Joset suspect?

Denis took a deep breath to center himself, fighting to counterfeit a calm he did not feel. He had known ever since he began his studies that his charade would have to be perfect, but now he began to doubt his abilities, and that thought was dangerous. For a Deryni even to apply to the seminary was absolutely forbidden, and if he were to be caught now, it would mean death by fire. But *Jesu,* seven years of absolute, complete control?

He would have to concentrate more on his shielding, and pray that it would be good enough. His fellows and his teachers would see him as arrogant and aloof, but better that than discovery. Still, at least he could talk to

Brother Mearad; after all, Joset had practically ordered him to!

Mearad bade the young student sit at a table near the window; then, hiding a smile, he took a large folio from the racks and placed it in front of him. The boy opened the book at random and began to leaf through its pages. In the space of a bare few moments he began to wonder whether the arrogance he proposed to hide behind was all that much of a construct. The prospect of a thousand years' worth of dialectic was certainly enticing. But now that the presumptive Talmud student was actually faced with the text itself, he wondered just what he was letting himself in for. He stared at the totally unfamiliar letters until they swam on the page before him and coalesced into the shape of a monster that defied even Deryni imagination.

"Brother. . . ." Denis cleared his throat and tried again. "Brother Mearad, can you help me learn this?"

"Young Arilan, do you have any idea what you are asking? Even were you to begin your Hebrew studies now, and finish all the courses in the curriculum, you would be no closer to reading these pages than a child who has mastered the alphabet could read the Psalter. This is not even Hebrew, it's Aramaic—a related language, true enough, but as different from Hebrew as Koine is from classical Greek. Still, I do have some Hebrew knowledge, though not as much as your masters, and if you wish, I can teach you your letters—the 'aleph-bet'— and then, mayhap, a psalm. That way, you may judge for yourself how hard the study will be. And either way, the experience may do you good."

Denis did not stop to speculate what the usually gentle monk meant by that last. His eyes fairly glowed as Mearad settled his rotund frame on the bench next to him and began what would be the first of many hours of study.

*   *   *

DENIS BIT HIS tongue to stifle the curse that had been
about to escape his lips as he bent over a page of a Hebrew psalm. Not only did the letters track perversely from
right to left, but many of the letters were surrounded by
small dots and dashes, almost impossible to see, but which
could make a total difference in both sound and meaning.
On more than one occasion, Denis had been sorely
tempted to use Deryni learning techniques, but he was
wary of showing sudden progress after so many hours of
slow, plodding study with the ever-patient Mearad. He
was left with no choice but to learn the way students always do—one mistake at a time.

Once he dared a Deryni probe in Father Joset's direction and was not really surprised to find that the old priest
was keeping himself informed of Denis's progress. Indeed, it seemed that Joset took a fair amount of pleasure
in the difficulty that the arrogant young whelp was having
in his attempt to improve upon the curriculum his betters
had devised for him. Denis felt no small relief that he had
not betrayed himself as Deryni, though just now he was
sure he was betraying himself as woefully stupid instead.

"Brother, does anyone ever really do more than hobble
through all this?"

"Patience, young Arilan, patience. Hebrew is simply
one of the many tasks set before you, and it is no less
learnable than any other knowledge. The Jews use it as
their language of prayer just as we use Latin, and any one
of their children can read it fluently by the time they are
five or six. Do you think yourself no less capable than
that child?"

The rebuke was gentle enough, but it stung, and Denis
tasted bitter tears of frustration as he bent himself once
more to the task of sounding out the psalm, letter by stubborn letter.

FOR ALL HIS efforts, Denis never completely mastered the Hebrew tongue, though he did gain proficiency.

But though he conceded that point, old Father Joset nonetheless took perverse pleasure in reminding Arilan that for all his skill, he was still no closer to penetrating the mysterious Talmud of the Jews. Even so, it was one more accomplishment to come to the attention of notables beyond the seminary walls, and when at last Arilan was priested, there was a definite, though discreet, competition for his services.

Now, a junior priest on the archbishop's staff is still only a junior priest, but even so, he has certain privileges, and among them is relatively free access to the best libraries. So it was that Father Arilan found himself—again—staring at another page of strange letters that kept threatening to blur before his eyes.

Handfire, he thought, *would be so much easier on the eyes than these candles!*

But he dared not conjure even the smallest spell within the confines of the library. What if he were distracted and a fellow priest walked in? They were all instructed to look for the signs of Deryni in hiding, and handfire was one of the surest giveaways.

And distracted he could easily be. Here was a challenge that simply would not bend to his will. Never before had Arilan been faced with anything he could not learn, if by no other means than sheer diligence and perseverance. His air of superiority had never really been so much intellectual arrogance, as the certainty that there was no knowledge that would not yield to deliberate, determined pounding.

Until now.

When first he went to Brother Mearad, he had been unschooled and untutored in the special skills that he would need. Now he was proficient in all of them, and *still* that page of text would not yield up its secrets! Who *were* these Jews, whose writings so baffled and enticed him? Where could he find them? Would they teach him? Could he trust them with his yearnings?

It was an unusually pleasant day for early spring, and

Denis yielded to its temptations. He closed the stubborn book—indeed, he almost slammed it shut in frustration—and replaced it on the library shelf. Then he made good his escape to the priory garden. The scent of flowers and the warmth of the sun worked their quite un-Deryni-like magic on him, and Arilan felt his anger begin to fade under their gentle ministrations.

The hammering of a woodpecker broke his reverie. He blinked and shook his head, startled at the loudness of the noise so close by. He looked about, seeking its source, and discovered that the little bird was not simply feeding, but nesting.

Arilan sat entranced. He watched the tiny creature struggle to make a home for itself in the trunk of the proud and stately elm. And despite its awesome size, the huge tree gradually yielded up a small space within itself to the persistent petitioner. In like manner had the church yielded up a place for Denis within her own sacred precincts. Why, then, would the Talmud not in its turn yield to him as well? Was he not as persistent, as deserving, as that woodpecker?

Still, it was a beautiful spring day, and he was determined not to spoil it. It was, after all, a gift from God just as surely as was his love of learning.

I really should get out and see this city. I need to breathe fresh air. I deserve it, after eating all that library dust!

Arilan quit the garden, the priory, and the cathedral precincts altogether. He wandered into the streets of Rhemuth with no clear destination in mind. It was market day, and the streets hummed with all the normal activity of a town at work. Oxcarts were everywhere as farmers, having sold their produce in the early morning hours, now made their way back through the city gates to their homesteads. As he walked, Denis suddenly realized that, all unawares, he had followed one such cart into an unfamiliar precinct of the city.

The history of Rhemuth, like that of any substantial

city, could be read upon its streets. Neighborhoods that had once been prosperous fell slowly into decay and disgrace, as their buildings became too old or too unfashionable to be worth the expense of repairing them. Arilan recognized this neighborhood as one such, though he had never been here before or heard its name.

He was brought up short as he spied the ruined carcass of a burned-out church, half-concealed by other buildings all around it, all of them in disrepair. From the looks of the church's locks, the doors had not been forced. Indeed, the building seemed totally ignored by the locals who crowded all about him. Even a cursory inspection revealed this old church to be completely abandoned, and to all appearances it had been so for many years. Strange, indeed! The locks that stood solitary sentry at the great doors of the old building were so rusted that they would not have discouraged anyone who had the slightest desire to enter.

Odd! No city is without her poor. Why should anyone shun a derelict old church?

And as he framed the question, the answer struck him with such force as to stagger him under its assault. There—under the grimy masonry—the remnants of an old Camber symbol! The attempts to remove or at least deface it were obvious. But the passage of time had enacted a small revenge, for the dust and dirt of centuries had settled into the crevices and so revealed it once more to the discerning eye. This had been a Deryni church! This desecrated ruin of a house of God had been raised in the memory and veneration of the only Deryni that even humans had admitted was worthy to be a saint—at least for a time.

For one brief moment, a rush of emotion overwhelmed the young Deryni priest who was now the sole spiritual heir to Saint Camber. Years before, centuries past, others like himself had humbly, willingly, publicly dedicated their lives to the service of God and Church. And now. . . .

A single tear welled up in his eye, and only the harsh

years of discipline, both priestly and Deryni, kept him from sobbing openly in the street.

"Good day, Reverend Sir," said a voice behind him.

Arilan whirled about in total surprise, his almost-tear forgotten, and found himself facing a man who might once have been tall, but now was stooped from years. His hair, years ago a flaming red, now showed wide swaths of gray. A somewhat scraggly beard completed the picture, and it, too, showed the effect of many passing seasons. The bright colors of fall were fading, and winter settling in. The man stepped back a bit at Arilan's sudden movement, but cleared his throat and continued gamely on.

"You'd not be thinking of starting a congregation in these puir old bones of a church now, would you?"

Arilan by now had recovered his composure. A quick reading of his questioner revealed a gentle, inquisitive soul; nothing more. The situation was awkward, but not dangerous. And the old man's question was so unexpected that he could not help smiling.

"Why would I want to do that, good sir?"

"Well, as I understand it, Reverend Sir, Christians are required to attend church in the area in which they live. But, I assure you, no Christians live in this neighborhood. And those few people of your faith who do pass this way avoid this old church as if it were the gate to Hell itself."

Denis laughed in spite of himself.

"Have I made a joke now, Reverend Sir?"

"Not at all. But you see, this was a Deryni church, and undoubtedly deconsecrated centuries ago. I had no idea this church had ever even existed, but it is nothing more than an old wreck now. And please, call me 'Father,' if you would. 'Reverend Sir' is for monsignors, not ordinary priests."

"Forgive me, Rev—Father, I did not mean to give offense. It's just that none of your kind . . . excuse me, none of the clergy have ever taken an interest in this district. I've heard about the Deryni since I came to Gwynedd,

but I never met one before." Denis's gasp went unnoticed
as the old man continued blithely on. "Is it true what they
say about you, that you can turn water into wine?"

Denis felt his cassock clinging to him as he broke into
a cold sweat. All those years of careful hiding, of per-
fecting his disguise, and a casual remark by an unsus-
pecting stranger had exposed his most treasured secret.
He tried to recover.

"You don't seem to understand. There are no more Deryni priests. They were all barred from sacred service two
hundred years ago, at the same time this church must have
been destroyed. There are no Deryni priests!"

"Of course. I see now," said the old man, in a tone that
sounded thoroughly unconvinced.

Denis thought it best to change the subject fast. "Tell
me, if you would, why you think there is no need of a
church here?"

"Because, Rev—Father, those of us who live here are
mostly Jews."

Who were these Jews? Where could he find them?

Denis offered up a quick, silent prayer to the God who
had directed his steps at this time, to this place, to this
old man. Taking a casual tone so as not to betray his
excitement, he said: "I had no idea. And are you yourself
a Jew?"

The old man smiled briefly. "Well, yes, that I am."

"Then tell me, if you would, if you know anything
about one of your books called the Talmud?" Denis tried
not to hold his breath as he waited for the answer.

But the old man did not answer him at once. Instead,
he peered more closely at the young priest standing before
him trying unsuccessfully to conceal his eagerness. Reb
Elias the tailor dealt every day with gentiles in the course
of business, and this was no ordinary gentile. And although he had never met a priest before, he sensed somehow that this was no ordinary priest. The tailor closed his
eyes and allowed himself to step briefly onto the plane of
inner vision, of *yetsirah,* the Kabbalistic level just above

the world of the outer senses. The image of Arilan on the
plane of formation was still heavily cloaked, but he could
feel a great power there, still unformed, still unaware, but
with no inclination toward evil. What was its desire, then?
Reb Elias opened his eyes and spoke to Denis in a quiet,
unsuspicious tone.

"Well, Father, the Talmud . . . now the Talmud is a lot
of books. A lot of laws for the Jews to follow, nothing to
interest a Christian. What use is the study of the Talmud
to a priest?"

Denis, in his turn, looked hard at his interlocutor. The
older man's probe of him had been so subtle he was almost convinced he had only imagined it. But he knew
instinctively that this question was a test. How he answered it would determine much of his life.

"All knowledge is a gift from God," he replied. "We
are merely its custodians while we live. Besides, study is
never wasted."

Reb Elias nodded to himself. Again he closed his eyes
and *Looked* once more at the priest. The power was still
cloaked, but he sensed the eagerness to learn, to drink in
learning for its own sake, tugging at the leash. Knowledge
in this man's hands could never be misused. With his eyes
still closed, as if in meditation, he said: "I do not know
who you are. But it is not without purpose that you are
here. 'He will fulfill the desire of those that fear Him.' "
The last words were said in the Hebrew, and Reb Elias
smiled when he *Saw* that Denis understood him. He
opened his eyes and continued.

"I will tell you what you must do. Follow this street to
the next corner, then turn left and walk until you come to
an alley with a badly broken slate at the edge of the road.
Turn left again and go to the fourth house on the right;
that will be Rabbi Kefir's house. He can help you find
what you are looking for. Go in peace. God bless your
quest."

Arilan turned away to face the church for a moment as
he sought to recover his composure. All unlooked for, the

answer was nearing his grasp! A pity—the hour was late, almost time for Vespers, and although as a priest he had far fewer restrictions on his movements than as a seminarian, still his presence for the major offices was expected. He would have to make time to visit this rabbi— Kefir?—another day.

Denis turned back to bid thanks and farewell to the older man, only to discover that he had vanished into the crowd, as quickly as he had appeared. With one last glance of longing, Denis looked over his shoulder at the old church. He was about to retrace his steps back to the cathedral when it suddenly occurred to him that in an obviously Deryni church it might just be possible that there would be a Portal. He knew of other ecclesiastical Portals, some of them in surprising locations; his brother Jamyl had made particularly sure he knew about the one in the cathedral sacristy, should he need to flee in an emergency.

In an outwardly unhurried manner, Denis made his way along the outer wall of the nave toward the area where the chancel ought to have been. He found there a small door leading into what was probably a sacristy or study. A quick probe revealed that the door was locked only with an iron bar. Now, if he could just lift it a few scant inches . . .

Denis focused his will and pushed hard against the bar behind the door, willing it to move upward. Being out of practice and overeager, he succeeded not only in lifting the obstructing bar but in sending it halfway up the wall. The resulting clatter almost made his heart stop.

He looked carefully around him, chiding himself for not having done so before, but no one seemed even to be in sight. The old church must have been falling apart for years, and the neighbors had grown used to the occasional noise within. He cautiously eased the door open and found himself indeed in the study. His enthusiasm at his success was somewhat diminished by the mouthful of spiderwebs he inhaled as he pushed his way in.

Denis sneezed and spat out a wad of black soot. As the accumulated dust of centuries rained down on him, he looked around him. Even in the fading light, he could see that the walls were fire-stained, and exposed brick showed through the charred and crumbling plaster. All but a small corner of the roof had burned away, and the few cross-beams still in place were blackened with soot and smoke. The faint twilight showed the barest outline of the sacristy walls and remains of the altar without. Had the devastated interior not so resembled a church as did the outside, Arilan might not have mustered the will to go on. As it was, he simply sighed and cast his mind about, searching, his feet feeling their way slowly through the littered debris.

He almost missed the tessellated border that marked the Portal, but a tingle at his feet prompted him to look down. Falling to his knees, he brushed away the charred remnants of carpet and other, less identifiable remains. As his hands uncovered the mosaic pattern beneath, he could feel just the faintest surge of power still remaining. Probing as best he knew, he could find no trace of a trap or special setting. Perhaps the church had burned too quickly, or else there had been no one there who knew how to destroy a Portal. In any case, this was a Portal meant for general use, and was now dying. But it was not yet dead.

Unheeding of the possible consequences, the young priest reached into himself and released power into the matrix. The sudden pull from the Portal almost stunned him into unconsciousness as it wrenched at his life force. Only with great effort did he manage to pull himself free.

He lay gasping in the dust for several minutes before he could stagger to his feet, out the sacristy door into the fresh air. He leaned against the old church wall, chest heaving, until slowly his breathing returned to normal. As he stumbled along the cobblestone streets back to the cathedral, he was grateful for the cover of lowering darkness that hid the grime still clinging to him; indeed, he looked more like a charcoal burner than a priest. By the time he had reached the cathedral, Vespers were long since over.

He slipped unnoticed into his chambers, and knelt in reverent prayer. Alive and whole—thanks be to God!

SEVERAL DAYS PASSED after his encounter with the tailor before Denis found the time to visit the rabbi, and then only after Vespers, when it was already dark. He discovered that chance, or a benevolent God, was kinder to him than he knew. The Jewish community of Rhemuth, though small, was still the largest such in Gwynedd, and the only one where he might find a Talmud scholar. It had started about a hundred years ago when a few Jews came as traders from the Moorish lands. They had been allowed to stay and do business because of the spices and silks they were able to bring, and also, the differences between them and the Christians were not so apparent when the Church had Deryni to persecute. As time passed, their families followed them, as well as others from the south—not many, but there were those who were tired of the hot deserts, and would put up with and even welcome winter cold and spring rains in Gwynedd.

They had no need of priests, of course, and Denis doubted he had ever met a Jew before the tailor came and spoke to his soul. How would their rabbi react if a priest came calling? Although relations between the Church and the local Jews had always been civil, still there was some uneasiness on both sides, and they tended not to mingle.

Thus Denis had decided to dress in ordinary clothing. Later, if all went well, he could reveal himself as a priest, for by then it would not matter; he either would have been accepted or not. He and his brother Jamyl were nearly of a size, and he had borrowed clothing from him before. In fact, now that he thought about it, he could make a complete outfit from the clothes still in his room. Breeches, boots, a shirt of homespun, a cloak, and finally a cap to conceal his tonsure were all that was needed. Something of a little boy still lived inside him, and it was not without a little boy's sense of adventure that he snuck out a side door of the priory and retraced his steps to the old ruined church. From there he followed the remembered directions to Rabbi Kefir's door.

The house itself had nothing to distinguish it from any other house in the Jewish quarter. Nor was there any light in the windows that he could see, but he went up and knocked anyway. He waited. A small light grew in the window, like that of a candle coming closer. Then there came a voice from the other side of the door.

"I'm closed already, it's nighttime! Bring me your shoes tomorrow, I'll fix them in the morning."

Shoes?

"I didn't come about any shoes. I was looking for the rabbi."

"Oh, it's a problem you want fixing. Well, for problems I am open . . . always open. Wait just a minute."

When the door opened, Denis was briefly spellbound. Like all pious Jews, Rabbi Kefir never shaved. But unlike so many, his beard was not some scraggly, stringy pittance, but a great full bush of a beard. It rolled luxuriously off his chest, almost to his waist. It was mostly white now; the rabbi had lived many long years, and bore every one of them in his beard. His fingers played in it constantly, stroking it with the ease of long familiarity and love. For the rest of his life, Denis would never forget that first sight of the rabbi's fingers in that magnificent beard.

"So. What can I do for you?"

Denis ignored the question.

"I don't understand. If you are a rabbi, why did you want to fix my shoes?"

The rabbi was amused. "A rabbi also has to make a living, yes? You think maybe they pay me by the *bracha*?"

Denis was not used to hearing Hebrew spoken, and it took him a second to remember that this was the word for blessing. The rabbi noticed his hesitation.

"You don't mind my asking, you're not Jewish, are you?"

"No. No, I'm not. Do you mind?"

The rabbi shrugged, a complex movement in which his shoulders went one way while the beard went another. His eyebrows, either of which on any other man's face would have made a decent mustache, shot up briefly.

"Mind? No, I don't mind, it's just—you shouldn't mind my saying it—a little odd for a Christian to come to me with a problem. You have your own priests for that, you know." He paused again, then seemed to make up his mind all at once. "Well, come in, come in, I can't help you while you stand on one foot in the street. Come, sit in the study, and we'll see what I can do for you."

Arilan, now thoroughly bemused, stepped across the threshold and closed the door. The only light in the room besides the candle in Kefir's hand came from beyond the door on the far wall, but he could see well enough to tell he was in a cobbler's shop, and not a high-class one at that. Benches and scraps of leather lay everywhere, and he had to pick his way carefully around them as he followed the old rabbi to the far door. He was not entirely convinced that this whole undertaking was not a mistake. How much could he learn from a man who made his living fixing shoes?

The door led into a kitchen and eating area, poor but well kept. The old man's wife was the only other person in the room. She looked up startled as Denis walked through the door, then relaxed as she saw her husband come in behind him.

"Eh, Gittel, I have a young man with a problem. We'll be in the study; make us a bit of mulled wine, would you?"

Gittel said nothing, but nodded in agreement and smiled at Arilan. He tried to smile back.

"Now, my young friend, come this way." The rabbi pointed to an open door to his left and again gestured that Arilan should follow him in. There was a lamp on a desk inside, and the rabbi used the candle to light it, then blew the candle out.

In the slightly brighter light of the lamp, Arilan got a
better look at his surroundings, and gasped in spite of
himself. More books than he had ever seen outside a seminary! He was shaking as he made his way over to one
of the shelves. His fingers moved of themselves over the
spines, tracing the letters that he had painstakingly studied
for so many years.

Jesu Christe, so many books! Maybe he *can* help me!

Only with some difficulty did he will his heart to calm
and his breathing to slow, but there was no controlling
the glow in his eyes as he turned back to the rabbi. The
old man had been watching him, growing more puzzled
by the moment.

"Who *are* you? What do you want with me?"

"I—"

"You're a priest, aren't you? From the archbishop's
staff?"

"How . . . how could you know that?" Denis was more
than a little frightened. How could the old man have seen
through him so quickly?

Dear God, does he know I'm Deryni, too?

"Here, relax, you're as white as a sheet. No harm in a
priest, you know, it's just that I wasn't expecting one. As
for how I knew, well, among you Christians only a priest
would recognize Hebrew letters, and only someone bright
enough for the archbishop would be so fascinated by
them. So sit down and don't be so upset." He raised his
voice. "Gittel! Some wine already! Our young friend
needs a mug of wine!"

Gittel appeared at the door, a mulling poker in her
hand. "Calm yourself, I'm making it! You can't wave
your hand and shout 'Wine' and there's all of a sudden
wine! It has to warm up yet!"

She disappeared behind the door and returned immediately with two filled mugs. She handed one to Arilan
with a smile, then gave the other to the rabbi. She tried
to scowl at him, but in the end the smile won.

"Don't be too late, hmm?" she said softly. "You've had

a long day." She closed the door behind her, leaving the
rabbi and the priest alone in the room.

Arilan wrapped his hands around the mug more to
warm his spirit than his body. He drew in a deep breath
and let it out, little by little. When he had calmed a little
more, he sipped at the hot wine. He felt the rabbi's eyes
on him through the whole performance, but the old man
said nothing, merely blowing on his own wine to cool it
a bit, and then he, too, sipped at it.

They remained this way, in the same room but each
alone with his drink, a few minutes more. The rabbi broke
their silence.

"So. You are better now. I did not mean to startle you
like that. Now tell me, my young friend—you do have a
name, by the way?"

Arilan blinked, a smile forming on his face. "Yes, of
course I do. It's Denis." Harmless enough; Denis was a
common name.

"Very well, Denis—Father Denis, I should say, yes?"
Denis nodded. "I am Rabbi Kefir. 'Kefir' means 'young
lion' in Hebrew, but I expect you know that?" It was not
really a question. "My parents had rather fanciful notions
when I was born. Of course, I am at best an old lion now,
but I still have my mane"—he was stroking his beard
throughout this speech—"and it is a little late to be changing my name at this time in my life."

Denis warmed to the rabbi. He was reminded of old
Brother Mearad, who had been so patient with him as a
student.

"Well, you know, monks often take a new name when
they enter the monastery. They leave their old name behind with the rest of the world. But we priests usually
keep the names we were born with."

"Ah yes, you priests. You are, forgive me, a little young
to be a priest yet, not so?"

Denis flushed. His appearance was going to cause him
problems for some few years yet, until he acquired the
look of maturity that years of study deserved. He wished

briefly that beards were in fashion, and that thought caused him to smile again. Belatedly he remembered that he was still wearing his cap, and took it off now to reveal his tonsure.

"I assure you, I really am a priest. I may be a little young—twenty-two, actually—but my teachers were pleased with my studies, and gave me dispensation. I am quite thoroughly ordained!" A small smile of satisfaction accompanied that last, the ordeal by *merasha* still vivid in his mind.

The rabbi smiled in turn, though in his case it was harder to tell; the beard all but swallowed his mouth.

"Umm-hmmm. Your teachers have trained you well. I have from time to time talked with some of the seminarians here, and many of them are fine scholars. And you seem to know more than enough Hebrew to fulfill your priestly duties. So tell me, what brings a priest to see a rabbi?"

The rabbi's voice did not change as he asked this question, but Denis felt again that same feeling of being tested as when that other Jew had found him staring at the church. Prodded by that memory, he realized once again that only the truth would serve.

"I was walking near here a few days ago—I'd never seen this part of town before—and I met a man who told me I should come to see you. I don't know his name."

"A man, hmmm? One you did not know? Why should this man send you to me? Perhaps you had better begin at the beginning. It says in the Talmud"—Denis twitched before he could stop himself—"that all beginnings are difficult. But then, it seems we have already begun."

Rabbi Kefir sat back and waited, the mug of wine forgotten and cooling in his hand. The other hand sought its customary refuge, in the rabbi's beard. The sight of that hand stroking the long white hairs over and over, up and down, up and down, had a calming, indeed hypnotic effect on the nervous priest. He took a deep breath and told the rabbi everything: how he had first heard of the Talmud, the rebuffs from Father Joset and the kindnesses of Brother Mearad, the fascination that had never left him to master this strange, impenetrable learning. He barely retained the presence of mind not to reveal that he was Deryni as well.

At length Denis fell silent, and looked up to find Kefir smiling at him.

"Denis, my friend, do you realize, do you have even the slightest idea, what you are asking? Even for someone who has nothing else to do, the Talmud is a lifetime's study. Someone such as yourself, a full-time priest, with obligations, with superiors. . . ." Rabbi Kefir shook his head, and Denis sat back in dismay. He looked around the room, his heart sinking lower and lower with each succeeding book that caught his eye. He almost missed Kefir's next words.

"But, you know, it is not necessary for you to *master* the Talmud. Perhaps what you really want is to become friends with it." He let Denis absorb this new idea, then went on. "And that, my young priest friend, is enough, and more than enough, for one day. The hour is late, and even if you are young, I am not, and I need my rest. Gittel will be angry with me as it is. Perhaps you priests have the right idea after all, not getting married." But he smiled as he said this, and Denis knew he did not mean it. He had sensed the love Kefir and Gittel had for each other, and if he was at all envious, it was because he had married the Church, and when the Church became angry, it was for reasons other than love.

"Now, can you come this Shabbat—Saturday, that is— in the afternoon, perhaps?" Denis nodded. "Good. Very good. Come then, and I will introduce you, and you will begin your friendship with the Talmud."

The wine, the lateness of the hour, the tension, had all gone to Denis's head. Barely suppressing a yawn, he nodded once again and let Rabbi Kefir lead him through the darkened cobbler's shop out into the street. He never remembered how he made it back to his room.

*   *   *

"**N**OW TELL ME, what is the Talmud?"

Denis and the rabbi were seated once more in the rabbi's study, the bright light of a Saturday afternoon shining even through the one small and poorly glazed window that was all the room afforded. Denis, having barely sat down, almost stood up again in his surprise at the question. Then he relaxed as he realized that this was again a test, this time to discover not whether he was worthy to study at all, but to find out where his study should begin.

"I was taught that the Talmud is the record of the arguments of the rabbis on questions of law, covering about a thousand years or so, maybe up until about the eighth century."

"Well, that is true enough, as far as it goes," replied the rabbi, "although the last of the recorded discussions— a better word than arguments—more likely took place around the year 500. But the Talmud is more than discussions, or even arguments, on the law. 'Talmud' means study, after all, and in a real sense the Talmud is studying how to live, how to function in the world."

This was not quite what Denis was expecting. However, the eager young dialectician he had been was older and more mature now. He was interested in the broader world, in study for its own sake, not just in finding out new ways to win a debate.

"The old man who sent me here said that the Talmud is full of laws for the Jews to follow."

"Again, that is true enough. We can find in the Talmud a law, or at least a recommendation, that we can use to answer practically any question of how we should behave, what we should do and what we should not do. And this applies to our dealings with man as well as with God; we do not really separate our lives into heavenly and earthly parts. 'A life should always be lived for the sake of Heaven,' " he quoted. "Let me give you an example." He reached behind him to one of the shelves and pulled out a book. "This is a small part of the Talmud, called *Baba Metziah,* one of the sections on the laws of property. Like most of the Talmud, it is written partly in Hebrew, but mainly in Aramaic. You are aware of the difference?"

Denis nodded. "I have, of course, studied Hebrew, but the priests and monks were always telling me that Aramaic was different, though they never explained."

"Aramaic was the common language of the people in the days of the Talmud. In those days, Hebrew was used mainly for prayer, and only educated people could understand it. It is much as Latin is used today. So, parts of the Talmud—the basic statement of the law, what we call the *Mishnah*—are in Hebrew, while the rabbinic discussions about the law—the *Gemarah*—mostly use the language they spoke in, which was Aramaic. But the two languages are close enough that you should be able to get a taste."

Again, Rabbi Kefir was steering Denis away from the temptation to master this foreign skill. Denis sensed this and, though disappointed, was resolved to learn as much as he could. *Even if I can never finish studying it, I can be—what did he call it?—a friend to this Talmud. Certainly better than being a stranger!*

"Here, for example, is the opening line of this tractate: *Shnayim ochazin b'tallis,* two men come, that is, come to the court, holding a tallis—a prayer shawl, which means any garment or loose object. One says 'I found it' and the other says 'I found it.' One says 'It's all mine' and the other says 'It's all mine.' Now we assume that there is no proof who is right, no other evidence. So the law says that you make one swear that his share is not less than half, and make the other swear that his share is not less than half, *v'yachluku,* and they divide it, which means that they sell the object and divide the money. So far, you can follow the Hebrew, yes?"

Denis had been noticeably quiet during the reading. "I can make out the words well enough, but so much of the thought is missing. It seems you had to explain every other word. Is it all like this?"

The rabbi laughed a little. "I'm afraid most of it is worse. This is one section we often start with, because it is easy to explain. But there must always be someone to explain it. It is said that if the Talmud were left unstudied for one generation, it would be lost forever, for no one could ever understand it again."

He pointed to the shelf behind him, to a row of about thirty large volumes. "You see these? Each is one volume of the Talmud." He began pulling down books at random. "Here is *Sanhedrin*—the laws of the High Court; this one is *Chullin*—clean and unclean foods. Ah, this one might interest you—*Berachot*—on the nature and kinds of blessings, prayers, and so forth. There are others; I do not have a complete set. There is probably none in all of Gwynedd, but we make do. And yet, for all its size, it is still condensed; too many years, too many people with something to say. Jews do like to talk, you know." He paused for effect, and they both laughed.

"Now you see how the Talmud can be used? If two people come to me as a judge and ask me to decide which of them owns a certain thing they both found, I have a basis now to make a ruling. That's what a rabbi is, after all—a judge for the community."

"Yes, of course," Arilan replied. "That explains some of the references I read in my studies. And we on our side have the canon law by which we live, though I've never heard of it getting so specific as to rule on the division of a garment. But you are right: I think I would find the section on blessings more interesting—if we might?"

"Certainly. Each tractate is different, has different concerns, and it would be good for you to try different tastes. So let us take *Berachot*—Blessings. We believe that everything comes from God, and therefore when we use anything of God's, we have to thank Him. Here"—the rabbi opened the volume at random—"is a section on the blessings for fruits. Now different fruits have different blessings, and so the first question is: what distinguishes among them?"

The two of them bent their heads over the page, filled with columns of strange letters arranged in fantastic patterns, one explaining, the other asking. Just when the fading light was about to force a halt to their study, a knock on the door startled them.

"Kefir! *Nu*, it's late, you have to make *Ma'ariv* yet!" Gittel was calling her husband to get ready for the evening prayers.

"So late already! When I was younger, Shabbat would never end, it seemed to go on forever. And now, when I could use a longer Shabbat. . . . You see what age does to you, Denis? You want my advice, stay young; you'll live longer."

"Kefir!"

"All right, all right, in a minute! Denis, you will come next week, we'll continue, yes?"

Denis wouldn't have missed it for the world.

ᛗONTHS PASSED IN this fashion. If Arilan's superiors noticed his frequent absences on Saturdays, they said nothing to him. He was careful to be seen at all the major services and most of the minor ones. Whenever he could, he would leave the cathedral precincts through a little-used but serviceable door in the library, so that his fellows would think he was still in there studying, and he would not even have to run the risk of being caught at a Portal that only Deryni could use.

Whether he finally came under suspicion—perhaps he was thought to be seeing a woman, not unheard of—or whether it was all just a coincidence, he never did find out. But one day in autumn Denis was summoned to the archbishop's office. As he knelt to kiss the episcopal ring extended to him, he was outwardly calm but inwardly trembling like a leaf.

"My son, I have just received a letter from my brother

of Valoret. He reports that he has need of a priest to help
with a new parish and he has none to spare. He asks me
to lend him someone, and my first thought was of you."

"M-me, Your Grace?"

The archbishop smiled. "Yes, Denis, you. Your scholarship has grown since you came here, but we feel you
need experience of the wider world. You should minister
to a flock, learn their problems, hear their confessions,
know their souls. A stint as a parish priest will serve you
in good stead. You will accept, Father?" There was a
touch of steel in the archbishop's voice as he spoke; archbishops do not expect ever to be refused, especially when
they are offering a chance for promotion. Denis knew that
if he ever wanted to advance in the hierarchy, there could
only be one answer.

"Of course, Your Grace!"

"Excellent. Go to your room and pack; you'll leave
tomorrow."

"To—tomorrow, Your Grace?"

"Yes, yes, tomorrow. The letter from Valoret was delayed in getting here, and His Grace of Valoret is not a
patient man. The sooner you are there—with my letter of
introduction—the easier you will get on with him."

Denis sighed—but only to himself—and knelt again.
"As you wish, Your Grace."

In the whirlwind, Denis had no time even to pen a note
to Rabbi Kefir explaining his change in circumstance. He
had missed sessions before, but always he had been able
to get word to his teacher, so that the rabbi would not
expect him in vain.

And there were still so many questions!

ARILAN ARRIVED IN Valoret and made his obeisance to his new superior. While on the road, he had had
an idea—there was a portal in Valoret, so Jamyl had once
told him, though how his brother knew that, he had never
explained. He could use it to get to the old Deryni church

near Kefir's house. With God's help and good timing, he would still be able to continue his lessons.

Saturday, Arilan finished his morning prayers and asked if he might be allowed to spend the afternoon in meditation. The archbishop frowned; sooner or later Arilan was going to have to get used to being a parish priest as well as a scholar. But he let Denis go. With stealth and his Deryni senses extended to the maximum, Denis made his way to the sacristy and the Portal he prayed was waiting for him there. He probed for and found the familiar tingle that told him a working Portal was in place. He stepped into position and was about to form the Words of transfer when a thought stopped him: *The old church will surely be empty, but what if there's someone here when I come back?* The sacristy was little used except at the times of services, but there was always the off-chance that a priest or a servant might come in just at the wrong moment, and discover everything.

Denis almost gave up his plans at that moment, but then had another idea: if he could take an instantaneous sweep of his surroundings and be ready to transfer back to the church if he was not alone, he could still hope to avoid detection. The energy involved would be enormous, but he was young and had youth's quick reflexes and recuperative power. Just for practice, he set himself a test: he would transfer to the church, sweep it, and flick back to Valoret; then, just as quickly, he would transfer back to the church again. He set the patterns in his mind and began.

Denis managed this feat—barely. He all but collapsed on the floor of the church, swaying on his feet and breathing in great gasps.

I can do it if I have to, but I certainly hope I'll never need it!

In his confusion and relief, he barely noticed the cobwebs in the old church, nor how they clung to his clothes as he brushed them off and pushed his way to the sacristy door.

Outside, in the alley, he paused again to catch his breath, and then quickly made his way through the streets of the Jewish quarter to Rabbi Kefir's house, where the rabbi was, as usual, waiting.

"Denis! Come in, come in. Somehow I wasn't sure you would make it today. But come in, sit."

As he spoke, the rabbi led the way to the study. But instead of opening the tractate they had been working on before, Kefir took a chair opposite Denis and studied him for a long minute. Just as Denis was beginning to get alarmed at the silence, Kefir looked down and heaved a long sigh.

"Denis, Denis, my friend . . . I appreciate your enthusiasm, your love of learning, but do you not realize the risk you ran? It's not worth it. You know, Jews have died for the Talmud, for Torah, but there is no reason for you to do so. I think this game has gone too far, and you must stop it now."

Denis blanched. "What—what do you mean? What risk?"

Kefir sighed again. "You didn't notice it was raining, not ten minutes ago?"

This time Denis's heart almost stopped. The rabbi saw it in his face, but continued. "You come here, it's at least half an hour from the cathedral, in pouring rain, and not only are you not wet, you have dust on your clothes! Did you walk between the raindrops? On the other hand, if you came from somewhere else, where it wasn't raining, then of course your clothes would be dry. Ah, but to do that"—Kefir had out of habit fallen into the singsong pattern of the Talmud "—now how could you do that, except by magic? Deryni magic? I read my history; there used to be—gates? portals—portals—that Deryni could use to get from one place to another, and so they might miss the rain, they might not notice it had been raining. And if these portals are hidden, are not much used, then there would most likely be dust nearby. I suppose you found a portal not too far from here, yes?"

Denis could only nod.

"And of course Deryni cannot be priests, not since the Council of Ramos. So you must be one of a very few, very special, and maybe some other people died to get you where you are. Certainly you would be killed if they found you out. No, my young and foolish friend, I should be flattered, but youthful foolishness is not flattery, it is only foolishness. You take too many risks as it is; you do not need the Talmud so much to die for it."

He waited a few minutes for his words to sink in, then spoke again in a kinder tone.

"So. You are surprised again. I should ask Gittel to mull us some wine as before, but it is Shabbat and we do not cook today. Will some cold wine help, at least?"

Denis nodded mutely, and the rabbi went out into the kitchen, returning in a moment with two cups and a jug of wine. The two men sat again in silence. Denis forced himself to sip at his wine, not gulp it, even as he willed his heart to slow and his breathing to return to normal. The rabbi was still watching him closely—he always watched Denis closely—and his fingers as always played with his beard.

"An interesting trick, that. I wonder if I could learn it. But I suppose I would have to be a Deryni for that. A pity."

Denis looked up, startled; no human of his acquaintance had ever wished to be one of the "accursed Deryni."

"Well. Are you better now? Would you like to tell me about it? Since you are here anyway, we may as well make the journey worth something. Where are you now, by the way? They didn't send you away from Rhemuth because of the Talmud, did they?"

"No . . . no, I've been promoted, actually. I was sent to Valoret to get parish experience. It's not actually a promotion in itself, but the Church likes its scholars to know about parish life . . . about people . . . as well, if they plan to advance them in the hierarchy."

"So, they have plans for you. I am not surprised. You

have—you *are* a great promise." Denis blushed; for all
the times he had heard that, it still affected him. "All the
more reason not to throw it away. Tell me, what was it
that drove you to defy the Church and become a priest in
the first place?"

Denis looked down at the wine left in the cup and continued to sip it; it seemed to help. The rabbi refilled it and
sat back, listening, as Denis told him everything, even
things he had never told his brother before. The shadows
had grown long by the time he finished; the day was coming to an end.

"Well, well, you have certainly had a busy time of it!
Now I caution you again, do not come back here anymore! Not like this! The Talmud will still be here. Mark
my words, one day they'll send you back to Rhemuth.
The Talmud will still be waiting. And you have many
years of work ahead of you; you mustn't throw them
away!"

He never added the obvious—Denis's secret would be
safe with him. In a daze, Denis followed Rabbi Kefir for
the last time from the study, through the cobbler's shop,
and out to the front door.

"Go in peace, Father. May God bless and keep you
always."

"God bless you, Rabbi."

It would have made a strange sight if anyone had happened to see it: a priest and a rabbi standing in the street
blessing each other.

SEVERAL YEARS LATER, Arilan was still in Valoret, now a monsignor, and one day soon to be considered for the bishop's mitre. He was in his study when a
messenger came to his door.

"Monsignor Arilan?"

"Yes?"

"Forgive me for disturbing you, Reverend Sir. I have a
package for you, from Rhemuth."

From Rhemuth? From the archbishop?
"Thank you, my son. I'll take it now."

When the man had left, Denis opened the wrappings and was surprised to discover it contained one of the precious volumes of the Talmud. There was a letter with it, written in a frail hand.

Dear Monsignor Arilan: Kefir spoke often of your devotion to learning. He asked that this book be sent to you as a token of his affection. And of mine. Gittel.

Much of the Talmud is unspoken; the meanings as much in between the words as in them. Arilan understood—his old friend and teacher had died.

❄

DEO VOLENTE
1107

Our next story is another of those I don't think I could have written nearly as well myself. Its author, Sharon Henderson, is another of those splendidly talented writers poised for a launch into professional publishing; and like many of our contributors, she responded to an incident in one of the Deryni novels that spoke to her profoundly in her own heart of hearts. I think her own words best describe how this particular story came to be written:

"Most of this story just plain 'happened' as a complete entity, but there were two very important things going on in my life at that time.

"I had been taking Scottish country dance lessons with a local group in the Washington, D.C. area, and had gotten at least good enough to occasionally dance with the demo team. It was the first time I had substantively touched on the Scottish part of my family heritage, and I was a bit amazed at how quickly I became enamoured of those dances and the sprightly music that accompanies them. It seemed only natural to share the wonder of the experience with Duncan and Maryse.

"The second thing was of a significance even deeper, and which I had vicariously shared with Duncan McLain from the very beginning of my experience with the Deryni books. I had felt a vocation to ministry in my teen years, and was introduced to Katherine's works shortly thereafter. Duncan's dilemma as a man of deep and abiding faith—clearly called to be a priest and being a good one at that, yet knowing he is a member of the 'proscribed race'—means that he has had to flout local law and risk his life in the bargain. Let's just say that feeling Called, knowing the Source of that Call, and yearning to reply *Adsum, Domine!* from the depth of your soul was something I understood very well.

"After reading about Duncan's secret and tragic marriage, I spent a lot of time pondering what kind of girl she must have been, to inspire so great a love in so pious a young man. And how hard it must have been for Duncan to spend that summer torn between two great, intense loves—vocation and Maryse—with no recourse to either Alaric or his brother Kevin, to whom one would assume he might usually turn for advice. The more I thought, the more I had to know. Then one afternoon I sat down at the typewriter, and this whole story, in very nearly the form it is now, came out. Maybe someday I'll answer my own other burning question about all this: Why did Duncan never simply sit down with his mother and get her help?

"Since then, I've switched to learning the dances of my German heritage—and been ordained to the priesthood myself. What a long, strange trip it's been!"

DEO VOLENTE

❄

Sharon Henderson

Gorau nawdd, nawdd Duw
[The best-known protection is God's protection].
—ANCIENT GWYNEDD PROVERB

IT WAS COLD, kneeling there in the darkened chapel—
very cold—and Duncan McLain was trying not to take it
as an omen. He could not recall having been so distracted
from his prayers before. Whenever he knelt to share the
secrets of his soul with the God he adored, Duncan was
accustomed to a very special kind of experience, one he
had come to think of as perhaps unique to the race of the
Deryni. Every sensation of the body would retreat before
the sweet and overwhelming majesty of the Presence.
Duncan would, for however long he remained at prayer,
lose all but the most rudimentary contact with the mundane.

But tonight, though he tried, he could find no calm, no
special retreat. On this night above all others, such inner

agitation was a bad sign. Not that he didn't have reason
to be anxious, but still . . .

Duncan lifted his eyes wearily to the altar, which
glowed dimly, almost arcanely, in the only light available—Duncan's own solitary candle and the ruby shimmer
of the nearby Presence lamp—and shook his head.

"I don't understand," he whispered. "Why *now*? Why
at all, sweet Lord—but why now?"

He did not expect a graphic answer, such as Deryni
sometimes received if subtle use of their powers crept into
their worship, as it did with Duncan. He was, in fact,
relieved not to receive much more than the silence and a
hopeful feeling of being listened to. Duncan did not know
for certain if his nerves could have dealt with more than
that.

"They'll have to understand," he went on, resting his
damp forehead on the arms crossed before him on the altar
rail. "If we were just two people who fell in love under
normal circumstances, we wouldn't do this—You know
that! But it's gone beyond us. Almost too far beyond us
but—but . . ."

Duncan froze. There were footsteps outside the chapel,
dimly heard; he began to breathe again as the steps went
on past.

Just a guard. . . . It must have been just a guard. At this
hour on normal nights, Castle Culdi was heavy with sleep,
watched over only by the regular guards and the dreaming
stars above—but this was not a normal night. Duncan was
in a state approaching panic lest anyone find him here and
order him back to bed before the one he awaited could
arrive and their business be completed beyond the power
of others to interfere. Shuddering with the effort to calm
down, Duncan returned to his prayers—only to lose the
thread of them once more as he heard voices outside. Angry voices.

"It's insulting, that's what it is—bluidy impertinence!"

"He's a right to, Andrew," a second voice said placatingly. Duncan recognized them as the voices of his father's seneschal, Lord Deveril, and Andrew MacFergus, the household watch captain. "They've had a wrongful death—wouldn't matter if they were in the middle of the Anvil of the Lord, with nary a soul about for miles. They'd have a right to mourn their dead. Besides, His Grace gave them permission."

"It's bluidy eleven o' the clock!"

"His Grace gave them permission," Deveril repeated, a trifle less cordially. "I don't like it either."

"Too damn bad we aren't in the heart o' the desert," Andrew retorted, laughing unpleasantly. "Maybe there'd be a dust storm, an' the pipes'd seize up. Then there'd be nae problem!"

That's all you know about it, my friend, Duncan mused. *Pipes in the dead of night or no, there would still be a problem. . . .*

The footsteps and voices moved away, becoming ever fainter, replaced with silence. But very shortly there would be no silence, for a little while at least. The piper from Clan MacArdry had been killed fighting the Mearans—one of the first to die, they had said, conspicuous for his bright plaid and the sound of his pipes. He would not now be able to complete the teaching of his young apprentice—a sturdy lad of ten, still learning his craft. But every hour since the return of the clans early this morning, the boy had taken up a place on the walls of the castle, with Jared McLain's disgruntled approval, to skirl an ear-piercingly inaccurate but heartfelt dirge in honor of his clan's tanist, young Ardry MacArdry. Dead in the prime of his youth, killed by accident (his clansmen said murdered) in a tavern brawl over a serving wench. . . .

It did not matter that Jared, punctilious as always in his justice, had had the responsible McLain man tried on the spot and hanged. Earl Caulay MacArdry was not appeased. He had spent the whole day stamping about Castle Culdi, muttering ominous words about blood feuds and "damned uppity, murderin' bastards!" Men on both sides were all too ready to tussle at the drop of a border bonnet. Steel had been drawn with abandon already, and the sergeants had had their hands full to keep fights from breaking out afresh almost on the hour—hence, the reason the younger McLain laird prayed so desperately in the chapel, awaiting midnight and a far softer footfall than either Deveril or Andrew could ever make.

Duncan buried his face once more in the soft azure linen of his shirtsleeve and waited for the start of the untrained piper's woeful, sobbing lament. Each time he'd heard it, Duncan had been reminded how symbolic it seemed of what his once-orderly world had suddenly become—out of tune by a wee bit, some of the notes fumbled for, broken, misplaced but meant so lovingly. Love could mend all manner of things—at least that was what Duncan had been taught. Now he could only hope it would be able to mend even this terrible string of events.

Ready for it or no, Duncan nevertheless winced as the undignified squeal started up, that flattened-cat bawling which, for this piper, replaced the expected, spine-chilling opening drone a more experienced musician would have produced. There were a few solid, actually recognizable bars of music before the boy's fingers began to fumble over the more difficult first change, but Duncan could pick out the tune. It was the usually haunting "Lament for the Laird of Transha," penned many years before in honor of a MacArdry earl who had been much beloved of his people. That same laird was legendary among his folk, and everything from poems to prayers had been written in his memory.

Someone had even made up a dance and named it after that former MacArdry earl, for he apparently had been a jolly soul—Rantin' Aidan, he'd been called. The dance created in his memory was a happy one, in honor of the cheerful life he had led before his messy but heroic death. The MacArdrys tended to trot that dance out every chance they got—a stately strathspey, dignified but building subtly toward the brief, riotous reel that ended it. True to the visiting clan's reputation, "Aidan's Pride" had been danced right here at Culdi by request. Was it only a few short months ago, at the start of the summer, when Caulay had brought his folk here? Only then, with a banquet and a ball to celebrate their coming and toast the close ties of the Borderlands, which bade neighbors aid neighbors against common enemies?

Their precious dance became our dance, Duncan thought, mourning with the broken pipe tune for that long-dead Transha laird, for Ardry and his silly, fatal brawling, for the now-fatherless family of the man who was being called a murderer—mourning for himself and for Maryse MacArdry, the girl he had danced with, that first night.

His memories beckoned him over into a kind of half-miserable, half-hopeful day-dreaming about the night when he had learned there was more to life than books, scrolls, and pen nibs. While the music racketed on outside and the minutes ticked by toward midnight, Duncan McLain retreated weeks into his past through a prayerful Deryni trance as he struggled to understand this strange and wonderful summer, with the events that had brought him to this anxious pass. . . .

KEVIN McLAIN, THE young Earl of Kierney, appeared suddenly at his brother's side and dropped down onto the bench beside him, exhausted.

"Are you *still* nosing around in that old book?" he demanded, though it was obvious Duncan was in fact doing so. "You've scarcely moved from here all night!"

"The blazes I haven't," Duncan retorted mildly, glancing up with smiling blue eyes and taking in his brother's disheveled person. "I've danced with Mother and Bronwyn. As for not moving, I beg to differ with you. I've been out for a breath of fresh air twice."

"Yes, well, what a splendid lot of fun *you're* having, then!" Kevin mocked him cheerfully. He craned his neck to peer over Duncan's shoulder, trying to read the fine lines of script. "Must be a grand good book."

"Isn't," Duncan sighed. "I've never liked Livy. Talk about biased. And reading him direct from the Latin makes a mock of a perfectly good language, as far as I'm concerned. But I've got to do it sometime, so it may as well be got out of my way." He stuck a scrap of vellum into the book and closed it, half turning in his place to look at Kevin. "You seem to be having a good time."

"I'm fagged out," Kevin told him happily. "The MacArdrys may only be a little backwater clutch, but they certainly know how to have fun."

Duncan rolled his eyes ceilingward. There were times when he wondered just where his brother could possibly have picked up such a high-flown opinion of himself and everything connected with Clan McLain. A great clan they were, and a proud folk, with vast holdings and connections to some of the finest families in the Eleven Kingdoms. But Duke Jared himself displayed twice the understanding and thrice the diplomacy about such importance as did his eldest son and heir.

"I'm sure they'll be thrilled to know they have Your Highness's approval," Duncan murmured, his eyes twinkling. "Kevin, that arrogance of yours is going to make you burn in hell."

"Ahh, go on wi'you," Kevin retorted, giving Duncan a playful punch in the shoulder. "I'm harmless, and if you know that, so does God. Besides, you can pray me out of Purgatory when you're a priest."

Duncan cocked an eyebrow and said nothing, offering up only a quiet smile in reply. In any other late spring, he would have been still at school, preparing for the examinations he hoped would place him in the great university at Grecotha. But after a long, heartfelt talk with his teachers and a candid discussion of the facts of life

regarding Deryni—secret ones or no—with a certain ducal personage in Rhemuth, Duncan had decided to take
some time off to run through some extremely sobering
thoughts about his future. Just at this juncture, the future
of his plans for holy orders was suspended somewhere in
the realm of the nebulous hoped-for.

"I'd certainly try, anyway," he finally said, trying to
look doleful and world-weary. "But you've got a lot to
answer for, in the Hereafter."

"Silly twit," Kevin muttered, and wrestled the younger
boy off the bench onto the floor. He managed by sheer
force and superior size to pin Duncan to the wall beside
them. "Cry forfeit, sirrah!" he demanded.

Laughing, Duncan gave in and was released. As they
got to their feet and dusted off their finery, the two young
McLain lairds realized they were being watched indul-
gently from nearby.

"I had hoped someone would convince you to unwind
a bit, *bach*," Duchess Vera McLain murmured, joining
them to pluck a bit of rushes out of Kevin's brown hair
and tweak Duncan's rumpled plaid back onto his shoulder. "However, this wasn't quite what I had in mind!"

"I wouldn't have hurt him *too* badly, Mother," Kevin
said with wide-eyed innocence, an impression he immediately spoiled by grinning at the stepmother who had
raised him since toddlerhood, and given him Duncan as
the brother every man needs by his side. "I was just tired
of looking over here and seeing him flipping pages, rather
than treading measures!"

"So was I, darling," Vera told him. "Duncan, your father would like you to take a more active role in helping
to host our MacArdry guests this evening. Since you
won't be riding out with them on the day after tomorrow,
you'll be largely responsible for certain duties here at
home all summer. No one will know that, if you hibernate
in the corner with Livy."

Duncan made a face at the closed book. "Suetonius,"

he pleaded in the general direction of the ceiling, spreading his arms wide in a gesture of entreaty. "Why couldn't it have been Suetonius?"

"Why couldn't it have been Martial!" Kevin retorted. "His poetry to their history, anytime. C'mon, brother, let's go. There's got to be a pretty girl among those people somewhere, and you're not a priest yet!"

Duncan suffered himself to be led away, glancing over his shoulder at his mother as Kevin hauled him back toward the center of the hall. Vera only nodded, understanding all her son had not said—and would not have said to anyone, save either to the compassionate human father who tried to understand, or the Deryni mother who understood all too well.

It's all right, my dear, she whispered into Duncan's mind. *We've got all summer to sort things out. For now, just enjoy yourself!*

Duncan shrugged and went on. Enjoying himself—well, that might be a difficult prospect. He would a hundred times rather have been in Rhemuth at court in the company of his cousin Alaric Morgan—also Deryni, and now Duke of Corwyn. But there was no excuse for the Duke of Cassan's younger son to be at court without Jared himself present.

"Well—there you are!" Jared said jovially when Kevin had deposited Duncan at the foot of the dais where the duke and Laird Caulay MacArdry, the Earl of Transha, were seated in splendor before their two clans. "I'd about given you up for dead."

"No, sir, only hibernating," Duncan said politely, sidestepping the elbow Kevin directed at his ribs and managing to give his father a filial bow. "I pray you pardon me if I've seemed disinterested. I was wading through Livy."

"Ach, great God," Caulay MacArdry growled. "That's a divil of a thing to set a laddie like ye after. Ye'll no be bringin' those books wi' ye on campaign, I daresay!"

Duncan glanced at Jared; the duke nodded slightly. With permission to address the earl so given, Duncan bowed to Caulay.

"I'm afraid I won't be coming on campaign, my lord," he explained, "so the books will be staying behind with me as well."

"Not coming!" Caulay leaned forward, peering at Duncan with disconcerting directness. "Och, aye, I'd forgotten. Ye're the one that's t'be a priest, then. A fine calling, that—somewhat passing tame, but a fine calling."

"If God wants me for a priest, sir, I'll do my best to satisfy Him," Duncan said quietly.

"Well, then, for now ye'd do best to satisfy yerself," the earl roared, laughing. Duncan decided he had never seen such an unremittingly cheerful man in his life. The fellow reminded him of Father Christmas, all big and jolly. "There's dancin' to be done here, lad, and a son of McLain, even though he's to be a priest, mustn't bury himself under those foreign ancients so long as the music still plays an' there are pretty lassies wi'out partners to turn 'em!"

Laird Caulay rose from his seat and descended all three stairs of the dais with one great perfectly balanced step. Taking Duncan by the arm, he led the boy over to a small knot of ladies gathered around the end of a table of sweetmeats.

"I've brought ye a fine young fellow, my lasses," the earl announced as Duncan glanced back at his own father with an expression half-amused, half-resigned. Jared saluted him with a raised goblet, unmistakably commanding him to get on with the hosting duties Duncan would have to carry out all summer in his sire's absence. "Since no MacArdry girl should be partnerless when they dance 'Aidan's Pride,' I'll gie this McLain lordling over to my own daughter, and order the rest o' ye out after his clansmen!"

The girls giggled among themselves, whispering, then

broke away as if choreographed and went to find partners. This left Duncan blushing a trifle and weighed down by Caulay MacArdry's tree-trunk-like arm about his shoulders, facing the lovely, placid girl he remembered being introduced to earlier that day. She smiled at him, a sweet mixture of sympathy for his embarrassment and pleasure at the thought of dancing with someone other than brothers and cousins of her own.

"Her name's Maryse," Caulay said, pushing Duncan closer. "An' his name's Duncan," he announced to his daughter.

As Duncan bowed slightly in greeting and the silver-haired girl gave him a gravely polite curtsey in return, Caulay turned to bellow orders at the musicians.

"And the children here will head the set!" he finished, happily oblivious to the looks both Duncan and Maryse gave him behind his back.

"Have you ever danced 'Aidan's Pride' before, Laird Duncan?" Maryse MacArdry whispered in a clear sweet voice that made Duncan think irrationally of church bells.

He managed to swallow past a lump in his throat and shook his head.

"No, I'm afraid not, Lady Maryse," he said, matching her polite formality. "But since his lordship has given us the top of the set, perhaps you could talk me through it?"

"Of course," Maryse said, and smiled conspiratorially as Duncan took her hand and led her to the dance floor, nearest the musicians as custom required for the top of the set. "I think this is his idea of a jest. But I also think we can do him over and out—I saw you dancing with your cousin, my lord. We can be confident."

Duncan only nodded, unable to think of anything clever to say. He was a good dancer—he had felt called only to be a priest, not a hermit—and knew there probably wasn't a single figure in the dance he had not run across somewhere in a different piece. As Maryse talked him precisely through the measures, he could picture the whole dance

in his mind. When the music struck up and they bowed
to one another in the opening *reverence,* Duncan stepped
forward without hesitation to accept her hand for the beginning cross-and-cast. . . .

She was like a feather, Duncan thought, smiling and
staring blindly up at the glowing crucifix above the altar.
We were perfect together. Like mirrors, covering exactly—
never out of step, never off time. . . .

Laird Caulay had the grace to be pleased, even though
he had tried to see to it the McLains were outdone in that
precious MacArdry dance.

*Three times more that evening we danced—and then
the night was over, and I was so angry I'd wasted all that
time with Livy—stodgy, prejudiced Livy!*

He pounded a fist halfheartedly on the altar rail, still
smiling, his gaze transfixed by the gleaming gold of the
cross.

Her own father brought us together, he thought. *We
were made for one another, to mend the rift between our
families. I know we were. And marriage can be a kind of
special service to God. A sacrament of devotion—to
peace, to each other, to service in sweetness, all our days.
We could even name our first son Ardry, for her poor
ridiculous brother, and so the lost son would live
again. . . .*

Outside, the stumbling pipe music had halted. Duncan
shook himself mentally, trying to come back to the here
and now, trying to listen for the whispering softness of
Maryse's footsteps—for it was she whom he awaited in
the deserted chapel. It must be nearing midnight, the hour
they had agreed upon. Duncan could not be certain of how
much time had passed, but he had been here alone since
just after the eleventh hour.

They would have to be quick, once she arrived. Father
Anselm, the assistant to the McLain family chaplain, Father Lorcan, would be coming in shortly after midnight

to pray at Matins. Not too long after that, the household would be stirring in earnest, for Laird Caulay had roared his intention not to be under Jared McLain's roof for one moment longer than was absolutely necessary. They would be leaving, all of them, even Maryse—even after what she and Duncan planned to do here. But there would be time enough later to tell the two families of this night's work.

Duncan hauled himself up wearily to a more erect and respectful position. He did not want to be held sluggish in his prayers.

"Heavenly Father," he whispered, staring once again toward the altar, "forgive us for this subterfuge. But we cannot turn to any *but* You! No one else will listen to us—no one else could understand!"

He fumbled inside his shirt for the gilded silver crucifix he always wore, and as he did, he scratched the back of his hand on the lion-faced brooch that bound his plaid upon his shoulder. Biting his lower lip against the brief stab of pain, he rearranged his bright tartan and clutched both hands around the cross and its chain.

Duncan planned to give his brooch to Maryse, as a bridal token. If the world had not gone suddenly crazy and they were free to declare their love, he would have much preferred to give her the McLain crest ring he wore on the little finger of his left hand—but for now, the distinctive but innocent-looking brooch would have to do. She could wear that as his secret wife in far greater safety of keeping that secret than she ever could wearing his ring. Time enough for that later.

Thinking of the brooch and its new-won significance led Duncan inexorably back into the tugging compulsion of his heady memories—the memories that had been engulfing him all this long miserable day since the two clans had come home snapping and snarling at dawn, all too eager and ready to draw steel on one another for the least imagined cause. And even as he continued to pray with

an ever-increasing sense of urgency as midnight approached, his inner being tumbled headlong into the very
recent past as only a Deryni could so tumble, reliving
those moments with all their sweetness and pain. . . .

HE WAS SUPPOSED to be reading, working his way
through the long-term school assignments he had been
given to keep him occupied while he made his all-
important decisions about the future. Maryse was supposed to be embroidering, putting row after intricate row
of Border knotwork on a shirt she had made for him. And
after a fashion they were both doing just that—but in
another way they were not, for every so often they would
catch one another in a sidewise glance.

They shared the embarrassed laughter at being mutually
caught, and tried to get back to work. But it was hard, so
very hard. In the warm spring sunshine of this clearing
deep in the great Arduin Forest, after a delicious picnic
lunch and all the running about they had been doing in
the fresh air, it was difficult to imagine any other task but
daydreaming with and about one other.

After a while Duncan gave up the pretense of concentrating on the book he had brought along. Lying on his
stomach at Maryse's feet, a little to one side of her, he
rested his chin on his hands and gazed up at her, watching
her work. Her needle moved with precision, up and down
through the fine cambric with little, barely audible plops
as the design grew. Sleepy-faced McLain lions worked in
brown silk threads lounged among interlaced vines of
green and azure, highlighted with silver and sprouting the
occasional Cassani rose.

But it was not the exquisite handwork that had Duncan's attention. He had already seen it, admired it, told
her he could scarcely wait to wear it. He was much more
interested in Maryse herself, as exquisite a piece of crafts-
manship, he was ready to swear, as he had ever seen. He

decided he had never seen her look so beautiful, even dressed as she was in boys' clothes, the better to ride in— castoffs of Duncan's from the previous summer. He had grown only a little more than a handspan in height beyond the wearing of the tunic, hosen, and shirt. But his chest had deepened and his shoulders broadened just enough that his lady mother had given a jaundiced eye to almost all of Duncan's wardrobe before calling in the tailor.

It was not unusual to see a nobly-born lass in such garb. Duncan's own cousin, Bronwyn de Morgan, occasionally would dip into the clothes press where all their outgrown clothing was put for distribution to the poor, and wore either Duncan's hand-me-downs or Kevin's—but Duncan could not recall finding her beautiful in them. Cute, perhaps. But never so beautiful as Maryse looked now, even to having her silver-blond hair tied back with a ribbon, so it would not stir against her face in the breeze as she worked.

"I thought you were reading," Maryse murmured, glancing up from her work—but she did not look directly at the young man lounging beside her.

Duncan grinned. "I *am* reading. I'm reading the most beautiful lyric poetry ever written in all the world. You may think I'm looking at you, but I'm really reading such beautiful poetry that the Lord Llewellyn would want to set you to music. Have I told you within the past five minutes that I am in love with you?"

"Oh you," she demurred, turning to look at him. "You're impossible, did you know that?"

"Probably," he admitted, nodding. "In fact, very likely. But if I am impossible, then you have to be incredible. I mean it. You are absolutely the dearest, most beautiful person I know. I can hardly wait for our fathers to come home, so we can be married."

"We shall have to wait, nevertheless," she reminded him, blushing at his compliments. Something about that blush touched Duncan in a way he had not realized he *could* be touched, and his easy grin faded into something more contemplative as he watched her. From hairline to the gentle curve of her young bosom, just barely concealed by the open collar of the shirt, Maryse's skin was a pale, glowing pink, which deepened slightly as she realized the intensity of his gaze.

"Duncan—" she began, then broke off to stare at him in her turn. There was something about the look on his face, his blue eyes wide and back-lit by the love he felt for her, his smile wistful and set on slightly parted lips as if he had been about to speak—something Maryse was sure she would carry in her heart as a precious memory for the rest of her life.

"Duncan?" she repeated. "What is it?"

"I was just thinking of how I love the sound of your voice," he said softly, moving to sit next to her, their shoulders just touching. "Your Border accent on all those lowland words. You're beautiful all over. I love everything about you! Do you know what?"

She smiled at his enthusiasm and bent her head to return to her embroidery. "What?"

He gestured expansively. "I wish the summer would never end! That way, we could have every day like this forever."

"If the summer never ended," Maryse said practically, "our fathers would never get home from Meara—and we'd never be married."

"We could tell our mothers," he said, rolling over onto his back once more, putting his head in her lap so she could not work. He smiled up at her a little ruefully. "But then, I suppose you're right. Mothers are allowed to be sympathetic and advisory, but in the end it's one's father who gives permission."

"Then you'll be patient?"

"I'll have to be, won't I?" Duncan sat up just enough to take one of Maryse's hands and kissed the palm of it.

She could feel the warmth of his breath against her skin; smiling, she bent to brush his brown curls with her own kiss.

"You don't have to like it," she whispered. "But I'm afraid you do have to be patient."

Duncan lay back in her lap with an exaggerated sigh and closed his eyes. "Maryse—"

"Yes, my darling?"

"I want a daughter just like you," he said, slipping over into the daydreaming he had been doing so much of lately. "Will you do that for me? Give me a sweet little daughter, who's just like her mother in every way?"

"As soon as we are wed," she promised, "I shall do what I can to give you such a daughter. But when she is old enough to have a husband—whom you shall pick for her, of course, and whom I shall have to approve—you'll be lonely, and you'll hate the man who takes her away. Even though he'll be a perfectly nice young fellow."

"Nonsense," Duncan snorted. "He won't take her away. I'll give them the manor next door."

"I see. And what about sons? Don't you want sons? Most men do, you know."

"Of course I do," Duncan told her. "I want lots of sons. You can't have failed to notice that Clan McLain isn't exactly overblessed with males."

"You're enough for me," Maryse said, and kissed his forehead.

"Well, thank you," Duncan said, "but I'm afraid my lord father would reluctantly disagree with you." He spread his arms wide, as if he could with words alone people the clearing with the few McLain men in the immediate line. "My father was the only surviving son. Both my grandfather and my great-grandfather were sole surviving sons in their generations! And now there are only Kevin and I. Not what you'd call a horde."

Maryse's face became quite still, and she gazed at Duncan, her amber eyes wide. "If you had become a priest, only Laird Kevin would marry and have sons," she murmured. "Oh, Duncan—are you *certain* you'll not regret this?"

He sat up to take her into his arms, his expression grave. "I've told you already, Maryse, I'd already been having doubts about the rightness of taking holy orders before I met you. It *is* against the law of both the Church and the land for Deryni to do so—no matter how strong the calling. And even if those laws are wrong, it would still be wrong for *me* to flout them. It's rendering unto Caesar, I suppose."

"What if you had *not* met me?" she persisted, resting on his shoulder. "What then? Would you have flouted or rendered?"

Duncan smiled a little at her choice of phrasing. "I have a feeling I'd have flouted," he told her. "It's difficult to say just when I first realized it—but it seems a very long time ago that I felt my vocation. God alone knows how many Deryni have broken that law and kept their secrets over the years—and only God really knows if it's a sin for them to have done so. The Church certainly thinks so, and they've burned enough of us for it. But now you're here and we'll be married, so it's a sin I'll not have to worry over."

"Do you think they'd have found you out—the bishops and all?"

He shrugged. "Who knows? It's not the sort of thing one *could* hide forever, I suppose. Having powers with which to act makes it harder to stand by and do nothing. So mayhap this is God's way of letting me know this isn't the time yet for Deryni to be in the Church."

Duncan gave a crestfallen sigh, thinking of the sensations that came over him during Mass—watching Father Lorcan and Father Anselm handle the holy things, participating in the miracle that turned the mundane into the divine, and hoping that someday he, too, could stand where they stood within the magic circle of the chancel, in the nearer Presence of the Lord.

"There will be an answer to all this someday," he said at last, speaking as much to himself as to Maryse. "I know there will be."

"It isn't fair," Maryse sighed, hiding her face against his tunic. "You'd have been such a *good* priest—you're so good, so kind, and you know so much! And being Deryni—well, that'd probably have made you even more able to serve God that way. But no—they don't *want* Deryni priests, and they'd kill any they found! That's the real evil."

"I won't disagree with you," Duncan told her, smiling wistfully at her vehemence. "Look you, though—perhaps things will change one day. King Brion openly supports my cousin Alaric, and everybody knows Kevin will eventually marry Bronwyn—even if she *is* Deryni. Between the Morgans and the McLains, we aren't exactly talking about powerless families—and that's where change has to start, among the folk responsible for the keeping of the kingdom. Maybe I could even admit to what I am, now that there's no reason to keep the secret. In another generation there'll be two Deryni dukes, with a king who is their friend.

"And who can say how many other great families have Deryni blood in their lines? Maybe someday a son of ours can openly be ordained a priest, his blood and power no secret. That'll be enough for me—as long as I have you."

The diatribe had become sermon-like as he sat there beside her, his blue eyes glowing with the seldom-voiced hopes he held for his race. Maryse said nothing further, not wanting to cast clouds over their day; some of their discussions about his bypassed priesthood had gotten too heavy to be borne in happiness. Sensing the reason for her sudden silence, Duncan subsided, slumping down beside her once again, putting his head back in her lap.

"At any rate, that's old ground between us," he murmured, smiling. "We were talking of our future—the one we can be relatively certain of. Shall we have lots of children, Maryse?"

"Oh, of course," she laughed, gesturing airily. "We have to have lots of sons, and at least one daughter—though to be fair, I'd like to have one girl for every boy."

"We're having a family, not trying to make up an eight-couple dance set," Duncan teased her. She cuffed him playfully.

"Never mind, you," she retorted. "We'll have all sorts of nice, well-mannered Deryni children. And Kevin and Bronwyn will, also. They'll all grow up together, won't they?"

"Yes, and when Alaric gets married . . ." He paused, grinning. "Huh—fancy Alaric, so settled down!"

"Fancy *you* settled down, more belike," Maryse teased in return. "You were about to say that when he gets a wife, his children will be cousins and friends with ours, a whole family house full of beautiful, talented children. Everyone will be unable to help loving them—and they'll bring about a whole new future for all the Deryni people."

"God help us," Duncan whispered, rolling his eyes heavenward. He couldn't help snickering. "You're going to be *busy,* my love!"

"With all due respect, my lord," she replied, bending to kiss him on the tip of the nose, "*you* are going to be busy. *I* am going to be with child. Often."

"Tell me about it," Duncan pleaded, hugging her around the waist and burying his face in the folds of the old tunic, scented with her perfume and the sweet smell of the lavender she kept among her things. "Tell me what it will be like for us when we've married."

It was a question they had gotten in the habit of asking one another after the fashion of a game, over the course of time since they had realized their love was more than infatuation. And because Duncan would always be, in some secret part of him, priestly in nature, it had become a kind of replacement litany for the ones he now never expected to recite at the altar of God.

"We'll be married in St. Teilo's, and I shall wear the McLain nuptial crown with my veil," she recited dutifully, as Duncan closed his eyes and drifted easily into a light, aware trance, visualizing the scenes of which she spoke. "I shall be gowned all in white samite and silver tissue embroidered at the hems with McLain roses, and pipers will play for me as I come into the church. You will be there waiting for me in cloth of silver and sky-blue silk, and there will not be two happier people than you and I."

She spoke on, her voice low and soft. They would live at Uiskin in Cassan, she said, tending estates Duke Jared could not visit as often as he might wish, until the day when Kevin must take over the senior title. Then they would move down to the gentler climate of Kierney and care for things there, if Kevin and Bronwyn's eldest son were not yet of age to be earl. And no matter where they were—at King Brion's court or simply walking among the hills of home, everyone would say there were no people happier or more blessed in love than the Laird Duncan McLain and his own Lady Maryse.

In that quiet time Duncan discovered he was more in love than ever, listening as she became for him a kind of priestly being herself, celebrating their private mass of dedication with their own ceremonies and words of praise.

Marriage, he thought, *can be a kind of priesthood— can't it? Caring for one another as Christ Himself commanded—"Love one another, as I have loved you"—and wasn't marriage a stewardship, a using of time and talent, a fountain where one went to be refreshed from cares and the world, the better to serve again when called?*

And this Duncan knew was a priestly calling from which no prejudiced canon rule could call him to accounting or put him to death for daring to claim.

Enmeshed in the dreams, Duncan nevertheless came back to the real world with a start when Maryse tugged

a single strand of hair from his head. He woke and
touched a hand to hers, question in his eyes. Maryse
smiled down at him.

"Hello," she murmured. "Are they nice, these visions I
paint for us?"

"Splendid," he retorted. "Maybe I'll find a way to share
them with you someday. What are you doing to my hair?"

"You'll see," she responded mysteriously.

Duncan sat up a bit straighter, watching as she plucked
a much longer and lighter strand of her own silver-blond
hair and placed it beside his in her hand. She rose and
went to where their ponies had been left to wander at the
long end of their bridle ropes, cropping grass nearby on
the edges of the clearing. Maryse called to the animals in
her soft beckoning voice. They came to her readily—confused in their horsy way when she offered them no treat,
but only plucked a few hairs from the tail of each pony,
careful to keep them separate.

Returning, she knelt beside a wondering Duncan and
began to weave the little collection of hairs into a braid—
his pony's tail and hers, Duncan's hair, Maryse's hair.
When the little braid—defined in length by the shortest
strand, which happened to be Duncan's—was finished,
Maryse worked the ends together, intertwined to make a
ring big enough to fit the marriage finger of either of
them.

Duncan stared down at the simple band with its three
colors—black pony hairs, winding about one strand of
brown and one of silver, twining in and out of the design
like quicksilver.

"And what's this for?" he asked.

"Probably just a superstitious custom," she said, smiling calmly at his interest. "But you have to admit it's
uniquely ours."

She slipped the ring onto the third finger of his left
hand. Realizing what she was about to do, Duncan eased
himself to his knees beside her.

"I pledge myself to you," she whispered, looking Duncan in the eyes across their joined hands. "I promise that I, Maryse MacArdry of Transha, will marry you, Duncan McLain, at the nearest, most convenient time as can be arranged. And I further swear I shall do all in my power to make you a good wife, and be a good mother to your children. So help me God."

Duncan took the ring from his own finger, kissed it, and in his turn placed it on her third finger, left hand.

"I pledge myself likewise to you," he responded, reaching up briefly to brush away the tears that spilled over from her eyes. "I hereby promise that I, Duncan McLain of Cassan and Kierney, will marry you, Maryse MacArdry, as soon as can be arranged. And I further swear I shall be a good husband to you, and a good father to your children. So help me God."

He bowed his head over their entwined hands, his own eyes filling, blinding him with happiness. He kissed Maryse's slim fingers, one after the other. They embraced in the sunlight while, beside them, the ponies cropped their grass and the afternoon wore on. . . .

The memory brought fresh tears, happy tears, in spite of the revelations of the last few hours. Duncan felt inside his shirt cuff for a handkerchief, sighing when he realized he had forgotten to bring one in his haste for all to be as right as it could be, warring against the desire to be as inconspicuous as possible.

But then, a laugh just this side of hysterical escaped him, and Duncan buried his face in his shoulder plaid. Just how inconspicuous *could* the son of Jared of Cassan look, dressed in formal Border garb at midnight? A doublet of soft brown velvet embroidered with silver, the beautiful shirt Maryse had made for him—and eight yards of bright McLain tartan pleated about his body, pinned to his shoulder by the intricate brooch Maryse would shortly be wearing as the secret bride of a Deryni-born, Cassani-bred nobleman—scarcely an outfit chosen for a time of stealth and hopeful hurry.

Off in the distance Duncan heard the measured sound of bells tolling out the midnight hour. He stiffened momentarily, then grimaced at his own jumpiness. Of course. Those were the bells at Culdi Abbey, where the new abbot was all enthusiasm for the notion of upgrading standards. He had decided the resident religious of the abbey were a trifle lax, and so had ordered that all canonical hours were to be tolled five minutes early, to put everyone into the habit of getting to the sanctuary on time.

For Duncan's purposes, the early-ringing abbey bells were to be Maryse's signal. The guard changed at midnight, and though, under the circumstances, no one was likely to question the MacArdry's daughter having a desire to pray, if she were seen coming here, someone might get it into his head to suggest she would be safer praying in her own chamber.

But if she left that chamber just as the abbey bells finished tolling, she would make it to the corridor by the ducal chapel just after the early watch departed and the late watch went off the other way to secure the lower checkpoints. Then, just as the bells of St. Teilo's, hard by the outer wall of Castle Culdi, were ringing in the true midnight hour—if all had gone according to plan—Maryse would be here.

Duncan managed to get his laughter under control, but his smile did not fade. This was not the wedding he and his betrothed had imagined for themselves—not by a long shot. Kevin would not be standing by Duncan's side at the altar, nor would Alaric. One was in his bed, deeply asleep, exhausted from the long, miserable ride back from Meara, and the other—

Duncan allowed the image of his handsome blond cousin to form before his eyes, and his smile became wistful. Alaric would be in his bed at Court, dreaming appropriate dreams for a young Duke of Corwyn, serving the

king both as loyal vassal and as Deryni sorcerer. It was
not likely Alaric would be dreaming of what his cousin
was about to do! And there would be no splendid wedding
clothes, no rich ceremony, nothing that would call attention to the fact that anything out of the ordinary was happening—not yet.

But when the madness was over and Duncan and Maryse were married with all the trimmings in a real wedding,
it would all be different. They would have the nuptials
they had dreamed of, then. Jared would be there, proud
and magnificent, Duncan's first and most enduring hero.
His beloved mother Vera, his brother, both of his cousins,
all of Maryse's kin—they would be there. And maybe
even the king—and all the McLains, all the MacArdrys,
and—and. . . .

"And please, dear God, no more fighting between
them," Duncan breathed aloud, closing his eyes and letting the happy pictures form in his mind. A real wedding
day, a happy wedding day—better pipers playing than that
sad, unlearned boy on the battlements—and St. Teilo's
crammed to the vaulting with beautifully dressed guests.

"Gracious Father, let there be peace—let Maryse and
me bring them peace as our gift of thanks for the love
our families have given us as children, now that we've
become adults!"

That day, whenever it came, would be the time for
cloth-of-silver and the sweet odor of incense. That day
would be the day for priests and princes, for the joining
of two clans and greater hopes of stability in the borders.
But this night—this night was a time for secrecy and private sanctity, for two young people just barely grown to
show more sense than those who called themselves men.
A night for bowing before the only reliable, unshakably
trustworthy anchor in this awful storm of half-heard
threats and rumors of violence to come. A night for Maryse MacArdry and Duncan McLain to give themselves to
God, and let Him make of them one flesh, forever.

Soon she would be here. Duncan rose from his prayers,

reaching down automatically to smooth the soft velvet of his doublet, with a quick look to be sure the sett of his plaid was correct—everything must be as special as he could possibly make it, until that wonderful day when he could *really* make it all right. He was a McLain, of the lords of Kierney and Cassan—and through his mother, a Corwyn of that ancient and great Deryni line—and he dared anyone to say this would not be a fit and proper union, nevertheless!

Bowing apologetically toward the altar for that moment of defiant pride, Duncan made himself comfortable in the front chair back from the rail and clasped his hands between his knees, waiting. His mind wandered, and he found himself gazing at the little roses and lions Maryse had embroidered on his shirt cuff. It made him think of the huge heraldic arras mounted on the wall, downstairs in the great hall—the one behind which he and Maryse had hidden, holding their breaths, waiting—had it only been a few hours before? It felt like years, many long years. . . .

"It's a' the fault o' yer damned, brawlin', undisciplined kin!" Caulay MacArdry had roared, his accent coming even thicker than was his wont for all the pain in him. "Me boy—m'fine, braw boy lies dead! An' ye prate of lettin' be! Let *be*!" The Earl of Transha uttered an inarticulate roar of incredible, angry grief. "You'd nae be speakin' so, were it a bairn o'yer own—so God's me witness, Duke of Cassan!"

Hiding behind that arras, holding Maryse's hand in his so tight it was a wonder she still had circulation, Duncan McLain winced. He had never heard so proud and exalted a title made to sound, by mere inflection, as if it were the worst of vile insults. He waited, scarcely daring to breathe, for the explosion that was sure to follow such an outburst. Jared was a man of incredible patience, Duncan knew, but the entire household was so tense that the very air in Castle Culdi felt about to explode like a poorly set Deryni spell. The duke could only take so much. Saint

Teilo himself could scarcely have been expected not to turn berserker!

Low, controlled, impossibly even, Jared's voice cut across the heavy silence.

"I fully expect to hear in your next breath that the justice which has been done is not enough," His Grace of Cassan said. It was difficult to read any kind of emotion into that cold, exact tone. That was the McLain's way, in anger, in politic handling of a bad situation with no clear solution. Duncan could imagine him standing there with hands clenched into fists, those fists resting on his hips as he stared back at his grieving neighbor, enduring the unfair accusations that grief had made Caulay make. Blue eyes hard and glittering as midwinter ice, a look of uncompromising control on the handsome face—that whole appearance and aura Jared exuded at times like this, a sensation of severe and princely patience neither Duncan nor Kevin had ever been able to look in the eye; a Jared so different, all one could rationally do was beg forgiveness and hope he would soon return to normal. Duncan felt a stab of pity for Laird Caulay, but suspected even the Duke of Cassan at his least sociable would fail to penetrate the pain of losing a son so senselessly.

"Would you have me deliver up one of *my* sons for your killing?" Jared went on—and Maryse clutched harder at Duncan's hand, her fingernails cutting into his palm. "Or would you rather pursue this notion of a blood feud—which would have the same result in the end? Caulay, for the love of God, be reasonable! Will more killing bring Ardry back from the dead? I beg you—let be! The man who killed him has been himself put to death. Your son, though not wed or a father, will still be wept over by a woman and children—my man *had* a family, and they are now fatherless. Why can that not be enough for you?"

"Because," Caulay said, his voice now as low and as cold as Jared's—but throbbing with such an intensity of anguish that Duncan turned and hid his face against Maryse's shoulder, unable to bear that anguish battering against his Deryni sensitivity—"because m'son *is* dead, and as ye say, I canna hae him back. Because I willna forget, tae th'end o' me days, 'twas a McLain what killed him. Border blood, Cassan, spilled by Border hand. Low-lander though ye look tae be, moreso wi' every season ye spend at the Haldane's court, e'en ye canna forget that memory runs long in th' hills."

"You have my sympathy then, for all your blindness," Jared said, sighing. "But mark my words—if you come back to the territory of the McLains with armed men, seeking retribution where it's already been made, we will give you such a fight as to be sure the hills will never be able to forget. For if there's one thing I cannot abide, it's a man with a head on his shoulders refusing to use it."

"We canna let them do this!" Maryse said in a hissing whisper, her breath soft against Duncan's cheek. He raised his head with some difficulty and gazed blearily at her in the dim light, there in the crawl space behind the arras.

"What can we possibly do to stop them?" he whispered back. "Walk out between two armies of our kinfolk, beg them to stop, get killed, and fuel the fire?"

Maryse laid a finger across his lips. They heard the sounds of footsteps and receding voices; their fathers were leaving the hall still arguing, their aides following close behind, doubtless glaring suspiciously at one another. Maryse peeked around the side of the ornate wall-hanging; the room was clear in moments, and she stepped out into the brighter light of the hall, pulling Duncan after her.

"Are you all right?" she asked quietly, peering into his face with concern. "You look terrible!"

"I can imagine." Duncan swallowed hard. How many times had his mother warned him about his shields? How many times had she told him the power of emotions—especially human ones, where there was no conscious recognition of the need to be in control of such things? Too many times to count.

Duncan covered his face, pressing the heels of his

hands into his eyes. Quickly he applied a Deryni spell to banish the fatigue that was washing over him and raised his shields just enough to bolster against the undirected anxiety floating about the house.

"Don't worry," he told Maryse somewhat tardily, with a sheepish smile. "It'll pass in just a moment."

"And the priests say being Deryni is a thing of the devil," Maryse snorted, with some heat. "Fine lot of good it'd do a person, to belong to the devil and get no benefit of it."

"Never mind that," Duncan told her, taking her by the hand to lead her out of the hall and into the corridor. Putting a finger to his lips, he motioned her to silence. He chanced a quick look around the doorpost, then hurried to the stairs, taking Maryse halfway up before she stopped him. They flattened themselves against the wall.

"It's certain the devils are at work in this house, and not because there're Deryni here," Duncan whispered, gazing at her with miserable eyes. "There's nothing we can do to stop them, if our fathers get involved in a blood feud—and you know what happens to our chances of ever getting married, in that case!"

"But don't you see?" Maryse insisted, taking Duncan by both hands, clutching insistently at him as she looked up, her little face set and fierce. "That's just it! If we *were* married, there'd be no need for feuding. They'd be kin— far deeper kin than the neighbor bonds of the borders!"

Duncan pondered this in silence. Was there a chance— even a slim one—that if the suggestion were offered, it would forestall the feud? Caulay had lost a son—that was true. But wasn't giving one's daughter in marriage never so much the losing of that daughter, but the gaining of a son? A son lost, a son gained, and no need for a feud . . . ?

"And it isn't as if *my* father would be losing nothing and gaining all," Duncan whispered, continuing his thoughts aloud. "After all—he had planned on having a son in the Church—though he's said, time and again, that the choice was mine."

"The Duke of Cassan can surely spare the benefits to be had from a son high-placed in the Church," Maryse said, with curious impatience. She tugged urgently at Duncan's sleeve. "Do you think it would work? Could you talk to your father?"

Duncan made a face. He gave the notion a thought then discarded it, shaking his head reluctantly. "Did he sound like a man in a mood to listen?"

Maryse sighed and shook her head. "Neither of them did."

The two stood there in silence, desperate, riding the edge of panic and trying not to fall over into complete despair. Duncan suddenly dropped Maryse's hands and pulled her into his arms, embracing her with a fervor he scarcely knew he possessed.

"I *cannot* lose you!" he whispered. "I just can't. And I won't. This is ridiculous! Can't they see—haven't they got the faintest idea. . . ."

"Duncan!" Maryse pulled back from him. Her eyes were wet with tears—but she was smiling. "That's just it. Can't they see? Of course not—they haven't been here all these weeks! But our mothers can. Surely it can't have escaped *everyone's* notice, that we're in love!"

For a moment the faintest glimmer of hope, the smallest suggestion that there was some logic in the world after all, crept back into Duncan's face. Of course some had noticed. Bronwyn had seen them kissing just the other day, standing between their ponies in the yard, where they thought themselves safe from prying eyes—but Bron had been in an upstairs window. She'd mentioned what she had seen, and Duncan blessed her for a sense far beyond her years—for it had not been with preadolescent teasing. Rather, there had been a curiously adult sympathy, mixed with a healthy dollop of her sisterly romanticism, when she had flung her arms about him and joyfully shared the secret.

"I think it's wonderful! Oh, Duncan, I *do* love her so

much—I never had a sister before! It'll be so sweet—so romantic!"

He had given her a chaste kiss on the forehead, and in great relief swore her to secrecy—but now, as he thought about it, there were many others in this castle far more observant than dear little Bronwyn. Surely someone else must have noticed—if not two rather indulgent mothers, then why not a serving maid or a waiting woman? It was just possible. . . .

"My mother might see the merit in it," Duncan said very quietly. "But Maryse—my mother is not in mourning for the death of a son."

Maryse's face fell. The tears started afresh, this time for the older brother she had so idolized—and who had all unwittingly, by his regrettable liking for the ladies, wounded the hopes of future happiness for his little sister. A happiness Maryse felt certain he would have more than approved of, were he still alive and none of this nightmare happening; but he was not, and the nightmare grew more terrible with every passing hour.

"What shall we do, then?" she asked, resting her cheek against Duncan's shoulder. "Oh God, what *are* we going to do!"

"First of all, we are *not* going to panic," Duncan told her firmly, a desire to protect her welling up in him as her tears trickled down his neck. "There's got to be *something* we can do—and we'll figure it out."

"W-we could wait until it all blew over," she sniffled. "It might only take a little while—a y-year, perhaps. . . ."

Duncan actually blanched at the thought of enduring a year—possibly longer—in silence. Maryse apparently didn't like the sound of her own suggestion either, for she uttered a little strangled sound of agony and hid her face deeper in the folds of his shoulder plaid. The sad, tiny sound bounced off the old stone of the stairwell, and hearing it echo was more than Duncan was willing to bear in patience.

"We're not going to wait," he said, trying to sound

resolute—but in fact scaring himself with his own sudden presumption. "We're both of an age to make up our own minds. We've made them up to be married and exchanged our own promises. If those promises really mean a thing to either of us—well, this is the time to follow through with them. If we cannot, then we mustn't have been serious."

She slowly raised her head to stare at him, her amber eyes moist and confused. "What are you saying?"

Duncan swallowed audibly. "I'm saying we should get married," he said, his boy's voice failing him behind the adult words. Blushing, he cleared his throat. "Tonight. Before this foolishness can go any further, we ought to just get married."

Maryse's eyes widened in astonishment and hope. She glanced guiltily up the stairs, then looked back at Duncan.

"Can we do that?" she whispered, half scandalized and half giddy with the daring of it. "Who would marry us? Your father's priest or mine? Which of them would be more likely to consent, under the circumstances?"

Duncan licked at lips that were suddenly quite dry. His eyes were pale with nervousness as he stared blindly over her shoulder, peopling the blank wall with a scene of every possible reaction, once this mad, wonderful deed should become known. Bishop Bradene, the master of Grecotha and one of those certain that Duncan would someday make a splendid priest. King Brion. Alaric. Two pairs of parents. Kevin, Bronwyn, the whole spectrum of McLains, MacArdrys, and all the families tied into each clan. . . .

"We don't need a priest," he whispered hoarsely, his heart doing a slow, sickening roll at the uttering of such a sentence. "Since we'll be properly wed later on, when they know and can't do anything about it, we won't need a priest tonight. I was only just reading about it this past term—I had a session on canon law."

"That canna be right!" Maryse protested weakly, her expression of hope wilting as she began to suspect despair had unseated the reason of her young beloved. "No priest? How could we be truly married without one?"

"It's called *per verba de praesenti*," he told her, the Latin phrase sounding reassuringly authoritative. "A vow spoken before witnesses. It's got the same force as a wedding before a priest—though it has to be truly consecrated later. Folk up in the hills do it all the time, in places where there's not a regular priest and they have to wait until one rides through."

"Who can we have as a witness?" Maryse asked, suddenly all practicality. "And where and when ought we to do this? It's got to be tonight, true—but where?"

"The only witness I can think of who'd be sure not to tell is Bronwyn." Duncan sighed. "And she'll never do— she's not of age, so she can't be called to testify for us."

Maryse looked at him oddly. For a young man who had just shot down their only choice for a discreet witness, Duncan did not sound like someone at the end of his hopes.

"What are you thinking?" she asked, taking his chin in hand and making him look at her. "You have the strangest look on your face—like you were just staring at angels."

Duncan brought himself back to reality with some difficulty. His face was terribly still, his eyes backlit by a kind of incredible hope; he placed his hands on Maryse's shoulders.

"That's what comes of having as a betrothed someone who's studied to be a priest," he said, a slight smile finally coming to his lips, making him look a bit less strange. "We'll marry one another in the ducal chapel—midnight's probably best, it's a special, holy hour anyway, and the witness will be there waiting. For that matter, He's there now—He always is, that's what makes Him so exactly right."

Maryse could hear the capitalized letters in his words. "God—as a witness?"

He gripped her shoulders more tightly, giving Maryse an affectionate little shake.

"Don't you see, Maryse?" he insisted. "God is the only one we *can* trust. He'll never betray us, He's completely outside the squabble between our fathers, He grieves for both of the deaths that threaten us, even as we do. We'll exchange our vows before Him, in the presence of the consecrated Host stored on the altar—and by all the saints, Maryse, there's no better, higher Witness in all the Eleven Kingdoms we could call!"

He smiled suddenly. "Besides—who could possibly say God had lied, to say we were well and truly married?"

Maryse punched him in the shoulder. "Who could call Him to the account?" she demanded. "Don't run the risk of blasphemy, Duncan, please!"

"I'm sorry. I'll be properly penitent—just as soon as I stop feeling so giddy." But he did sober up, in the next heartbeat. "So, what say you, Maryse MacArdry? Will you marry me tonight at midnight, in my father's chapel, with none present save ourselves and the one Father we can depend on not to pull us apart?"

"I will," she said simply, quietly, her words more mouthed than spoken, so soft he could barely hear her. "But—when they find out, won't they have us annulled?"

"They'll not be able to, if the marriage is consummated," Duncan said, amazing himself by getting the words out so calmly and unhesitatingly that it seemed less the tremendous emotional implication that it was, and more the rational contemplation of two adults in love, awaiting their marriage.

Maryse blushed, her fair skin going pink from the bosom of her gown to her hairline. "Oh."

Duncan kissed her on the lips tenderly, calmly, giving no hint at all that his heart was racing. It was madness, what they were going to do—madness and therefore love, love and therefore holy.

What would his parents say? What would they think at school, at court? Would the king approve? Would *God* approve? Madness. Sheer, wonderful madness!

"You'd best be getting back to your mother before

you're missed," Duncan told her, nevertheless embracing her as if he never meant to let her go. "The guard changes at midnight, and they check the corridor near the chapel first. So start out from your chamber when you hear the bells at the abbey ringing out the hour—they always chime five minutes ahead. By the time you get to the chapel, the guards will have gone. I'll be waiting."

"It won't quite be the wedding we imagined, will it?" Maryse said quietly, feeling only a slight twinge, sharing as she did with Duncan a strange maturity that seemed to have crept into them over just the last few minutes. "All furtive at midnight, with nobody around save ourselves and the good Lord."

"I will make it up to you—I swear I will," Duncan declared. "For now, we'll just have to think of it as a sacrifice toward the sanity of our loved ones. But as soon as it seems right to tell them—as soon as things are calm enough that we don't provoke more nonsense in the telling of it—everything will be just fine. . . . We'll have our pipers, our kinfolk, and all the things we dreamed of."

His apparent confidence was infectious. Maryse was smiling as she rounded the top of the stairs and kissed her fingertips to him. She never saw Duncan lean up against the wall of the stairwell, letting out a held-in breath of anxious relief, closing his eyes the better to find some kind of calm in this quite mad world. There was no way to tell what manner of storm they might provoke by taking this drastic step.

All Duncan knew—and suspected Maryse shared—was the name and the power of the storm they had unleashed in themselves. And any bard could have told them what they already knew: Love had a habit—indeed a reputation—of not always being a gentle spring rain. . . .

The bells at St. Teilo's had just begun to ring out for the true midnight hour when Duncan sensed more than heard the approach of Maryse's soft footsteps outside the chapel. His breath caught in his throat. With a pleading, anxious glance toward the altar, he scrambled to his feet

and hurried to the huge carved door. Maryse's presence
was readily detected by nerve-heightened Deryni senses,
and Duncan called her name softly as he pulled the un-
locked door open to the right.

She stood there framed by the dim light in the corridor,
gowned in pink. About her neck she wore a *shiral* the
size of an almond, hanging from a fine leather cord. Her
silver-blond hair was bound back off her forehead by a
metal circlet decorated with little, intricately worked flowers, and each flower had as its center a tiny golden gem,
just the color of Maryse's eyes. Those eyes stared back
at Duncan with a combination of nervousness and defiance as he took her by the hand and drew her into the
deeper dimness of the chapel narthex. Together they silently closed the door.

In the flickering glow of the ruby and sapphire votives
banked to either side of the doorway, Duncan enfolded
Maryse into an embrace, giving her a quick, reassuring
hug before holding her off at arms' length to search her
pale face.

"If you listen hard enough, you can almost hear the
pipers," he whispered. "It takes even less imagination to
realize we're making the only rational response to this
terrible situation. Are you ready?"

"Aye," she replied, a faint, hopeful smile coming to her
lips. "Let us go up to the altar—we oughtn't to keep our
Witness waiting."

Duncan swallowed hard and nodded, doing his best to
prevent her from seeing just how anxious he was—how
fearful that despite all their care something would still go
amiss. He suspected that Maryse, too, was hiding similar
worries.

Following a day of misery and an evening of reflection,
the unexpected finish of a springtime of learning and love,
it had all come down to this—the time to prove that love
was the brightest flame in this dreary world, just as the
bards said. It would mend the loneliness in two young
lives, and unite two Border families—but more, it would

stifle the likelihood of a blood feud and all the terrible
ramifications of such a thing. Duncan felt a sense of peace
beginning to well up inside him; he reached for Maryse's
hand once more.

"We will be so happy, you and I," he told her, his gaze
straying back to the waiting altar, to the golden crucifix,
to the crimson splash of light that was the symbol of the
Presence they were about to approach. "A short while of
parting, a little more of working things out—then forever,
and the making of all our daydreams."

"Peace, love, and children," she murmured, nodding.
"Yes—we're going to be very happy."

She gave Duncan's hand a squeeze. Solemnly they
paced the aisle together, their footsteps silent on the thick
Kheldish carpeting. They made their obeisance to the altar
and knelt, bowing their heads to pray privately.

Duncan's prayers did not take long. He had made most
of his petitions already, in the hour he had spent here
alone. He offered up a heartfelt entreaty for assurance they
were doing the right thing, then signed a cross upon his
chest and waited until it seemed Maryse might be finished
with her own devotions. After a moment or two he cleared
his throat and fastened his eyes on the Presence lamp with
almost blind intensity. This was the hour of commitment—
the start of the dream, the first step toward a return to
peace.

May all their strife be put to rest in our love, he
thought. *God's will be done.*

He reached up to unclasp the stiff pin backing his
brooch, and worked it free of the bright tartan folds. It
felt light but tingling with portent in his hand, and Duncan
thought, *Like the protection of God, it weighs nothing, yet
means all. . . .*

He turned solemnly to begin the words of love and
binding. One flesh forever, protected by the love of God
and made braver thereby—one could do worse than face
the future so. It was impossible to know what that future
would hold—but at this moment such was not their con-

cern. It was all in the hands of Fate, waiting on the will of the good Lord.

Deo volente, Duncan thought, and turned to take in his the hand of the woman he loved.

※

DHUGAL AT COURT
1116

As frequently happens, the author of this next story became caught up in a possible back-story regarding an incident to which I'd only alluded in passing—in this case, a childhood recollection of Dhugal MacArdry, who became such a close friend of young King Kelson. Again, the author herself speaks most eloquently of how her story came to be written:

"I was home from college for Thanksgiving weekend in 1984 when I discovered *The Bishop's Heir* on the shelf of a local bookstore. Delighted to find a new and unexpected Deryni book, I took it home immediately and devoured it. I particularly liked Dhugal and having another character near Kelson's own age to complement the adult characters introduced in the first Kelson trilogy.

"The scene that really sparked my imagination for this story was the scene in the royal crypt when Dhugal remembered King Brion's kindness to him after he'd dropped the full platter of pheasants the first time he'd served the High Table. I wanted to know more about that particular incident. A small boy carrying a very large, heavy tray of food sounded like an accident waiting to happen. So how was Dhugal entrusted with it? Was it the oversight of a moment in a hectic, crowded kitchen, or was something else going on?

" 'Therein lies a tale,' I thought. The questions and ideas would not leave me alone, and I finally wrote the

original version of 'Dhugal at Court' during the summer
of 1985. At that point, I had never been to a convention,
had no idea that *Deryni Archives: The Magazine* even
existed, or that it had ever occurred to other fans to write
a Deryni fan fiction story. The thought of meeting Katherine in person then seemed about as likely as a private
audience with the Pope. I just kept thinking guiltily as I
wrote, 'Is this *okay?* Can I actually *do* this without the
copyright violation police coming to cart me off?' I was
having far too much fun writing the story to stop writing,
though.

"In 1997, I discovered via the alt.books.deryni news-
group that Julianne Toomey had inherited the editorship
of *Deryni Archives.* In the intervening years, I had taken
several creative writing classes at Foothill College from a
marvelous teacher, Laura Schiff, who is sadly no longer
with us. I thought 'Dhugal at Court' would make a good
contribution to the fanzine and dug it out of my files. I
still liked it very much even after not looking at it for
more than a decade, and after all the writing techniques I
had learned from Laura. I still rewrote and polished it
extensively until it reached its present form, although the
basic story remained the same. The dogs in the climactic
scene came running into the story without my consciously
having whistled for them. Once they were there, it was
one of those 'of course' moments. No self-respecting dog
would lie politely under a table with a dozen roast pheasants splattered all over the floor within easy reach."

DHUGAL AT COURT

✣

Melissa Houle

THE LORD CHAMBERLAIN of Rhemuth Castle pounded the floor with his great staff. "My lords and ladies, Their Majesties, King Brion and Queen Jehana, and His Royal Highness, The Prince Kelson!"

Crowded at the back of the great hall with his father and older brother, Dhugal MacArdry knelt at once, but cautiously lifted his freckled face to watch. The king and queen cast everyone who had gone before them completely in the shade. Dressed alike in scarlet, gold, and brilliant white, with ornate jeweled crowns on their heads, they were everything that was regal and splendid.

But it was Prince Kelson who caught and held Dhugal's attention. In Dhugal's world, everyone of any importance was an adult, so he'd assumed the Crown Prince of Gwynedd must be a grown man, too. But the prince was just a boy; and no more than a year or two older than Dhugal, at that. Dhugal straightened on his knees and craned his neck for a better look as the prince passed. He stared at Kelson's rich scarlet silk tunic and the silver coronet on his head until a jerk on his wrist yanked him down again.

His father glared a warning and even his brother, Michael, scowled at him. Dhugal knew that only the nobility kneeling around them had saved him from a box on the ear.

He curled down in shame. He'd been staring at the prince as if he had no more wit than Wat, the simpleminded shepherd boy.

I'll never make a good page, Dhugal thought miserably.

He wasn't happy about becoming a page at King Brion's court, but he hadn't been asked if he wanted to do it. The children of Lord Caulay MacArdry, Chief of Clan MacArdry and Earl of Transha, were expected to do their duty. He would remain a page until he was eleven or twelve, when he would be promoted to the rank of squire.

After that, he'd be assigned to the service of a knight until his own knighting at eighteen. But he'd have to earn both of those promotions; nothing would be given to him. Dhugal dared not fail or he'd disappoint everyone at home, from his father down to the kitchen maids and stableboys. His disgrace would be the more absolute for being the chief's son. Respect, like rank, had to be earned.

Ten years, Dhugal thought and couldn't suppress a sigh. The decade of lowland service stretched before him like a prison sentence. It was actually a little longer than ten years, since he wouldn't be eight until early in the New Year.

Christmas Court dragged for Dhugal. He couldn't see or hear anything that went on in the hall, as all activity was centered at the far end. He was also hemmed in by adults against one of the huge pillars that supported the roof high above everyone's head.

"Wake up, boy!" Caulay muttered in his ear, giving his arm a shake. "Th' pages go forward next. Hurry now, or they'll leave ye behind!"

Dhugal scuttled through the crowd and stepped into the very last place in the double line of new pages, and marched forward with them. With his view of the great hall now unimpeded, he stared up and around in amaze-

ment. It was twice as high and wide as the great hall of
Castle Transha, and at least three times as long. A red
carpet runner lay like a woolen road over the middle of
the stone floor, leading straight to the royal dais and the
two canopied thrones. They looked an intimidating distance away.

To either side of the central aisle, Dhugal saw richly
dressed men and women against a background of tapes-
tries, evergreen garlands, and burning torches. Far over-
head, he saw heraldic banners hanging from hammered
wooden beams. A green gryphon surrounded by an embroidered gold bordure on a black silk background caught
Dhugal's eye in particular. He wondered which family
that one represented.

"Boy!" a woman's voice whispered urgently. She
waved a beringed hand toward the front of the hall. "The
other pages will take their oaths without you, if you don't
hurry!"

Dhugal woke up and, realizing he was alone, galloped
after the others now lining up before the dais steps. He
came to an undignified stop beside them, although at least
he remembered to bow this time.

He straightened, wondering if anyone had noticed, only
to meet Prince Nigel's fierce gray glare. He was the only
boy standing upright in a row of bowed backs.

Dhugal went down again as if hinged at the waist. He
didn't dare look up again. He wondered if the prince
would have him arrested and marched off in chains in
front of everyone. Next to disgracing the Clan like *that,*
failing in his duty was almost good.

"Kneel," Prince Nigel commanded.

Dhugal dropped to his knees with the others, then cautiously lifted his head. For the first time, he dared look
up at the king. His Majesty was surveying the pages lined
up before him, one hand stroking his black beard and
mustache.

Dhugal looked down again. He couldn't be sure, but he

thought the king *might* have been concealing a smile behind his hand.

After Dhugal had recited his page's oath in unison with
the other boys and had received his scarlet leather page's
livery, he was free to study the royal family on the dais
again. The king and queen sat on their matched thrones
while they watched Prince Nigel and occasionally leaned
over to speak to one another in low tones. Prince Nigel's
wife sat with her two sons off to the left of the queen's
throne.

Dhugal quickly looked away from them after he saw
the older of the two boys watching him with amused contempt. Instead, he turned his gaze on Prince Kelson, sitting on a carved wooden bench to the right of his father's
throne. The crown prince looked to be a very grand young
person sitting there, but not haughty. He studied the row
of new pages with his face full of friendly curiosity. When
his gray eyes met Dhugal's amber ones, Prince Kelson
grinned.

Dhugal immediately grinned back, forgetting for the
moment the vast gulf of rank that separated a minor Border earl's second son from the Crown Prince of Gwynedd.
He knew a friend when he saw one. They were too far
apart to speak, though. All too soon, Dhugal had to return
to the back of the hall with the other new pages.

HOURS LATER, DHUGAL leaned against a pillar at
the side of the great hall and yawned wide enough to
make his chin wobble. It was now so late that even the
privilege of being up past his bedtime had lost its charm.
He had to wait, though, while his father talked to yet
another of his neighbor lords. At least Dhugal could see
much more of the hall, now that the crowd had thinned.

What he'd seen of tonight's entertainment had been
viewed in slivers between adult backs. Every now and
then, a juggler had tossed a ball, hoop, or flaming torch
high enough to be seen over adult heads, or an acrobat

had balanced on the shoulders of another, but that had been all. Evidently, the short and unimportant people at Court missed a lot of entertainment.

Dhugal dug his knuckles into his eyes and rubbed them to stay awake, yawning again. He shifted around the pillar to avoid the smoke from a burning torch over his head, then gasped. Prince Kelson sat on the side steps of the royal dais, scarcely ten paces away.

Dhugal stared harder when he realized the prince was talking to Morgan. Dhugal's father had pointed out the tall, fair-haired duke earlier that evening with the express warning that Dhugal was *never* to annoy him, for Morgan was Deryni.

Dhugal was far too curious to look away, although he knew that eavesdropping and spying were inexcusably rude. He'd never seen a Deryni before in his life. His father's warning put Morgan in almost the same danger category as wolves and bears.

Morgan looked disappointingly undangerous right now, however. He sat casually on the steps beside the prince, his ducal coronet lying beside his feet. He listened to Kelson with respectful attention, as if the boy were his own age. Dhugal couldn't hear Kelson's voice, but the conclusion of his story made Morgan throw back his head and laugh. The prince looked pleased and proud and not at all frightened of Morgan.

Then both Kelson and Morgan jumped to their feet at the queen's approach. She set her slender hands on Kelson's shoulders and glared at Morgan, ignoring his bow. Dhugal strained, but still couldn't hear them. The queen and then Morgan looked angry.

Morgan bowed again, although this time his salute was directed at Kelson, then scooped up his coronet, and left in a swirl of black and green court robes. When he was gone, the queen turned Kelson to face her, one hand under his chin. He listened to her with a face full of mutiny. She seized his arm and pulled him up the dais steps with her, still scolding him as they went.

Another huge yawn blinded Dhugal, though he wanted
to keep watching.

"Och, if I dinnae get this laddie to bed, he'll spend the
night here with the castle garrison!" Caulay announced in
Dhugal's ear, making him jump. "We'll talk more on this
matter tomorrow, Laird Erskine."

Dhugal yawned and stumbled all the way back to their
rooms, but once he was tucked into his cot, he was no
longer so drowsy. He caught his father's sleeve with one
hand when Caulay started to turn away.

"Da, do ye think Prince Kelson would ever play with
me?"

Caulay settled back on the edge of Dhugal's cot and
took his hand. His face was serious and kind, and Dhugal's heart sank. It was the way his father always looked
when he had something unpleasant to explain.

"Dinnae expect to see much o' the prince, Dhugal,"
Caulay began slowly. "There's a great difference between
the son o' a Border earl and the Crown Prince o' Gwynedd. His Highness does nae take his lessons in the
schoolroom with the ordinary pages, an' I'll warrant His
Majesty controls whom the prince befriends."

"*I* know," Dhugal argued. "But His Highness must be
allowed to play with other boys *sometimes.*"

"Aye," Caulay agreed. "He's no prisoner. But His
Highness's days are planned to the last hour, an' everything he does is watched. Everyone at Court has ideas
about how their future king should behave. I dinnae think
their ideas run to the crown prince playin' with the sons
o' Border lairds."

Dhugal sighed his disappointment. He would probably
never be allowed even to speak to Prince Kelson then, let
alone play with him.

Caulay leaned down and kissed Dhugal's forehead,
wine strong on his breath. "Go tae sleep now, Dhugal.
Maybe ye won't play wi' His Highness, but there'll be
other lads for ye tae befriend. I'm off to find yer brother

before he drinks himself under some table." He rose and left, taking the candle with him.

Dhugal turned on his side and stared at a square of moonlight on the floor. He was quite sure Prince Kelson had smiled at *him* and that he wanted to be friends. But they were both surrounded by adults, Kelson even more so than himself. If the king didn't want his son to play with the son of a Border earl, that was that. There would be nothing that Dhugal or even Caulay could do to change his mind.

"For the first year spent at Court, each new page will have one of the older pages as a roommate," Prince Nigel decreed two weeks later.

Dhugal shivered in the cold of the early January morning and tried to quell his homesickness. The Epiphany celebrations were over, and Dhugal had seen his father and brother start on their journey home an hour ago. He and the other new pages were gathered in the refectory hall of the pages' dormitory. Across from Dhugal and the other new boys were an equal number of pages in the ten- to twelve-year-old range.

"Your roommate will help you learn the routine here," Prince Nigel continued. "It is his responsibility to teach you the rules and to make sure you're awake, dressed, and tidy in time for inspection before breakfast each morning. After that, he will make sure that you know where to go and when for the rest of the day. In short, he is here to help you learn the duties of a royal page.

"*Your* first duty is to keep the room you share clean and to arrive punctually for your lessons and practice sessions. You will now be assigned a roommate and they will show you to your rooms."

He picked up a list and began reading off names.

"Dhugal MacArdry, your roommate will be Nicholas Murdoch."

Nicholas Murdoch stepped forward, and Dhugal's heart

sank. His new roommate was a tall, burly boy with dark brown hair cut in the pudding-bowl style all the other pages wore. By special permission from Prince Nigel, Dhugal had been allowed to keep his coppery red hair in its customary Border braid.

Nicholas had the beginnings of an underbite; his brown eyes were squinty and set close to either side of his broad, upturned nose. His face's most natural expression was one of belligerence. He looked across—and down—at Dhugal with obvious scorn.

"Well, don't just stand there. Pick up your things and come along." Nicholas sighed. "I *would* get a lump like you."

Dhugal followed him up a narrow spiral stair, tottering under the load of his saddlebags full of clothes, his heart full of foreboding. At the top of the stair was a long, bare hallway with a row of identical doors opening on the right. To the left was an equally long row of small windows looking down on an empty, snowy courtyard.

"In here," Nicholas barked.

He opened a door midway down the hall and stood aside to let Dhugal precede him. It was a narrow little room with a single small window set in the wall opposite the door. Identical iron bedsteads with matching wooden trunks at their feet took up most of the bare stone floor. A small wooden table stood between the two beds, under the little window. Dhugal stood still in dismay for a moment, remembering his father's comfortable rooms with regret.

"Ding-dong!" Nicholas crowed from behind as he seized Dhugal's coppery braid and yanked it hard enough to make Dhugal's eyes water. The younger boy dropped his belongings on the floor.

"An' how's me bonnie wee lassie today?"

"I am *not* a girl!" Dhugal yelled, stung. "All the men in Clan MacArdry wear a Border braid!"

"Then every man in Clan MacArdry is a sniveling *girl*!" Nicholas sneered. "Just like you!" He let Dhugal go with a shove, then kicked his things out of his way to the left side of the room.

"That's *your* bed and trunk, and don't let me catch you touching my things with your dirty hands."

Dhugal opened his trunk in silence and began unpacking. He took out his kilt first; he wouldn't be allowed to wear it while on duty, but the sight of the MacArdry tartan cheered him a little.

"Long hair, now skirts," Nicholas mocked, looking at the kilt. "And you still say that the men in your clan aren't girls?"

"Only men wear kilts," Dhugal retorted. "Tougher men than you!"

"What do I care what a lot of jumped-up peasants wear?" Nicholas asked. "Yes, you Borderers are next door to serfs and peasants—don't try denying it! And your father's not *nearly* as important as my grandfather, the Earl of Carthane."

Nicholas leveled a thick forefinger at Dhugal and poked him hard and repeatedly in the chest, driving him back until he was pinned against the wall with Nicholas looming over him. The older boy's voice was soft, with a nasty edge.

"A *real* earl, with real lands, not like that table-sized earldom where *your* father lords it over a lot of smelly, ignorant barbarians in skirts."

"We're not ignorant and we're not barbarians!" Dhugal's face was hot with outrage from the insults both to his father and his Clan.

"But you wear skirts, and you do smell. *Tcha!* To have to play nursemaid to a little worm like you!"

Their relationship deteriorated after that. Aside from waking Dhugal every morning with a splash of icy water in his face, Nicholas gave him no help with learning his bewildering new routine. After Dhugal had been disciplined several times during the first week for breaking rules, being late for lessons, or showing up in the wrong place altogether, he realized that Nicholas had deliberately misled him and stopped relying on him for any kind of practical help.

All the new pages endured mild hazing during those first weeks at Court, but Dhugal saw that *their* roommates also protected them from too much rough treatment. Nicholas and his three closest friends went after Dhugal with awful enthusiasm. Dhugal's bright red Border braid, his freckles, his Highland accent, and their estimation of his low status as a Border chieftain's second son provided his tormentors with endless amusement. They sought him out during their scarce free time until Dhugal began to feel like a hunted rabbit.

It never occurred to him to ask Prince Nigel or any other adult for help. At Transha, any child over age five who couldn't fight his own battles got little help and no sympathy. He assumed the same rule applied in Rhemuth, and doubly so. Every night before he went to sleep, Dhugal tried to think of a way to get back at Nicholas for all his insults and trickery, but there was always the problem of Nicholas's superior age, size, and allies. Physical revenge was simply impossible for one thin eight-year-old.

Dhugal was usually too tired to lie awake for long, in any case, for his new life exhausted him both physically and mentally. The daily drills in riding, swordsmanship, and archery were all right—he'd learned those skills well at Transha. He could read, write, and do simple arithmetic, so the more academic side of life in Rhemuth was also tolerable. His hardest lessons by far were learning his duties as a royal page. According to Prince Nigel and his assistants, there were an infinite number of "wrong" ways, but only one, very specific "right way" to perform each task.

And I do everything the wrong way first, Dhugal mourned.

He was the slowest learner among the new pages, and it couldn't be denied. Perfection was demanded of every boy, no matter how many times he had to practice a job to get it right. Dhugal was still working on the "correct" way to deliver messages when the other new pages had graduated to the proper way to offer basins of hand-washing water to nobility after they had dined. His slow progress amused Nicholas no end.

Dhugal saw Prince Kelson at least two or three times a week through his first two months at Court, but the prince was always hurrying somewhere in the company of his tutor or his squire. Kelson waved and grinned in the friendliest way every time he noticed Dhugal, but they hadn't had time even to say hello since Christmas Court. Although technically a page himself, Kelson led a very separate life from those of the ordinary pages, just as Dhugal's father had warned. As a first-year pupil, Dhugal never had practice sessions with Kelson, who had begun his own training four years before. Once in a while, Dhugal glimpsed Kelson while the prince practiced his riding, fencing, or shooting. Dhugal proudly noted that Kelson could do all of these things as well or better than boys older than he was, but it made the distance between them seem far greater.

"STOP!"

Dhugal lowered his bow and turned to bow, although it was more like a cringe. Until just then, all his concentration had been centered on his shooting. He'd taken the last target at the far left end of the archery yard on this overcast March afternoon. The last time he'd looked, Prince Nigel had been walking in the opposite direction, but now he stood before Dhugal looking as tall as a bell tower. Prince Conall, Nigel's eldest son, stood at his father's left and studied Dhugal with disdain. Nicholas Murdoch stood at Prince Nigel's right and looked smug. Prince Nigel himself was frowning.

Dhugal gulped and dropped his gaze to study his boot toes. He had no idea why Prince Nigel should be displeased with him, but he was sure Nicholas had something to do with it. It *couldn't* be his archery, for he'd just placed three of his last five arrows into the gold.

"Nicholas tells me you always shoot left-handed," Prince Nigel said. "Is that true?"

Dhugal's jaw dropped and his heart followed as he looked up at the prince in dismay.

"Well? I asked you a question, boy. I expect an answer!"

"Yes, Your Highness," Dhugal confessed in a bat-squeak voice.

"Not in Rhemuth you don't. There are no left-handed knights in His Majesty's service. Starting today, you'll learn to shoot right-handed." He plucked Dhugal's bow out of his hands and gave it to Conall to hold, then reversed the archery glove and wrist guards on Dhugal's hands. The other pages nearby stopped their practice to watch and listen while someone else got scolded.

"Try it now," Prince Nigel said, and handed the bow back to Dhugal.

Dhugal knew an order when he heard one. He picked up an arrow and nocked it to the bowstring after two clumsy tries. Holding the bow in his left hand and the bowstring with the fingers of his right felt all wrong and backward as he bent the bow, but he dared not disobey.

His first right-handed shot made a brief, wobbly flight and the arrow buried its head in the damp earth at least a yard short and wide of the target. Behind him, Conall and Nicholas sniggered while the other watching pages looked at one another, grinning.

"That will do," Prince Nigel told them crisply. "It's no easier for Dhugal to shoot right-handed than it would be for the two of you to shoot left-handed."

"Now, all of you." The prince gestured to the other pages and raised his voice. "I want to see arrows hitting those targets! You'll never improve without practice, and God knows, you *all* need to improve!"

The other pages scattered like leaves before a winter wind. Soon the archery yard was full of the whir of arrows flying and their thumping into the targets.

Nigel turned back to Dhugal. "Try another one."

Dhugal's next shot struck the bottom edge of the target, but not with enough force to stick. It dangled for a second, then dropped to the ground. Dhugal groaned.

Prince Nigel touched his shoulder briefly. "Don't be discouraged, it was only your second try. You have the makings of a fair archer in you. You just need more practice."

*Y*OU HAVE THE *makings of a fair archer in you.*

Dhugal repeated Prince Nigel's words over and over in his mind later that afternoon while he groomed his pony. His first afternoon of shooting right-handed had deteriorated from inadequate to disastrous by the end of the archery session.

All at once, Dhugal threw the brush down and leaned against Chestnut's barrel, his cheek against her rough coat for comfort. He squeezed his eyes shut, determined not to cry, even though he was safe from observation here at the humbler end of the royal stables.

He couldn't resent Prince Nigel, even though his decree had ruined Dhugal's shooting. Stern and exacting taskmaster though he was, Prince Nigel was also very fair and very patient. In his two months at Court, Dhugal had never seen him punish anyone without hearing all sides of the story first, or humiliate any boy. Everyone strove to earn the sparse words of praise the prince doled out. Even the qualified praise he'd given Dhugal today was something to treasure.

Dhugal retrieved the brush, then resumed his grooming while Chestnut ate her hay. He felt the heaviness in his chest and stomach slowly diminish. The smell of hay and horses and the small, contented sounds they made never failed to soothe his spirits, no matter how unhappy he might be. The royal stable was the one thing that had made his life at Court bearable this winter. He'd made friends among the grooms and stableboys far more easily

than he had among his peers. The only trouble was that
Chestnut would never look as if she belonged here. She
was bear-shaggy, although now that it was March, she shed
enough hair to coat Dhugal's clothes every time he
groomed her.

Dhugal finished his grooming and patted Chestnut's
neck in farewell, regretting his disloyal thoughts. Although he longed for a real R'Kassan horse like those the
king rode, he knew he could never have one. Such a horse
would be badly suited to life in the Highlands, even if the
price were within his father's means.

At least in Rhemuth, Dhugal could *look* at fine, blooded
horses as much as he liked. He left Chestnut's stall and
walked boldly up the long aisle toward the opposite end
where the royal horses were stabled. It was a shorter walk
back to his quarters from that end of the stable, so he had
an excellent excuse for a visit. Knowing he could be
trusted around horses, the grooms allowed him to go
where he pleased here. Dhugal rounded the last corner
then stopped and stared in his surprise.

Prince Kelson stood at the stable door feeding pieces
of broken carrot to a tall gray stallion and a fine bay pony.
A groom stood by waiting to take the horses, but his presence barely registered in Dhugal's brain at the sight of
Kelson miraculously standing still and unattended. He
started toward the prince eagerly, already beginning to
speak.

Kelson didn't notice him, but the prince's companion
did, and turned his fair head, resting cool gray eyes on
Dhugal—who turned and scuttled back around the corner
to safety, his heart pounding with fright and disappointment.

How could he have mistaken Morgan for a mere
groom? Kelson was *never* unattended. Dhugal listened for
footsteps, dry-mouthed with fear but the duke didn't come
to investigate.

"Come, my Prince," he heard Morgan say. "It's later
than you think. I don't want your mother believing I've

gone and turned you over to Wencit of Torenth. That would be a legitimate grievance."

"She's *always* fussing," Kelson sighed. "And Father said I could go riding with you today."

"You and I and your father know we went riding," Morgan chuckled. "I'm sure your mother thinks I spent the afternoon luring you to your damnation instead." Their voices and footsteps faded out of Dhugal's hearing.

Resigned, Dhugal started back to his own quarters. After encountering Morgan, he was embarrassed and frightened at having dared to approach Kelson. As far as his mother was concerned, the eleventh commandment was "Thou shalt not presume." Would Morgan speak to Prince Nigel about him? Or worse, to the king? Looking down at his horse-hair-covered clothes as he walked, Dhugal realized he didn't look like the sort of child anyone would invite to befriend a prince. He'd have to hurry to get changed and tidied up before supper.

To Dhugal's great relief, Nicholas was not at home when he returned. He opened his own trunk to get out a clean shirt and saw his extra pair of scarlet hose lying on top of the pile of his freshly laundered clothes. He snatched up the hose and, after standing in the doorway to listen for Nicholas, he opened Nicholas's trunk and substituted his own clean hose for Nicholas's larger pair.

Dhugal eased the trunk lid closed without a sound, then stepped back over to his own side of the room and stuffed the purloined hose at the very bottom of his trunk beneath his kilt. Just in time, for he heard Nicholas's heavy footsteps coming up the turnpike stair at the far end of the hall. The trunk lid slipped from his fingers and crashed closed, echoing against the stone walls.

"You smell like a *horse*," Nicholas complained, coming in two minutes later. He sniffed loudly and pressed his handkerchief against his nose and mouth in a show of disgust. "Even worse than usual. What a filthy grub you are!"

"That's why 'm washing," Dhugal explained, though

indistinctly. He bent over the basin scrubbing his face hard, his heart pounding. Had Nicholas realized that the crash had come from their room?

"You *ought* to have washed in the stable trough," Nicholas sneered. "Mind you fetch me a basin of clean water when you're finished. I won't use any that's touched *your* dirty face. You MacArdrys are better suited for a life as grooms rather than knights, anyway. No breeding to speak of."

"STUPID COW OF a laundress!"

Dhugal opened his eyes a slit the next morning to see Nicholas sitting on his bed, struggling to pull Dhugal's hose up his stocky legs. The older boy's face was red as the wool, his lower lip curled over the upper while his eyebrows were low and frowning over his muddy brown eyes.

Dhugal closed his eyes to keep from laughing aloud. "Whassa matter?" he asked, rubbing at his eyes and faking a yawn to hide his smile.

"That worthless laundress has given me the wrong pair of hose!" Nicholas indicated his legs, having managed to pull the hose up only over his knees. "I'll see she's dismissed for this!"

Dhugal bit his lip. The old laundress had been kind to him. He didn't want to see her dismissed just so he could get even with Nicholas.

"Wear your other pair."

"I *can't*," Nicholas grumbled. "Got 'em too dirty yesterday, and Prince Nigel is sure to notice." He grabbed the waistband of the hose and began his tugging and writhing all over again.

Dhugal dressed quickly and hurried out to the corridor, both to be ready for morning inspection and to avoid the risk of Nicholas noticing his amusement.

Nicholas was the last boy of all to emerge for morning inspection, Dhugal's hose shiny-tight on his heavy thighs.

Dhugal stood on his side of the door and stared straight ahead, afraid to glance aside lest he laugh. Even after inspection was over and everyone was dismissed, he had to work to conceal his laugher. There was an unattractive sideways wriggle to Nicholas's walk this morning, and he had to continually stop and hitch up the waist of Dhugal's hose as it threatened to roll down beneath his hips.

Everyone else watched Nicholas too. None of the younger boys dared laugh aloud at him, but they darted admiring glances at Dhugal. Even some of the older squires winked at him in passing.

Once Nicholas had disappeared down the stairs, Dhugal allowed himself a grin. He felt a warm surge of pride at his success. All the same, he was glad it was Saturday, and that his duties and Nicholas's would keep them apart for the rest of the morning. He would go riding outside the city this afternoon, Dhugal decided. Whether or not Nicholas realized Dhugal's trick between now and noon, he would be in a ferocious temper later on, making this an excellent day to disappear. Dhugal just hoped he'd have enough time to get to the stables before his roommate realized he was gone.

"DHUGAL!"

Dickon MacEwan came hurrying through the pages' refectory to where Dhugal sat eating his midday meal at the long table, at about an hour past noon. He had to squeeze past a group of older boys and jump over a bench to reach Dhugal's side.

"You mustn't stay here!" Dickon panted in Dhugal's ear. "Nicholas is looking for you and he's very angry. You have to hide quickly!"

Dhugal froze with a mouthful of half-chewed bread and cheese in his mouth.

"Come *on!*" the younger boy urged, tugging on Dhugal's arm. "I ran all the way here, but I think he saw me. We've got to leave."

Dhugal stuffed an apple in his pocket, then ran out with
Dickon. He stopped just long enough to grab his cloak
from its peg at the entrance before Dickon dragged him
outside with panicked strength.

"I have to get to my pony in the stable," Dhugal protested when the other boy tried to pull him across the
courtyard to the main castle.

"But he'll look for you in the stable!" Dickon's blue
eyes were round with fear.

"He'll look for me in the refectory first," Dhugal whispered, hurrying toward the stables through the garden
shortcut. Dickon's terror made him feel almost brave by
comparison, although his heart was pounding as if he'd
just run a race. "I have to get as far away as I can, as fast
as I can."

He posted Dickon to keep a lookout by the main stable
door while he saddled and bridled Chestnut. He was just
leading her out when Dickon came running, eyes wide.

"Nicholas is watching for you at the castle gate! You
can't leave without his seeing you!"

Dhugal swallowed hard, his earlier bravery fading. No
matter where he tried to hide within the castle or in the
gardens, Nicholas would search for him until he found
him. He didn't fancy spending his free afternoon cowering
somewhere waiting for Nicholas to find him and beat him.
Especially not on the very first bright day of spring, and
not now that he'd finally done something to truly merit
Nicholas's anger.

"What do we do?" Dickon whimpered.

"I'm going to try anyway," Dhugal answered. "I'm a
MacArdry. And I'll bet Nicholas can't run fast enough to
catch my pony.

"But don't stay here, Dickon," Dhugal added. "I don't
want Nicholas to know you helped me—and thank you
for warning me."

"Well, if you're sure," Dickon whispered, already turning away. "Be careful!"

Dhugal led his pony out to the stable yard and mounted,

heart thudding against his ribs with his excitement and
fear. Chestnut sensed his agitation and broke into a brisk
jog as soon as he was settled.

At the entrance to the main courtyard, Dhugal pulled
her up. No sense in just bolting into the open without
taking a look around first. He spotted Nicholas at once,
waiting by the gatehouse arch to Dhugal's right on the
side away from the entrance to the stable yard.

Dhugal sniffed at this lapse in Nicholas's strategy, although it worked to his advantage. He'd have to kick
Chestnut into a gallop right away, then turn her sharply
right and charge past Nicholas before the older boy had
a chance to recognize him. A bigger horse might not be
able to do it, but Chestnut was nimble.

Chestnut responded to his squeeze with a burst of
speed, hurtling toward the gatehouse passage like a well-
shot arrow. Dhugal clung low to the right side of her neck
lest Nicholas see and recognize him, and almost went off
over Chestnut's head as she stopped all at once to avoid
colliding with the two big war horses just emerging from
the passage.

It was a large party arriving, and they separated Dhugal
and Nicholas like a river of horses, men, and baggage
wagons. In his own frantic anxiety to be gone, Dhugal
counted at least a dozen mounted knights, then their lord
and a younger man, mounted servants, and half a dozen
baggage wagons.

"Now!" Dhugal urged Chestnut, with his heels as well
as his voice, as soon as the passage was clear.

She leaped forward, almost leaving him behind this
time as she veered sharply to the right around the corner.
Dhugal grabbed a fistful of mane and leaned down over
her neck, trusting her to carry him, for the moment.

Nicholas had been waiting for his chance too, and he
was running hard to catch them up from behind, his fists
doubled up and his face red with anger.

"Keep back!" Dhugal shouted over his shoulder. "She
kicks!"

Chestnut's hooves thudded over the drawbridge planks then clattered on the cobblestones, too fast for Nicholas to catch them. Looking back over his shoulder, Dhugal saw Nicholas standing at the end of the drawbridge, hands on hips, watching him go.

"Free!" Dhugal crowed in triumph. He slowed Chestnut's gallop to a more moderate trot for maneuvering through the crowded city streets.

"WILFRED, THERE'S ANOTHER horse in Chestnut's stall," Dhugal called to a groom hurrying past. He stood bewildered in the stable aisle with Chestnut unsaddled and impatient for her evening feed. It was almost sunset, and the stables bustled with the evening chores.

"Eh, I know, Dhugal, laddie," Wilfred said. "Chestnut can manage out in the long paddock for one night, can she no? She's got a good thick coat."

Seeing that Wilfred was both busy and weary, Dhugal didn't object. A cool spring night in lowland Rhemuth wouldn't bother his pony in the least. She had endured far worse weather in the Highlands.

"Of course she can. But where did all these other horses come from, Wilfred?"

"Duke Jared McLain arrived two days earlier than we expected," Wilfred grunted. "We've spent all afternoon runnin' about tryin' to find stablin' for forty extra horses. There's not an empty stall in the royal stables tonight, and that's with a good two dozen down in the long paddock." Wilfred ran a hand through his coarse graying hair. "It wouldnae have been a problem if we'd just had time to send the mares an' foals—" Wilfred broke off and grinned at Dhugal, shaking his head.

"I'll just take Chestnut out then," Dhugal said, turning to lead his pony down to the long paddock.

"Wait, lad," Wilfred said. "Seein' as you've been sportin' about puttin' Chestnut out for the night, will ye do

me the favor of bringing Moonshadow in from her paddock on your way back?"

"Moonshadow?" Dhugal gasped. "But—"

"Ah, it's no 'but twenty feet from the paddock to the
stable," Wilfred teased. "There's not many lads I'd trust
to tend *that* one, but I daresay you'll manage her this
once." He pressed a leather halter and coiled lead rope
into Dhugal's hands. "I certainly wouldn't trust that young
brute who was here earlier to touch her."

Dhugal's joy over the unheard-of privilege of tending
Moonshadow evaporated at once.

"Who was here earlier?" he asked anxiously, already
sure of what Wilfred would say.

"That Murdoch lout—Nicholas, I think." Wilfred
shrugged. "Young fool could see we were busy, but he
stood about underfoot, pesterin' us to tell him where
you'd gone. Finally the chief groom sent him about his
business, and he hasnae come back."

"Wilfred!" a deep voice bellowed from down the corridor. "There're horses to be fed. Get on with it!"

Dhugal swallowed, and hurriedly led Chestnut out of
the stable and down to the long paddock. Several horses
were already there grazing on piles of hay spread upon
the damp ground. Dhugal turned her in quickly, only
pausing long enough to make sure the gate was securely
latched. Then he walked up the path toward Moonshadow's paddock. He looked to either side of him and over
his shoulder every few steps along the way, expecting
Nicholas to rush out at him from every dark corner.
He had only postponed the reckoning with Nicholas, he
knew, and the thought of what would happen before he
was allowed to sleep tonight made Dhugal's stomach
cramp with fear. After a whole afternoon to think about
Dhugal's trick, Nicholas's revenge would only be the
worse for having been delayed.

Once he reached Moonshadow's paddock, however,
Dhugal forced himself to be calm, lest he frighten the
mare. Moonshadow approached him, her pale silver coat

shining in the dusk. Dhugal let her sniff his hand, his fear
waning simply at being close to her. She dipped her head
obediently into the halter he held, so that all Dhugal had
to do was buckle it at the side and lead her out.

He walked slowly beside her on the short way back to
the stable to make this incredible privilege last, as proud
as if he were escorting Queen Jehana herself. For Moonshadow was the queen's favorite saddle horse, a birthday
gift from the king the previous autumn.

She was purebred R'Kassan, bred in the stables of the
King of R'Kassi himself. According to Wilfred, if horses
could be royal, then Moonshadow certainly was. She was
a perfect example of her breed, her head being small, her
wide forehead tapering down to a delicate black muzzle.
Her large brown eyes were both gentle and intelligent,
and her small sharp ears were expressive of her every
mood. From her arched neck to her slender legs and proud
tail, every detail of her conformation confirmed her flaw-
less breeding. Her mane, tail, and legs were iron gray, as
were the large round dapples on her neck and rump that
had given her her name. All Dhugal's fear temporarily
fled, his eight-year-old heart lost to a perfect R'Kassan
mare.

The next second, something heavy and fast-moving
struck Dhugal from behind, knocking him face-first onto
the muddy path. Moonshadow reared and whinnied
shrilly, yanking her lead rope out of Dhugal's hand,
though he clutched for the knotted end to keep hold of it.
He heard her gallop away, but could not tell in which
direction, with Nicholas pinning him to the ground on his
stomach.

"You little sneak!" Nicholas growled at Dhugal. "Let
me catch you taking my things again, and I'll—"

"Lemme go!" Dhugal cried. He squirmed hard, lifting
his head to see where Moonshadow had gone.

Nicholas slammed his head back down and held it
pressed to the dirt.

"You're not going anywhere! I'm going to *get* you for

what you did today. Humiliating me in front of the arch-bishop and the queen!"

Even with his left cheek pinned to the muddy path, Dhugal kept squirming mightily to get away, but gave it up with a cry of pain when Nicholas grabbed his left wrist and twisted it up behind his back. He was really afraid now, but more on Moonshadow's account than his own. Where had she gone? He couldn't see anything except Nicholas's right knee and a few blades of grass growing at the edge of the path.

"I'm going to give you two black eyes and a bloody nose!" Nicholas announced, his voice full of ominous pleasure. "But first, this."

He leaned down closer to Dhugal's face and let a thin rope of spit spill out between his lips. With his arm twisted behind his back and his head held down, there wasn't a thing Dhugal could do to evade it. He closed his eyes in revulsion, but there was no escape. Something wet and disgusting touched his cheek and was then withdrawn.

"Lemme *go*!" Dhugal cried, and made another frantic wriggle to escape. "I've got to find Moonshadow!"

"You're an even bigger baby than my little brother," Nicholas said, sounding disappointed. "Screaming about a little spit! But if you're ready for me to start hitting you, just say so."

"Stop it!" a new voice called from somewhere beyond and above Dhugal's head. "Leave him alone, Nicholas!"

It was a boy's voice, but it carried authority. Footsteps passed behind Dhugal's head, but all at once, Nicholas's weight was lifted from his back at last, and his left hand was free again.

"You haven't changed much, have you, Nicholas?" asked a second voice. "Still picking on boys who are too much smaller than you to have a fair chance."

Dhugal still lay huddled on the path, too stunned to move yet.

"He deserved it, Richard!" Nicholas spat. "He's a thief and he tricked me. I had to teach the little sneak a lesson!"

"After living with you for two months, he probably had a lot of reasons to do what he did," the voice Nicholas had addressed as Richard answered. "His Highness doesn't like seeing his friends treated this way."

Dhugal finally dared look up at the words "His Highness" and "friends." Prince Kelson stood at the stable door with his back to the lantern light, so Dhugal could not see his face. But there was no doubting it was the prince. Dhugal climbed to his feet and bowed, but Kelson paid him no attention for the moment.

Dhugal turned to see what had become of Nicholas. A tall, dark-haired squire had Nicholas's right arm twisted behind his back just as Nicholas had done to Dhugal. Richard's other arm was locked around Nicholas's neck from behind.

"I *don't* like seeing my friends hurt," Kelson agreed as he walked toward them. "And my uncle doesn't like seeing younger pages bullied by the older ones. You've been warned about that before, Nicholas. You know that if my uncle were to find out, you'd be sent home from Court. You'd have to wait an extra year to be knighted."

"And since he's not here, I suppose you'll tell him?" Nicholas scowled at Kelson.

"I *could* do that, and I probably should," Kelson said, nodding. "Or I could tell my father. But I don't think I will—yet."

"Then, *what*?" Nicholas asked.

"Every page in Rhemuth would be happy to see you sent home Nicholas," Kelson said in a cool voice. "But there's someone I could tell who would be even better than my uncle."

"Your mother?" Nicholas sneered.

"That's 'Her Majesty' to you, Murdoch!" Richard snapped. He gave Nicholas's arm an extra hard twist. "Show some respect."

"Not my mother." Kelson shook his head. "She'd only have Uncle Nigel deal with you, and you'd be sent home for certain. I'll give you one more chance, but if you keep bullying Dhugal and the other pages, I'll tell General Morgan, and he'll turn you into a *toad*!"

With the light coming from the stable door, Dhugal could see the fear that swept over Nicholas's face at Morgan's name.

"He'd never do that!" Nicholas blurted.

"He won't if you promise to leave Dhugal and the other younger pages alone from now on," Kelson said. "If you'll swear to that, you won't have to *worry* about what Morgan will or will not do." The prince smiled at Nicholas, well pleased with his reasonable solution.

Dhugal wanted to laugh at Nicholas's angry, frightened face, but kept silent so as not to draw Nicholas's attention back to him. They still had to share a room tonight, after all.

"All right," Nicholas ground out between clenched teeth.

"Swear it," Kelson insisted.

"I swear to leave Dhugal alone from now on," Nicholas grunted. "Let go of my arm, Richard!"

"What about the other pages?" Kelson said.

"I swear I won't bully the other pages, either." Nicholas forced the words out as if they hurt him.

"Very well," Kelson said. "You can let him go, Richard. But remember, Nicholas, if you go back on your word, I *will* tell General Morgan, and he'll fix you!"

"Run when I let you go, Murdoch, or I won't be responsible for what I do," Richard said. He released Nicholas and gave him a shove down the path between the paddocks. Nicholas ran, his heavy footsteps soon fading from their hearing.

"That's that," Kelson said, dusting his hands together. "Are you all right?"

"Uh-huh," Dhugal nodded, staring at him, hardly believing who had come to his rescue.

"I don't think you'll have to worry much about Nicholas from now on," Richard told Dhugal with a friendly grin. "Nick's a coward at heart. All the Murdochs have a bullying streak, but he's worse than any of his brothers or cousins."

"He'll be better for a while after this. He's been reminded of what he stands to lose, if he keeps bullying other pages," Kelson agreed with a grin. "Are you sure Nicholas didn't hurt you?"

Dhugal flexed his stiff left arm. It ached, but that wouldn't last. His right hand was sore, too, where the lead rope had been yanked out of his hand. . . .

"Moonshadow!" Dhugal cried, and looked wildly around again. She was nowhere in sight.

"What about Moonshadow?" Kelson asked, completely bewildered.

"Wilfred let me bring her in from her paddock tonight," Dhugal answered, still looking in every direction, frantic with fear. "I was leading her in when Nicholas knocked me down, and he scared her. She got loose and ran away."

"Then we have to find her!" Kelson declared. "Father will be furious if anything happens to her!" He leaned closer to Dhugal and his voice dropped with the significance of what he said. "He paid the King of R'Kassi fifteen hundred gold marks for Moonshadow."

Dhugal stared at Kelson aghast. Fifteen hundred gold marks—he had no idea than any horse, even Moonshadow, *could* cost that much. If the little mare had fallen in the dark, lamed herself, perhaps even broken her leg, his father could never pay the king back. Had Dhugal beggared Clan MacArdry because he hadn't held on to her lead rope tightly enough?

"I'll get a lantern from the stable, my Prince," Richard said. "It's nearly dark now, and we'll need the light to find her. The grooms will help too. She can't have gone very far."

"And she can't get out the gates after sunset." Kelson nodded. "We should start with her paddock. Maybe she's run back there."

Dhugal turned and ran back the way he'd come, desperately hoping Moonshadow had, but the paddock was empty. His eyes were accustomed to the gloom now, though, and he saw neat, rounded hoofprints in the firm mud.

Not waiting for prince, squire, or lantern, Dhugal ran head-down, following those prints. He was too intent on them to truly watch where he was running, though, and when the hoofprints disappeared at the edge of a mud puddle, he lost his balance and fell in.

It was a very large puddle—more like a young pond— and cold, dirty water soaked Dhugal from head to waist. He only jumped up and ran around the edge searching for Moonshadow's prints. He found them again on the opposite side, and they led him to a little copse of birch trees at the edge of the parade ground.

Moonshadow reared in panic when Dhugal ran up to the trees. She backed swiftly away from him, her eyes rolling and her ears pinned back, then pivoted on her hind legs and cantered several feet away before she stopped to look back at him. Her eyes showed a white ring of fear in the deep blue twilight, but Dhugal was greatly relieved to see she wasn't limping and appeared unhurt.

He stood still and tried to think what to do next. He knew better than to try to chase a frightened horse, and Moonshadow could outrun him in seconds.

Perplexed, Dhugal stuffed his hands in his pockets. Under his left palm, he felt the round smoothness of his forgotten apple. Smiling, he pulled it out and cut it into chunks with his dagger. He returned all but one piece to his pocket, and walked toward Moonshadow one slow step at a time, offering her the bite of apple on his outstretched hand.

"Moooooooooonshaaaaaaaaaadoooooooooow," Dhugal crooned, making his voice as soft and coaxing as he could.

Moonshadow didn't run away this time. She stood where she was and turned her head toward him. Her ears swiveled forward and pricked at the sound of his voice.

"Moooooooooooonshaaaaaaaaaaaaadoooooooooow."

Dhugal kept walking forward slowly, calling her again and again in the same soft voice, willing her to listen. Just beyond her reach he stopped and waited, not moving his hand.

A twig snapped under her hoof as she stepped toward him, then her soft muzzle brushed against his palm as she took the apple. Her teeth crunched it as Dhugal slowly brought out a second piece. She ate that and another before Dhugal had the courage to grab her lead rope. Two more pieces were eaten before he summoned the courage to stroke her neck.

He was very glad he had a firm hold on her lead rope then, for her head jerked up. But it wasn't his touch that had startled her. Voices and footsteps were coming nearer, and lantern light made great swaying bars of light and shadow on the white tree trunks.

"It's all right," Dhugal murmured to Moonshadow, and fed her the last bit of apple. The tension went out of her and she prodded his chest with her muzzle for another treat.

"That's all, I'm sorry," Dhugal whispered. "It wasn't a very big apple." He began to lead her forward then, and she walked at his side, docile and quiet as they left the little copse of trees.

"Hurrah!" Kelson cried when they emerged from the tree trunks. "You found her!"

"Is she all right?" Wilfred's anxious voice called from behind the prince.

"I think so, but I couldn't really see in the dark," Dhugal answered.

"Let me take her, lad." Wilfred took the lead rope from Dhugal. "The sooner she's in her stall, havin' her feed, the better. I intend to examine every inch of her."

It was a longer walk back to the stable than Dhugal had expected. Although he hadn't noticed it earlier, his page's tabard was clammy wet in the chilly darkness. By the time they reached the stable, he was shivering all over and his teeth chattered.

Prince Nigel was waiting for them at the stable door, and he surveyed them all with impartial sternness as they bowed.

"All right, how did Moonshadow get loose to begin with?"

"Weel, Your Highness, young Dhugal here is a dab hand with horses. . . ." Wilfred quailed and fell silent under Nigel's angry stare.

"Bringing Moonshadow in for the night is your responsibility, Wilfred, not Dhugal's. This is no horse for a child to tend."

Dhugal swallowed hard, panicked to find the prince's stern gaze now bent on him. He opened his mouth but couldn't squeeze out a word.

"It wasn't Dhugal's fault, Uncle," Kelson spoke up urgently. "He wasn't doing anything wrong. Moonshadow was scared off because Nicholas knocked Dhugal down from behind. When Richard and I got there, Nicholas had Dhugal pinned to the ground on his stomach. Richard had to drag him off."

"Is that what happened?" Nigel asked Dhugal.

Still speechless, Dhugal nodded vehemently.

"He found Moonshadow, too," Kelson supplied. "He caught her and brought her back."

"Did you?" Prince Nigel raised his eyebrows at Dhugal. "This mare isn't easy to catch when she's loose." His voice was tinged with respect as well as surprise this time.

Dhugal opened his mouth to speak and sneezed instead. For the first time, Nigel noticed the state of his clothes and hair.

"Good Heavens, boy, what happened to *you*?"

"Fell in a puddle, Your Highness," Dhugal confessed.

Prince Nigel snorted softly, and it sounded almost like laughter. Then the stern prince was back.

"Don't just stand there, Wilfred, take Moonshadow to her stall! And Wilfred, as long as Moonshadow is perfectly sound, I won't mention this incident to His Majesty this time. For your own sake, though, this had better not happen again. Do I make myself clear?"

"Yes, Your Highness." Wilfred bowed, then hurried past with Moonshadow.

"Come along, Kelson," Prince Nigel continued. "I really came out here to look for you, not for loose horses. You're out later than usual, and your mother was anxious—she *is* your mother," Nigel added sharply, when Kelson rolled his eyes. "Now come with me and show her that you're still in one piece."

He laid an arm around Kelson's shoulders and turned away. Kelson grinned back over his shoulder at Dhugal in farewell.

Dhugal tried to smile back, although he felt lonely and forgotten. Kelson had helped him, first with Nicholas and just now with Prince Nigel. For a while, they had simply been two boys looking for a lost horse, but now Kelson was a prince again, returning to his palace and his true rank, leaving Dhugal behind.

"Well, come on, then, Dhugal," Prince Nigel ordered over his shoulder. "Don't stand about in the draught in those wet clothes of yours. There's nothing more useless than a page with a head cold."

Dhugal trotted forward, too amazed to disobey, and Prince Nigel laid a hand on his shoulder.

"Ah, Richard, there you are," he said when Kelson's squire appeared with a lit torch in his hand. "Hold that up so we can all see where we're going, please."

The four of them left the stableyard together. Dhugal walked quickly at Prince Nigel's side, thunderstruck and grateful. Anything to postpone his next encounter with Nicholas was welcome. Prince Nigel's hand was warm and firm on his left shoulder, but his fingers didn't grip in a painful way. Once or twice, Dhugal dared to glance up at his face, but he didn't speak, taking his cue from Kelson. They were walking down a wide, well-lit castle corridor leading to the royal apartments before Prince Nigel spoke.

"Tell me, Dhugal, has Nicholas been bullying you?"

Dhugal jumped at the sudden question. "Yes, Your Highness."

"I don't hold with complaining, but neither do I condone bullying. You ought to have told me, and I would have put a stop to it." Nigel's tone was kind, belying his stern words.

"I'm sorry, sir. I didn't know," Dhugal whispered.

"No, *I'm* sorry. I should have realized." Nigel shook his head. "I know what Nicholas is like with younger boys. But when you didn't say anything, I thought he was behaving himself for once.

"In any case, I think you'll be wanting a new roommate. And you'll *definitely* need a new pair of hose."

Dhugal was positive he'd heard a laugh in Prince Nigel's voice this time, but he didn't have long to think about it as the prince guided him and Kelson up a short flight of steps, then knocked at an elaborately carved door on the right side of the passage. It was opened at once by a serving maid, who curtseyed and stood aside to let the two princes and Dhugal enter.

"Kelson?"

There was a rustle of rich fabric and Queen Jehana appeared through a doorway across the elegantly furnished room. Two more maidservants were just visible behind her. Only the pressure of Prince Nigel's hand on his shoulder reminded Dhugal to bow to the queen.

He stared at her in amazement when he straightened. Her red-gold hair hung loose down her back over her pale green silk robe. The gown was trimmed with gray fox fur along the collar, sleeves, and hem. Even displeased as she was now, the queen's face was lovely.

"Nigel, you're not even *dressed,*" Queen Jehana sighed to her brother-in-law. "You'd best go at once and change your clothes. I'll talk to Kelson."

"You're not ready either," Prince Nigel pointed out. "Is Brion? Anyway, I've been out rounding up your lost sheep. Two of them, actually. Don't worry, I won't be late tonight." He bowed and left.

"Where have you been, Kelson?" the queen now demanded of her son. "It was inconsiderate of you to worry me when you know your father and I are dining with the archbishops tonight."

"I was only down at the stables, Mother," Kelson protested. "I never even left the castle grounds."

"Truly?" the queen demanded. Her eyes never left her son's face.

Dhugal's eyes never left the queen's face, though he knew it was rude to stare at anyone, let alone a queen. Her eyes were deep green—he'd never been close enough to her to notice before. She was tall and slender, and her skin was as smooth as cream over her facial bones. There wasn't a thread of gray in her bright hair. She was as beautiful in her way as Moonshadow was in hers, and she looked far too young to be anyone's mother.

"Truly, Mother. I had Richard with me, too," Kelson answered, meeting her gaze squarely. When her expression didn't change, he tilted his head to one side and smiled up at her.

This time, the queen's severity melted away and she returned Kelson's smile.

"All right." She reached out and smoothed his black hair back from his forehead. "But you still should have come back before dark."

The warm air in the queen's solar tickled Dhugal's nose, and he sneezed loudly before he could stop himself. The queen jumped, only having noticed him then.

"Who is this?" she asked.

"This is Dhugal MacArdry, Mother." Kelson was clearly glad for the change of topic.

Queen Jehana tipped Dhugal's face up to the light with a smooth hand under his chin.

"You poor child!" she exclaimed. "You're freezing and soaked. Kelson, take him back to the nursery for a hot bath and some dry clothes. He can have supper with you afterwards."

"Please, may he spend the night too, Mother?"

"Just for tonight," the queen agreed. "Tomorrow he must go back to his own quarters. Now be off, both of you. I must finish dressing." She turned away in a flash of pale green skirts and disappeared through the arched doorway.

"Come with me," Kelson told Dhugal as they left the queen's solar together.

"Will your father—will the king mind my spending the night?" Dhugal asked nervously.

Kelson frowned in bewilderment. "No. Why should he?"

"Well. . . ." Dhugal squirmed a little. Kelson was behaving as if they'd always been friends—and as if there was nothing at all extraordinary about what had happened between them tonight.

"Don't worry." Kelson grinned and threw an arm around Dhugal's shoulders. "Father won't mind. He lets me play with anyone I like, as long as it doesn't interfere with my duties or theirs. Come on. I'm starving, aren't you?"

Two hours later, warm and dry and wrapped in one of Kelson's dressing robes, Dhugal felt truly comfortable and content for the first time since he'd arrived in Rhemuth. He and Kelson sat in chairs before a blazing fire in Kelson's bedchamber, drinking hot possets of milk and honey while Richard turned down Kelson's bed. Dhugal stretched his toes toward the fire, heels resting on the bearskin hearth rug, warm inside and out. He was as full of well-being as he was of the fresh bread and venison stew he and Kelson had eaten for supper. Accustomed to the coarse, scratchy wool that Transha sheep provided, Kelson's borrowed robe felt wonderfully soft and warm against his skin. Being befriended by the Crown Prince of Gwynedd clearly had more practical benefits than mere protection from Nicholas.

The thought of Nicholas brought the trick he'd played to the forefront of Dhugal's mind.

"Why did Prince Nigel say I'd need a ɴʟw pair of hose?"

Kelson laughed and almost choked on a swallow of his posset. "You didn't see what happened?"

"No."

Overhearing them, Richard came to join them, laughing himself. "It's a shame you missed it, Dhugal. It was a brilliant revenge."

"Mother and I came downstairs at noon to greet Archbishop Loris," Kelson said. "Nicholas was there in the hall, too. When he bowed as we passed, his hose split right up his backside. Mother and the Archbishop and everyone else nearby got a *very* good look at Nicholas's bare behind!"

Dhugal clapped both hands to his mouth, crowing with delight. He was dismayed at the same time, as his revenge had been far more effective than he'd planned. Small wonder that Nicholas had been furious today, after being humiliated in front of the queen and the primate of Gwynedd at once. It was almost enough to make him regret having been rescued this afternoon. Being thwarted in his revenge would only make Nicholas more determined to get back at him as soon as possible.

Tomorrow, Dhugal thought, and shivered. He couldn't count on being rescued twice.

Kelson saw and understood, though. "You won't have to worry about Nicholas anymore," he said. "Uncle Nigel said he'd find you a new roommate, didn't he? Even if that didn't happen, Nicholas is so afraid of Morgan, he wouldn't dare try to hurt you after today."

"I doubt General Morgan would appreciate your having involved him in a page's quarrel, Your Highness," Richard told Kelson in mild reproof. "And I don't think even *he* could turn Nicholas into a toad."

"I don't think so either, Richard," Kelson answered, still cheerful and unworried. "But Nicholas doesn't know that. If he thinks the danger is real, he'll leave Dhugal and the other pages alone, and Morgan need never know a thing about it."

"He'll not find out from me, my Prince," Richard said. "A little fear will improve Nicholas's nature, I think."

"You should have seen him this morning, trying to pull on my hose," Dhugal chuckled. He screwed up his face and pantomimed Nicholas's tugging and squirming until Richard and Kelson were both helpless from laughter.

"Where did you go this afternoon?" Kelson asked, when he'd recovered enough to speak. "I was looking for you. It was the first Saturday I'd had free in weeks, and I wanted to play."

"I'm sorry, I went riding outside the city," Dhugal answered. "I was avoiding Nicholas. If I'd known, we could have gone together."

Kelson shook his head, his face full of regret. "No, I couldn't have gone with you after all."

"Why not? You said you had the afternoon free."

Kelson gave him a long, measuring look, as if to determine his trustworthiness. "You promise not to tell?"

"I promise." Dhugal leaned forward to hear what the prince would say.

"It's awfully embarrassing, but I'm not allowed beyond the castle gates without an armed escort and at least one of the Privy Council lords," Kelson admitted. "Usually, I can't seem to go anywhere unless half the Court comes with me. By the time everyone's mounted up, half the day is gone."

Dhugal nodded, disappointed but not surprised.

"It's all because I sneaked off to the Rhemuth Easter Fair with some of the other pages and squires last spring," Kelson went on. "I couldn't get anyone at Court to take me, so I went with them." He rolled his eyes.

"You wouldn't believe the *fuss* everyone made! Mother cried for hours, and Father ordered his elite guard out to search the whole city and fairgrounds for me. He confined me to my rooms for a week after I was found and brought back."

"It's because he was *worried,* my Prince," Richard reminded him. "There had been rumors of a Torenthi plot to abduct you. When it was discovered you were missing, everyone was afraid they'd succeeded. If you're not allowed to roam around the countryside on your own, you know the reason better than anyone else."

"If I'd known that at the time, Richard, I obviously wouldn't have *gone,*" Kelson argued. There was resignation in his voice, as if he'd long ago despaired of making his point of view understood. "I can't help it if no one told me about it."

"I wouldn't be sure about that, Your Highness," Richard scoffed. He gave Kelson a light, very playful cuff to the side of his head. "You generally find out what you want to know, whether anyone tells you or not."

"A prince must be informed," Kelson said, his expression smug. "That's what Father always says."

"Naturally," Richard teased, then winked at Dhugal. Dhugal smiled in return, although taken aback by the familiarity of Richard's teasing. The squire collected their empty mugs and left the circle of firelight.

"Anyway," Kelson returned his attention to Dhugal, "we *can* ride together outside the city if we take a pack of adults with us. But there goes the chance to do anything really fun." He looked at Dhugal wistfully. "You're so lucky."

"*I* am?" Dhugal glanced around Kelson's spacious, richly furnished room in amazement, mentally comparing it with his own plain quarters.

"Yes. It must be nice to be able to go off alone when you have a few hours free. *I* can't go off by myself without making everyone hysterical." He sighed.

"Father says the lack of privacy is all part of being a prince, and that I have to learn to live with it. But sometimes . . ." Kelson broke off and made a disgusted face.

Dhugal nodded slowly. He hadn't really thought about

this aspect of Kelson's life before. Friendly or no, the prince's life was still very much shaped by the rules of adults.

"I think it's best you go to bed now, my Prince," Richard said, coming back. "You're to attend Mass at the cathedral in the morning, and you know Her Majesty doesn't like it if you doze off."

Kelson shot from his chair and ran across the room to leap up onto his bed, making the featherbed puff up around him. Richard had laid a pallet at the foot of the big four-poster. Dhugal hesitated, wondering where *he* was supposed to sleep.

"Well?" Kelson called. "Aren't you coming to bed?"

Embarrassed, Dhugal climbed in beside Kelson. The bed was easily wide enough for three adults, so there was plenty of room for himself and Kelson. Dhugal lay and watched as Richard banked the fire and blew out the candles around the room.

"Night," Kelson yawned.

"Good night," Dhugal whispered in answer. Very soon, Kelson's even, quiet breathing told Dhugal he was asleep.

Dhugal lay wide awake but content, enjoying the luxury of Kelson's bed and the smoothness of the sheets under his cheek and his hand. He reviewed his day with amazement and satisfaction. He had taken his revenge on Nicholas, and had made friends with Prince Kelson at last, but he never had dreamed he would accomplish both on the same day.

Furthermore, he'd done something his older brother never had. For that matter, not even his father had ever dined privately with any member of the royal family and then been invited to spend the night. Living at Court now would be a very different thing than it had been through the winter. It might even prove to be fun.

WHEN HE RETURNED to his own quarters in the pages' dormitory after Mass the next morning, Dhugal found a clean new page's tabard and a new pair of scarlet hose lying neatly folded on his bed. Nicholas and all his personal belongings were gone. When Dhugal summoned enough courage to peek inside his trunk, it was empty.

A junior squire by the name of Peter MacEwan moved in with him the next day. Peter was a tall fourteen-year-old, with red hair and freckles of his own. He ordered Dhugal about and teased him, but did so in a good-natured way. Dhugal was used to the same kind of treatment from his older brother, so he didn't mind at all. Between the orders and the teasing, Peter taught Dhugal an amazing number of useful things about being a good page—helpful points that Nicholas had spitefully withheld. Peter protected him from too much rough play, too. Even Nicholas's friends left Dhugal alone now.

As Dhugal's homesickness waned, his confidence and ability increased. When they both had free time, Peter showed Dhugal around Rhemuth or they rode their ponies together beyond the city gates. If Dhugal could have seen more of Kelson, everything would have been perfect in those happy spring days. But to his disappointment, his contacts with the prince were brief and infrequent over the next month. Dhugal bore it with as much patience as he could, for Kelson's friendliness was undimmed when they did meet. It was simply that the coming of the good weather increased the demands on Kelson's already scarce free time.

Fortunately Dhugal's encounters with Nicholas were equally infrequent. The glares Nicholas gave him whenever they saw one another promised dire vengeance, but all Nicholas did was glare. Perhaps Kelson's threat to tell Morgan had cowed him, or perhaps it was fear of royal displeasure. Dhugal didn't really care about Nicholas's reasons as long as he was left alone. Not having to share a room with Nicholas anymore was a blessing in and of itself. He and his former tormentor never spoke, and their schedules were different enough so that they almost never saw one another.

By late April, Dhugal's fear of Nicholas had become a small black cloud mostly banished to the far horizon of his mind. With Peter's help, he had progressed far enough in the previous month to be permitted to serve at the high table for the first time at the Easter Feast. All Dhugal's concentration was focused on getting through the evening without making a mistake. He wasn't strong enough to manage the great heavy platters of food, so with the other boys his age, Dhugal hurried back and forth replenishing supplies of fresh bread, carefully replacing empty wine and ale pitchers with full ones, and removing dirty dishes. Between courses he brought hot water and towels to the table for hand washing, always being careful to serve the royal family first.

The queen recognized him, smiled at him, and gave his shoulder a gentle pat as she replaced the towel on his shoulder. The king paid no particular attention to Dhugal, but Kelson smiled and winked at him. Dhugal returned the smile but didn't dare speak, with both the king and Prince Nigel within easy earshot. Seeing Kelson in his red silk tunic and silver prince's circlet, Dhugal could hardly believe that this was the same boy who had rescued him from Nicholas's revenge. That he had eaten supper privately with Kelson and spent the night in his bedroom felt far from the realm of possibility.

Dhugal returned to the pantry just before the poultry course was to be served. It was noisy and crowded in the little room, between the cooks and the other servants, pages, and squires.

"I roasted these pheasants for Her Majesty and they must be served hot!" one short, sweaty cook shouted. He had a marked Bremagni accent. "Who is serving the high table? They must go out at once!"

He carried a huge silver platter covered with roasted pheasants.

To Dhugal's astonishment and dismay, that particular platter was suddenly thrust into his own hands, giving him no time to even try to refuse it. He staggered a little at the weight of it.

"Dhugal will take them for you, don't worry, Master Jules," Nicholas announced loudly from Dhugal's other side. "He's serving the high table tonight."

"But I'm not allowed—" Dhugal gasped in panic, staring up at Nicholas and seeing the squire's unpleasant grin of triumph.

"There's nothing Her Majesty dislikes more than cold food that ought to be hot!" the cook scolded. *"Va t'en, vite, vite!"* He shooed his hands at Dhugal, then disappeared into the smoky kitchen again. Even Nicholas deliberately turned his back.

Dhugal stared down miserably. His arms were spread as wide as they would go, to grip the handles at either end of the wide oval dish. Two dozen pheasants had been arranged in a tight circle, their intact heads facing inward and their black-barred bronze tail feathers spilling over the edge of the plate, those at the ends tickling Dhugal's wrists and hands. Fragrant gravy had been ladled over each bird and lay pooled beneath them. The tray was far too heavy for him to carry all the way out to the high table. It was all Dhugal could do to hold it level.

"Excuse me, I can't—" Dhugal tried to tell a passing servant.

"Don't just stand there, boy. Move! They're waiting at the high table!"

So Dhugal had to stagger out last in the line of servers. All the way up the passage he struggled not to drop his burden. Prince Nigel would be angry to see him totter into the hall carrying a load too large and heavy for him to manage, but Dhugal couldn't see any way to explain how this had happened in the first place. The best he could hope right now was that he'd make it all the way to the high table without an accident. Surely he could make Prince Nigel understand tomorrow morning.

His arms and back ached, but there was no sense in

retreating, especially not now that he was in the great hall proper. More than halfway there now. . . .

Keeping the pheasants steady as he ascended the steps to the royal dais commanded all Dhugal's strength and attention with nothing left over for his feet, hidden from his sight by the wide platter he held. Just before taking the last step up, Dhugal tripped, his left heel planted on the long pointed toe of his right boot. The platter tipped forward, sending the pheasants tumbling off in a gush of steaming gravy. Dhugal barked his shins painfully on the top step as he landed, still clutching the empty tray with both hands. The remaining gravy splashed backward over him, making him yelp. Unable to regain his balance, Dhugal rolled backward down the dais steps to land at the bottom with greasy roast pheasants all around him.

He kept his face down, eyes focused on the carpet, too frightened and ashamed to look up. Everyone had seen him fall, and they were all laughing at him. Not that looking at the carpet was very comforting. The gravy had made a terrible brown stain on the scarlet wool, and gravy-bedraggled tail feathers were strewn everywhere. Dhugal wished he, too, could soak into the carpet and disappear.

They'll send me home for certain after this, and in disgrace, too! he thought. *What will Da say to me?*

He had no time to worry about this, because a large, fierce wolfhound darted out from under a side table and seized the largest pheasant in its jaws.

"No! Drop it!" Dhugal cried.

The hound curled its lip showing long yellow fangs, and a murderous growl sounded deep in its throat. Dhugal jerked his hand back, terrified. Other dogs came running to snatch up the unexpected windfall. Dhugal scurried about from one to another, unable to stop any of the dogs from running off with their mouths full of pheasants. Two small spaniels were playing tug-of-war over a bird at the top of the dais steps. The Court was almost hysterical over this unplanned entertainment.

Dhugal's face was hot, he was out of breath, and he could not stop the tears that ran down his face. His humiliation was complete when he glanced up to see that even Kelson was laughing at him. The prince clapped his hands over his mouth and gave Dhugal an apologetic look, but this final betrayal was more than Dhugal could bear. He plopped down on the dais steps, head bowed in despair. It took all his determination not to sob with shame, right where he sat.

Then the hall went suddenly quiet. From above and behind Dhugal, someone cleared his throat with meaning.

Dhugal jumped up, and bowed low as he turned. King Brion was now standing at his place, leaning forward to rest his hands on the table.

"Are you hurt, boy?" The king's voice was mild, even gentle, but all Dhugal could do was shake his head, open-mouthed.

"That's good. Perhaps you could pick up the pheasants and take them back to the kitchen, then?" the king suggested.

Dhugal nodded, still bereft of speech.

"When you finish that, go change your clothes and wash up," King Brion ordered, sitting down again. "You're so covered with gravy and tail feathers, I can hardly tell you apart from the birds."

His eyes twinkled and his expression was kind. Nor could Dhugal mistake the undercurrent of amusement in his voice. The king turned and nodded to Richard, standing behind Kelson's chair.

"Richard, help him, would you please?"

With Richard's help, Dhugal gathered up the pheasants, Richard plucking half-gnawed birds from disappointed mouths and shooing the dogs away while Dhugal picked up those that hadn't been grabbed off the floor. He bowed to the king before fleeing the great hall, pheasants piled up anyhow on the platter.

"My pheasants! Ruined!" the Bremagni cook howled when Dhugal returned to the kitchen. He yanked the tray

from Dhugal's hands and stared at the remains of his birds
while two big tears rolled down his cheeks.

"I raised those pheasants from hatchlings myself, especially for Her Majesty," he mourned. "She never even
got to *taste* them!"

Dhugal hung his head, feeling almost as terrible as he
had in the great hall with everyone laughing at him. When
he finally dared glance up, the cook was looking at him
as if he contemplated threading Dhugal on a spit for roast-
ing. Dhugal fled.

Back in his room, Dhugal flung himself facedown on
his bed and sobbed. He *couldn't* go back to the great hall
tonight, or ever face anyone at Court ever again. Especially not Prince Nigel and the other pages. Even Prince
Kelson had laughed at him. He wanted to go home—
wanted to *be* home right now, although that was impossible.

Finally Dhugal wept himself empty. He stood and discarded his stained tabard and washed his face and hands.
The king had said, "Go change." He hadn't said anything
about "Go to bed." Clean and neat again, Dhugal sat on
his bed to wait for the king's summons, feeling like a
condemned prisoner before execution.

It was very late when the knock finally came on his
bedroom door. Dhugal was grateful to see that Richard
had been sent to fetch him.

"Is the king terribly angry with me?" he blurted.

"Come along. He's not going to *hang* you, Dhugal,"
Richard coaxed, laughing. "But it won't do to keep His
Majesty waiting."

Awful possibilities chased through Dhugal's mind on the
way, especially when he and Richard passed through
the now deserted great hall. Two serving maids were
on their hands and knees scrubbing at the stained carpet
on the steps of the royal dais. That must be why the king
wanted to speak to him; he'd ruined the carpet. There was
no time even to think about bolting, though, as Richard was

already knocking on the door to the withdrawing room behind the dais.

"Come in," the king called.

"I've brought Dhugal MacArdry as you commanded, Sire," Richard said.

Sick to his stomach from fear, Dhugal followed Richard inside and bowed when he did.

The king and queen, Kelson, and Prince Nigel were gathered inside, all of them watching him when Dhugal straightened from his bow. Queen Jehana darted toward him and clasped him in her arms, her cheek against his hair.

"You poor boy, there's no need to look so frightened," she soothed, and kissed the top of his head.

Dhugal could only blink in stupefaction. This wasn't in the least what he'd expected.

"No one is going to punish you, *are* they, Nigel?" Queen Jehana gave her brother-in-law a pointed look.

"I daresay Dhugal has learned a valuable lesson about not trying to carry platters too big and heavy for him to lift," Nigel agreed.

"I only wanted to make sure you didn't hurt yourself when you fell down the steps," the queen went on. "That was a bad tumble. You didn't hit your head, did you?" She pulled back far enough to look anxiously into Dhugal's face, briefly feeling at his head for lumps and bumps.

All Dhugal could do was look up at her and shake his head.

"Perhaps we should let Dhugal explain what happened," the king interposed.

The sound of his voice, mild and calm as it was, made Dhugal's knees go wobbly again. Queen Jehana squeezed his shoulders, then went back to sit beside her husband. They both looked at Dhugal expectantly.

He opened his mouth, unsure of where to begin. "I—I was in the pantry, Sire, and Nicholas Murdoch told the cook I'd take the tray of pheasants up to the high table. I

tried to find someone else to carry it, but no one would
listen, and I—"

The king stopped him with an upraised hand. "Start at
the beginning," he ordered. "I should have known it might
be Nicholas again. Kelson has told me about the way he
treated you, and he seems to think that Nicholas played a
trick on you tonight. What I want to hear is *your* account."
He smiled and made an encouraging gesture with his right
hand.

Dhugal told them the whole story and made a very
truthful account. It felt worse than confession to a priest.
He did not spare Nicholas in his telling, but nor did he
hide his own involvement in Nicholas's humiliation, and
finished with the evening's events in the pantry.

The king listened with polite attention and without in-
terruption. His calm expression underwent a remarkable
spasm when Dhugal got to the part about exchanging his
own pair of hose for Nicholas's.

"The Murdoch boys," the king sighed when Dhugal had
finished. "I'll have to speak to old Carthane this time,
Nigel. Nicholas has been given half a dozen chances already."

"It's partially my own fault," Prince Nigel admitted. "I
gave Nicholas a stern warning before I put him in with
Dhugal. When the lad didn't complain about him, I hoped
Nicholas was behaving himself for once. When I found
out the truth, I gave Dhugal a new roommate. Until tonight, I thought the problem had been solved.

"Still, you're right. As little as I like giving up on any
lad, I think we have to seriously reconsider Nicholas's
future at Court."

"I'll talk to Lord Carthane in the morning, then," the
king said. "All his sons and grandsons have been trouble-
some, but Nicholas has been the worst of the lot." He
shook his head in regret even as he smiled at Dhugal. "I
did hate seeing those beautiful pheasants go to feed the
dogs."

He rose and stretched, then tousled Dhugal's hair. "Per-

haps, Dhugal, you've also learned tonight that there's no
need to suffer in silence when someone treats you un-
fairly, hmm? You could have spared yourself two very
unpleasant months if you'd told Prince Nigel what was
really going on."

Dhugal gulped. "Yes, Sire."

"With that being settled, we'd all best retire for the
night," the king ordered. "Off to bed with you, Dhugal.
It's very late, and your day begins early." He gave Dhugal's shoulder a kind squeeze before turning to offer his
hand to the queen.

Dhugal bowed low as they passed him, giddy with relief. Kelson grinned and slapped his back in passing, and
even Prince Nigel gave his shoulder a friendly buffet on
his way out.

When they'd gone, Dhugal went back to his room, un-
dressed, and crawled into bed, all in a daze. It was a long
time before he slept.

"DHUGAL!"

Kelson's voice calling his name made Dhugal look up
from his archery practice the following afternoon. Kelson
darted toward him down the length of the archery yard.

"What do you think?" the prince demanded eagerly,
with a huge grin on his face. He pulled Dhugal off to one
side, out of earshot of the pages nearby.

There were any number of things Dhugal could think,
but from the way Kelson was grinning, he was sure it
wasn't bad news. Out of the corner of his eye, he could
see the other boys looking on enviously at his having
private conversation with the crown prince. He pretended
not to notice them.

"Nicholas has been sent home for a full year!" Kelson
exulted. "Father spoke to the Earl of Carthane this morning, and he and Nicholas are leaving for Nyford later this
afternoon." Kelson's eyes danced as he tried to muffle his
laughter. "I saw Lord Carthane come out of Father's study

with his face as red as Haldane scarlet." He snickered. "I don't think Nicholas will enjoy his journey home very much."

Dhugal just grinned, dizzy with joy. No more Nicholas!

Kelson stopped laughing all at once and gave Dhugal an apologetic look. "I'm sorry about last night," he whispered. "I really tried not to laugh at you. You must have felt awful, tripping like that in front of everyone." He bit his lip and looked down for a moment, but when he looked up, his eyes were sparkling.

"I couldn't help it, though. You *did* look funny, all covered with gravy and feathers, with your face scrunched up like this." Kelson opened his eyes very wide and pulled down the corners of his mouth, making his lower lip and chin wobble as if he were on the verge of tears.

Picturing himself as he must have looked last night, Dhugal could not help laughing at Kelson's mimicry. The memory had lost its sting with Kelson's apology.

"S'all right." Dhugal shrugged and smiled back. "I must have looked silly chasing all those dogs." They laughed together companionably.

"Kelson?" a man's voice called from the other end of the archery yard.

"Oh, Lord. Dhugal, I'm sorry but I've got to go," Kelson said, already edging away toward Morgan. "Morgan's promised me a fencing lesson this afternoon."

"Morgan is your fencing master?" Dhugal gaped. He turned to look and recognized the tall, fair Deryni lord waiting patiently by the entrance of the archery yard. Morgan raised his hand and beckoned to Kelson.

"He's not my regular fencing master, of course," Kelson replied. "He hasn't got time for that, but he's just about the best swordsman in Gwynedd. I always learn more from him.

"But I really do have to go now. If I keep Morgan waiting too long, he may say we haven't time for a proper lesson." Kelson tilted his head to one side, even as he started toward Morgan. "Do you have a free afternoon next Saturday?"

"Yes."

"Come to my room then, and we'll play," Kelson invited over his shoulder, grinning at Dhugal before he dashed away to join Morgan.

Dhugal watched the two of them walk away, well content, and answered Kelson's wave just before the prince and Morgan turned a corner and were lost to sight. Smiling, Dhugal picked up his bow again and nocked a new arrow to the string.

That Nicholas had been sent home was wonderful news, but that wasn't why the other pages nearby were frankly staring at him. There was envy in their faces and new respect. Most of them had seen him talking to the prince, and all of them had heard Kelson's invitation to come and play.

Pretending not to notice them, Dhugal pulled the bowstring slowly back to his right ear. He'd been practicing hard in the last six weeks, and his right-handed shooting was much improved, although it still felt awkward to him. With a deep breath, he released the arrow—which landed with a satisfying thump in the straw stuffed target.

Lowering his bow, Dhugal saw that he'd finally shot into the gold.

❄

AUTHOR'S NOTE: This fan fiction story was written before the publication of the signed, limited edition of the *Codex Derynianus* in 1998. I am now aware that the Murdoch family no longer rules in the County of Carthane. However, I thought it was appropriate for my antagonist, Nicholas, to be a Murdoch. In the two hundred years between Alroy and Javan's reigns and Brion's, it seemed possible that the Murdochs could

have improved from the villainous to the merely unpleasant. I have corrected what other errors and incon-
sistencies that I could, to be consistent with the *Codex,*
however.

THE FORTUNE TELLER
1116

Our next tale delves into some of the back story of the lovely Lady Richenda, later destined to become Alaric's wife and the mother of his children. But when Alaric first met her, she was another man's wife and the mother of *his* child—and before that, she very probably led a life much like that of most young women of noble family in that time and culture, whose future was determined, at least in the beginning, by the wishes of her parents. (We must remember not to judge past times by the standards of today. I've sometimes been questioned over my decision not to let my female characters abandon their feminine attire and swash their buckles with the men—to which I have always responded that I've tried to show women more as they would have lived in an admittedly somewhat idealized version of our own past, which means that they mostly would have kept to traditional women's roles.)

This certainly would have been the case among noble women, at least—and let's face it: the reason most authors don't write much about ordinary folk is that the nobles have the leisure made possible by their wealth to pursue "adventures," while the ordinary folk have to expend almost all their energy just staying alive and keeping their families fed and clothed and sheltered. In our own past, only a privileged few had the leisure and support to be scholars like Evaine MacRorie (consciously modeled somewhat on Margaret Roper, the daughter of Sir Thomas More) or Richenda or Rothana. And as for the distaff swashing of buckles—it would have been almost unheard of, and regarded as scandalous when it *was* heard of!

So we are obliged to speculate on what it might have been like for a girl of privileged background, contemplating her future in the terms usually set out for young noble women: to be wed to a man whose fortune and prospects would complement her own and hopefully lead to at least a slight advancement in social stature for her eventual children—for women were expected to reproduce, and often, and preferably male children, at least to start. Though the notion of marrying for love was rarely the prime factor in arranging a marital alliance, especially among the upper classes, I suspect that most couples at least came to feel a companionable affection for one another—and the ideal of having true affection and love grow within such an arranged marriage almost certainly was a dream shared by most young women approaching the age of marriageability.

So this next story is a glimpse into that time of dreams before marriage, as it might have taken place for Richenda. Within the canon of the Deryni universe, we never see her with her first husband, Bran Coris Earl of Marley, so we don't know how she felt about him before treason led him to his death. But from comments she makes, even while the treason is coming to light, we can surmise that they had found a comfortable *modus vivendi:* that he was a fairly gentle and indulgent spouse, and a good father to young Brendan; certainly, Richenda doted on her firstborn son. But before her marriage, when reality had not yet intruded and girlhood dreams could still be indulged, she and some of her friends might very well have visited a local fair and gone to see "The Fortune Teller."

THE FORTUNE TELLER

Ann W. Jones

"RICHENDA!"

She turned as hands gripped her arm, her face lighting in a pleased smile.

"Avisa! Where did you spring from?"

"I'm visiting my kinfolk here for a few weeks. Did you know Leonora was here too?"

"No, where?"

"She's staying with her aunt. Isn't it fun that we're all here at the same time? Could we arrange a meeting, Richenda? I do hope we can."

"I'd like that," Richenda agreed impulsively.

The two sixteen-year-olds linked arms as they walked along, Avisa chattering on happily, both of them disregarding their respective maids, who hurriedly joined forces to follow them.

"My uncle's kept me very busy this past year, but I still haven't met my perfect warrior," Avisa continued.

"No castle yet, then?" Richenda teased.

"No, but I haven't given up hope. Who knows? Whilst I'm here, I might meet *him.*" Avisa gave a lighthearted jump in the air, then recollected herself, smoothing her gown and drawing Richenda to a seat at the edge of the square. "I've noticed several tall, handsome men here. One of them must be a warrior with a castle. Uncle knows what I want. What fun it will be to stand on the ramparts, waving my kerchief to him when he rides out for battle."

She stood up and demonstrated, letting her pale lilac kerchief flutter from her hand. "Or," she slipped into a curtsey, "receiving him on his return, and perhaps even being presented to the king with everyone at court watching us." She resumed her seat, eyes shining with the vision of her future.

Richenda laughed gently. "You haven't changed at all. It won't be all bright gowns and courtly ceremony, you know. Think of the constant traipsing from battle to battle—the rain, the mud, the wounds. He could even be killed."

Avisa pouted. "Why do you always have to make fun of my dreams?"

"I don't mean to," Richenda assured her. "It's just that I have this very practical streak. I can't help seeing the dull side of things as well as the sparkle."

Avisa smiled again. "You were just the same with Leonora, I remember, when she said she intended to marry a rich husband."

"An earl, wasn't it?"

"Yes. And you said that if she *did* manage to find one, he'd undoubtedly be old and fat."

"Well, he would, wouldn't he?" Richenda giggled. "He'd *have* to be old, if he'd already got his title, a castle, and the wherewithal to stock it the way she'd like. And if they lived as regally as Leonora hoped, he'd soon be fat, if he didn't start out that way—and he'd almost certainly be too set in his ways to indulge in the dancing and festivities Leonora has planned."

Avisa joined in Richenda's mirth. "You're probably right. She'll never change, though. It's been parties and visits all year for her. Half a dozen titled men must be vying for her hand. I hear Father Idris nearly had a fit when he learned what she wanted to do with her life."

"Poor Father Idris, we must have been a sore trial to him," Richenda murmured, thinking fondly of the gentle priest who had been their tutor.

"I suppose so," Avisa agreed, "but I think he had a soft spot for Leonora, in spite of the number of times he scolded her about the sin of pride."

"Mmmm." Richenda looked across the square and considered her own plans for the future. She had always thought in terms of marriage and children—especially children. She'd always liked mothering other people's, even when little more than a child herself. In particular, she was fond of little boys—the way they puckered their mouths after a fall, trying not to cry, with grubby fists knuckling their eyes; the small hands circling the hilts of wooden swords as they fought mock battles with one another on the grassy slopes of her home.

Now, a year since leaving her friends and their daydreams, she knew about the future father of her children as well. "A noble marriage," her father had described it, when he summoned her one day not long ago, standing in front of the fire in the great chamber, hands clasped behind his back. "An earl, m'dear, nothing less for my daughter, hey? I'm sure you'll manage splendidly."

He had meant to be kind and reassuring, she knew, but at first she'd thought of her own careless words to Leonora—old and fat. Her concern must have shown in her face, for her father left his place and led her to a chair.

"Bran Coris, m'dear—as fine a young man as ever I saw."

"Young?" Richenda murmured.

"Certainly, certainly." Her father patted her hand. "And comely, too, hey?"

For a moment she couldn't believe it, but there was no reason to doubt him.

A countess—I shall be a countess, was her sudden thought, *and before Leonora, that's for sure.*

"Run along now and get ready, m'dear," her father
went on. "M'lord Bran dines with us this evening."

"Yes, Father."

She dropped him a dutiful curtsey and followed it with
a quick peck on his cheek, then ran from the room. After
dressing, she stared at her reflection in the glass. She had
taken great care: lifting and replacing gowns, fingering
and leaving headdresses. Her final choice had been a loose
gown of blue to complement her eyes, the hem embroidered with silver star-flowers that were also entwined in
her headdress.

Her maid had brushed her red-gold hair until it shone,
leaving it loose as befitted the young unmarried girl she
was. She sprinkled a few drops of the star-flower essence
on her hair, throat, and wrists; otherwise, her pale skin
was unadorned. She clasped a silver bracelet on her arm—
an inheritance from her maternal grandmother—and took
one last look at herself before descending to the Great
Hall. Her father, in his customary stance before the fire,
came forward to greet her, taking her hand and presenting
her to his guest.

Her first sight of her husband-to-be was reassuring. He
was not old *or* fat. He raised her hand to his lips; she felt
them touch her skin, followed by the prickly sensation of
his beard brushing her hand. It was not unpleasant.

"My lady."

His voice was vibrant. She lifted her eyes to look at
him; he was not ugly. His gold-flecked eyes were fixed
upon her; slightly rounded and a little protuberant, they
reminded her of the great golden berries that weighted the
branches of the tree under her window in autumn.

"My lord?" She was suddenly unsure if that was the
correct form of address—a pity Leonora wasn't here;
she'd have it down pat. Lord Bran smiled at her and drew
her to the table, waiting until she seated herself before
taking his place.

"Richenda, you haven't heard a word I've said." A tap
on her arm brought her back to the present.

"I'm sorry, Avisa. I was daydreaming. What did you say?"

"I said a fair is starting tomorrow at the field, and I hear there's to be a fortune-teller with it. Wouldn't it be fun if the three of us went and tested her? I'd love to know who I'm going to marry, wouldn't you?" Avisa was bubbling with her plan.

But I already know, Richenda thought, and hugged her secret to herself.

"Wouldn't you?" the insistent voice recalled her.

"What makes you think that this—person could tell us?" she dissembled.

"My kinfolk have heard of her before. They say she's very good. Do say we can go, Richenda."

"We'll see what Leonora thinks about it."

They parted after arranging to meet again the next day, and Richenda returned home. Over dinner she told her father about her chance meeting with Avisa and their plans to see each other again on the morrow, but she did not mention the fortune-teller. To her relief, her father seemed preoccupied with business and only nodded agreement.

That night, clad in her white linen sleeping shift, Richenda leaned her elbows on the casement ledge and looked out over the silvered shrubs and bushes below. She wondered if Marley was like her home, and resolved to ask Lord Bran about his country at their next meeting.

The following day she was up early but breakfasted alone; her father had already left to ride around his tenant farmers for the monthly report. As soon as she had eaten, she summoned her maid to accompany her and stepped out onto the broad path outside her father's hall. She and Avisa had agreed to meet by the fountain in the abbey gardens.

The morning was bright and warm, but she walked briskly, not wanting to linger in the streets. She found she was the first to arrive. The fountain was the centerpiece of the abbey grounds, set amid peaceful flowerbeds and

well-kept lawns. Richenda perched on the edge of the pool
and trailed her fingers in the water, disturbing the image
of her face reflected in it. The heady fragrance of the
flowers hung in the air and the bees drifted over them as
she thought how soon she would be a married woman,
beginning the tasks of caring for a husband and home,
putting aside childish joys and pleasures.

"Richenda?"

A light, girlish voice broke into her thoughts and she
rose, shaking out the folds of her dress. It was Avisa, and
close behind her another familiar figure.

"Leonora!" Richenda hugged her friend. "I'm so
pleased to see you again!"

Dark curls hanging nearly to her waist, Leonora was as
pretty as ever, a beautifully embroidered girdle emphasiz-
ing the slim waist of a gown cut in the latest fashion. She
looked almost like an angel as she pulled her friends to a
nearby seat.

"Richenda, isn't it exciting? Avisa's told me of the fair.
Shall we go to hear our fortunes?"

Somewhat to her own surprise, Richenda found herself
agreeing.

"I've thought of a good idea," Avisa said. "How about
all going dressed the same, and not telling her our
names?"

"Why?" Leonora asked.

"Because she might have heard of one of us and only
say what she thinks we'd like to hear, or what she already
knows," Avisa explained.

"I think that's a good idea," chuckled Leonora.

Avisa and Leonora left when all the details had been
decided, but Richenda stayed awhile longer in the abbey
gardens and watched the black-clad Fathers walking se-
dately in their cloisters, wondering how they could bear
to shut themselves off from family life. She understood
the workings of the Church and gave unstintingly of her
time and purse to aid it, yet she was often aware of some-

thing lacking, something missing in her religious observance.

Perhaps it stemmed from being Deryni. Perhaps humans related to the Church in a different kind of way. Occasionally she found herself wishing she might keep the old Deryni religious teachings her parents had taught her, but those had long been superseded, and the Church leaders were intransigent in their attitude to all things Deryni. At length she rose, called her maid to accompany her, and left the gardens for her home. Her father was waiting when she arrived.

"Lord Bran is here again," he told her as she entered. "He'll dine with us, of course. Do you like him?"

"Yes, Father." She would have obeyed him anyway, but it was a pleasure to do so this time. The Earl of Marley was attractive, and had paid her much attention on his previous visit, obviously pleasing her father.

"Come in here, we must have a word before dinner," her father went on, leading her into the paneled study. "About Lord Bran—he's not Deryni, you know."

Richenda lowered her eyes. Of course she knew that.

"And what is more, I'm not at all sure he likes those who are. Otherwise, it's a good match, though. I don't suppose I need tell you that some things are best kept secret, even from one's husband—unless, of course, his feelings should change in the future. You do understand what I'm talking about, don't you, m'dear?"

"I understand, Father."

The evening passed quickly. M'lord Bran was assiduous in his attentions, listening to her and seeking her opinion on everyday matters. She was also able to question him about Marley. He was very pleased to describe his homeland, telling her of the rich farmland and the livestock raised there. His eyes lit up when he spoke of Marley. His youth and charm were infectious, and she was content in knowing she would become his wife later in the year.

She did not go out at all during the following morning,

but gave herself to her tasks, checking the household accounts and inspecting the storerooms. After the midday meal, her duty done, she dressed in the fashion agreed by her friends—a long, plain white gown, loose hair, and no ornaments—and set off toward the field with her maid.

The others were waiting when she arrived, laughing together, but she suddenly felt much older than they were; perhaps later today she would confide her news to them. They walked side by side down to the fair, past booths selling every kind of produce, where plump goodwives picked and pinched the fare before they bought. A juggler was demonstrating his skills at another stall, and for a while they stood and watched the patterns he made with the balls he tossed aloft.

Pausing at another booth, Leonora bought some marzipan fancies and handed them around, including the maids in her generous gesture. They munched the sweetmeats contentedly as they wandered toward their target— a drab-colored tent amid the garish display of the other booths. There did not seem to be anyone around, so Leonora twitched aside the makeshift entry curtain. It was dim in the confined space.

"Come in, my dear," an ancient voice crackled.

"You first," Leonora said, backing out and turning toward Richenda.

"Yes, you first," echoed Avisa, stepping to one side.

Richenda lifted the curtain and entered. For a few seconds she could see nothing, until her eyes became accustomed to the lack of light.

"Sit down, my dear," the ancient insisted.

Richenda perched somewhat nervously on the edge of the seat opposite the beldame.

"Let me look at your hand."

Richenda laid her left hand palm upward on the table between them. The crone lifted it and studied it, tracing the various lines with a grimy finger. Richenda wondered how she could see anything in the dimness.

"Give me a coin, mistress, and I'll look in the crystal."

Richenda fumbled in her purse, produced a small silver coin, and laid it down. It disappeared quickly into some part of the voluminous garments of the crone who, almost at the same time, produced a glass globe and placed it on the table. She passed her hand over it, and Richenda saw that her nails were curved yellow talons.

"I see the letter 'M'—it means something to you, I think."

The words took Richenda by surprise. "M"—Marley, of course, the Earldom of Marley, her future home. She nodded.

"The letter 'M,' " continued the beldame, "will play a larger part in your future than you imagine, yet for a long time it will be obscured." More passes of the hands, this time accompanied by a low incantation. "I see a man with whom your future is inextricably entwined."

Richenda nodded again—the woman was *good:* foretelling Marley and now about to embark on a description of her future husband.

"He is tall and straight—his hair silver-gilt and his eyes, gray mysterious pools."

Richenda blinked. It was all wrong. Lord Bran was nothing like that. How silly. It was just foolish guessing after all; she knew her future. She rose and moved to the entrance. "Thank you, Mother."

"Wait, don't you want to know if you will have children?"

But Richenda was already outside. Nor would she tell the others what had been said.

"We'll talk after you've both seen her."

They nodded, for that was what they had previously agreed, and Avisa went in next. She was every bit as long as Richenda, and came out laughing and bubbling. Leonora went in then, and the others ate the last of the marzipan while they waited. They were unprepared for their friend's return. She erupted from the tent with hair flying and eyes blazing, as a shrill laugh hung in the air.

"Let's get out of here," Leonora said sharply.

She would not speak until they had reached the scented gardens of the abbey above the fair.

"Now, *will* you tell us what's the matter?" Richenda asked her.

"Do you know what she said about *me*?"

"No, we're waiting for you to tell us," Avisa pointed out. "We haven't got the Sight."

"Neither has she," retorted Leonora. "She said I wouldn't marry any man, but would be wedded to the Church. Me!"

Her friends laughed with her—it was absurd. Leonora, the plague of Father Idris, a nun? It was crazy.

"What about you?" Richenda asked Avisa.

"Oh, the usual kind of thing. I'm to marry within the year—a man of medium height, brown hair and beard, yellow-brown eyes, with money too. It could be true. . . ."

"But it won't be," Richenda said firmly.

"How do you know?"

"She was totally wrong about me—said a tall, blond, gray-eyed man would be my future."

"Well, he might."

"No, I know it isn't true. Listen." And Richenda told her friends her news.

They were silenced for a little, then Avisa clapped her hands. "Your description of M'lord Bran is just like the beldame painted of *my* future husband. She's obviously confused. Maybe I'll get yours. And who could imagine Leonora a nun?"

The gloom was broken. They laughed together and were laughing still as they parted to return to their respective homes.

All the same, Richenda found herself thinking of the incident in the months leading up to her wedding. The remembrance kept returning to her at odd moments. It was strange that the beldame had been so right about the letter "M" and so wrong about Lord Bran. Her unease deepened when she had word that Avisa was to marry the son of a neighboring lord—a brown-eyed, brown-haired youth with a small inheritance of his own. Thankfully she did not hear anything of Leonora other than the general reports of her usual gaiety and beauty.

Some months later, leaving the abbey after her marriage, Richenda came out of the dim interior into the light on Lord Bran's arm. Crowds of well-wishers were there, showering them with petals. As Bran touched his lips to hers in the time-honored custom, his carriage drew up. He released her, opened the door, turned, and lifted her into the conveyance before going to speak to the leading horseman. Apart from an uneasy rustling, the crowd fell quiet. Richenda looked around to see an ancient figure regarding her, dusty black garments chillingly familiar.

"I knew 'twas you all along, M'lady," wheezed the crone, laying her clawed hand on the open side of the carriage. "Didn't I attend your blessed mother when she was birthing you? Remember my words, M'lady. The letter 'M' is not what it seems—yet it still is important to you. And watch and wait for the gray-eyed man; he holds the key to your future."

She cackled briefly, pressed something into Richenda's hand, and disappeared into the crowd who parted to let her through.

Richenda was shaken. Seeing that Bran was taking his leave of Father Idris, who had conducted the ceremony, she risked a glance at the object in her hand. It was a stone, roughly carved into the shape of a gryphon. Puzzled, she had just enough time to conceal it before Bran came up and settled beside her. He called to the horsemen and the carriage moved off on the first stage of her new life as Countess of Marley.

�֎

LOVER TO SHADOWS
1121

The next story definitely falls into that category of tales I wish I had written myself, though I don't think I possibly could have achieved some of the insights in "Lover to Shadows." I think it took a man to tell this particular story—and tell it he did, most marvelously. What makes it all the more fascinating, besides its attention to military detail (its author is a military historian) and its sheer poetry (a formidable talent, here!), is that it's told from the other side, the point of view of the bad guys—who aren't really bad guys, of course; they're simply on the opposite side.

In specific, it's a story about Charissa de Tolan, the Marluk's daughter, and the mountain lord who loved her throughout the decade or so before the beginning of *Deryni Rising*. It's a totally different voice from mine—and more than just the difference between a male or a female storyteller, I think. It's a glimpse from the direction of the lands east of Gwynedd, where I've only recently gone myself, from the steppes straddling the border between Gwynedd and Torenth. I'm certain that some of the images Lohr Miller conjured in this story and another that he wrote were early influences on my own vision of Torenth.

So meet Christian-Richard de Falkenberg, who loved Charissa, the Shadowed One. . . .

LOVER TO SHADOWS

✥

Lohr E. Miller

. . . Put not your trust in princes, we are told. And you and I know the truth of that. Rumor holds that you play for Claibourne and the Riding. Fealty yields before the promise of a coronet; that is no more than the nature of things. You know that I cannot but wish you luck and great victories. But put not your faith in princes: the Hart no more than the Lion. There are loyalties beyond those of liege and man, and if it chances that the Eagles are brought down by Hart or Lion, there remains a place for you and those loyal to you. I think you know I could do no less.

Given this day at Caer Curyll, in the Year of Grace
    1121. . . .
The Lord Falkenberg to the Earl of Marley. . . .

THERE HAD BEEN three of the letters, each written in the Lord Falkenberg's thin, precise hand, each with a private seal burnt on with a Deryni signet, each sent out with a black wax seal bearing the crest of the Falkenberg

House: *Bran Earl of Marley; Lionel Duke of Arjenol; Nigel Duke of Carthmoor*. Each letter had made the same offer. The House of Falkenberg could field few enough retainers, but there were few safer places in the Eleven Kingdoms for a man to run than Caer Curyll, on its mountain above the northern seas. The couriers had gone out on May Eve, in the wake of the Duke of Cassan's defeat at Rengarth. By now the Furstan Hart and the Haldane Lion would be facing one another before Cardosa in what the chroniclers would call "a great murthering battle." The House of Furstan was not known for its great tenderness; and *gwae'r gorchfygedig—vae victis!*—had been the Haldane way since the Restoration. Soon enough the first fugitives would come staggering up the Rheljan spurs to ask sanctuary at Caer Curyll. And that, thought Christian-Richard de Falkenberg, offered its own set of temptations.

Falkenberg looked up from the pages of elegant Moorish script spread across his worktable. At New Year's he had refused Wencit of Torenth's offer to join the Enterprise of Gwynedd, and in the long waiting he had passed the days composing Moorish poetry, the phrases crawling right to left across the page.

What lute have I borne for pleasure/Whose strings have not been snapped in pain?

Soon enough, Furstan or Haldane. And there would be riders at his gate, breathless, afraid, asking his protection. Bran or Lionel or. . . . He looked into the stained-glass images encircling his solar and allowed himself the briefest flirtation with temptation.

Nigel Haldane was, he supposed, a friend, and to be treated so. But ah, if under tattered Haldane scarlet and gold Nigel arrived with his royal nephew and the king's champion. . . . Kelson Haldane could be sent to Beldour—in all honor, but a prisoner of state, nonetheless. To Beldour: only a king might kill a king.

But the Duke of Corwyn, now. . . . There had been no executions in Caer Curyll since his grandfather's time, when Michael de Falkenberg set the heads of half a hundred Eastmarch sailors on pikes along the sea road. But

the King's Champion of Gwynedd. . . . *What hope woven
from threads of light/On which dark did not fall?*

He closed his eyes and allowed himself to see Alaric
Morgan's body falling past Darklair Edge, spinning down
nine hundred feet to the surf and the rocks.

Bloody hell! Falkenberg tossed his pen onto the table.
That would be too neat a jest, even for Fate. And there
was no point in fantasies of revenge and bitterness. Last
autumn he had told himself that he could deny himself
the cankered pleasures of such dreams. *However much
Morgan deserves it.* All winter he had laughed into his
brandy: Morgan excommunicate, hunted by the Church
Militant; anti-Deryni rebels torching Corwyn manors; the
ducal capital at Coroth in rebel hands. *From one Deryni
to another,* he had called the toast at Passiontide: *Burn in
hell, Morgan!*

Well, Alaric Morgan would hardly come calling. He
wondered if, indeed, Morgan had ever heard the name
"Falkenberg." Likely enough, not. One of Wencit's lancers might drive an ashwood shaft through Morgan's armor—that could happen! But personal vengeance could
not.

He reached out for something black, cubical, polished.
Held close, it had an almost amethyst color and a liquid,
near-obsidian look. It had been white once: one of the
eight cubes of a Ward Major. Something done once, long
ago, in a summer when there had been charm and no end
of laughter in being able to break Wards Major.

He turned it to catch his reflection: Christian-Richard,
Lord Falkenberg of Caer Curyll. A broad, dark face, high-
cheekboned. Black hair cropped to an almost spiky short-
ness, a beard close-cropped round his mouth. An
expression set permanently in what Lionel d'Arjenol had
long ago called "wry contempt." Deep-set eyes of polished darkness under darker brows.

A face for brooding and affected passion, he knew. *Dil-
ettante. Failed poet. Late commander of mercenary cavalry, accounted—God knows why!—successful.* An *almost*

face: *almost* clever, not quite brave, *almost* handsome. Not the face of a potential banesman of the Duke of Corwyn.

Let us drink to the pawns on the Board. He raised the cube in mock toast. Almost someone. Almost handsome.

She had been there, a year ago, the rose light from the high windows of the solar giving a strawberry tint to the pale fire of white-blond hair that fell across her bare throat and shoulders as she sat wrapped in a great fur rug, toying with the burnt warding cube and laughing with him. . . .

Someone only for her, then. Her portrait was there: a charcoal sketch his second-in-command had done of her in the first summer back from the South. She had grown thinner in the years he had been in Bremagne and the Moorish lands—thinner and more regal. And if less innocent, then more possessed of irony and self-knowledge.

A portrait, then: a girl of perhaps twenty, long, pale hair parted in the center, flowing down across her shoulders. The fine, high lines of throat and shoulders set off a face full of elegance and determination. A dark band around her throat held a single small jewel. And eyes of incredible depth, cornflower-pale in the flesh: glacier, summer, mirror, all by turn. Beautiful, then: gentleness, warmth, elegance, irony, sensuality, power, cold reserve— all were there. She had pressed her signet to it, the coronet and lion's claws burnt into the parchment. And below, in her precisely flowing hand, her inscription: *For Christian, given with all my love—a caryad, Charissa.*

Caryad-heart-of-my-heart. Falkenberg wrapped the cube in long, thin fingers and pressed the edges into his palm. *Caryad. No bitterness,* he had told himself. *It dishonors her, to dream of a vengeance you cannot take.*

Under his hand, the cube was glowing with a dull violet fire, its surface grown chill to the touch. He turned his palm up and held it before his eyes, trying to center his mind in the cool violet light. In the Moorish lands he had sat with the Amir al-Jabal, the Lord of the Mountain in

Alamut, and learned to look into the light. *In clarity is wholeness.* Yes. *The mirror only, and the moment.* Yes. *But damn you anyway, Morgan.*

"My lord—?"

Falkenberg looked up from his cube. A tall man in blue and silver livery was at the door. His name was Brennan de Colforth, and upon a time he had been captain of the Tolan household troops. Colforth and perhaps a dozen of the two-score men Charissa had taken to Rhemuth as her honor guard remained free after Kelson Haldane's coronation, loose ends not yet dealt with by the Haldanes. He was *faute de mieux,* attached now to the Falkenberg standards. Colforth was watching the glow of the warding cube and the portrait of Charissa de Tolan.

"I'm sorry to intrude, lord . . ." He trailed off, embarrassed.

Falkenberg dropped the cube onto the table. "This isn't a shrine," he said, more sharply than he'd intended. There was something of expectation and hope in Colforth's face, and the sight of it left him tired. *I've failed them,* he thought. *I'm not what they bargained for.* "I'm not up here in mourning. What is it?"

Colforth jerked his head toward the eastern windows. "Riders up, lord. One party up Wenlock Edge from the Tolan road. There's another from the Fells; there's supposed to be wounded. Aurelian's gone out to meet them."

"Well enough." Falkenberg pushed his chair back. "Go put your squadron at alert and get a surgeon and a priest. Let's play the gracious hosts something well, shall we?" He reached for his gloves and stood up, the rose light staining violet across the dark blue velvet of his tunic. He reached under the spread of papers and extracted a heavy silver chain. He scooped it up and settled it over his head. The silver falcon pendant fell heavily against his chest. Not the silver circlet of his lordship, but formal enough. He refused to ask himself which of them it might be, down there. *Too long the free-captain,* he thought. *We all end up bleeding in the saddle, knocking at gates and cry-*

ing for sanctuary. And any morning was as good as any other for it.

He could, he thought, offer sanctuary to the fugitive, console the dying, give wine and sympathy to the exiled. All that came with holding a lordship like Caer Curyll. Only the waiting was hard.

He followed Colforth down the long winding stairs to the main court, drawing himself up to play the good lord, the sound of his boots hollow in the great stairwell.

THE ARROW SLAMMED hard into the center of the target and Falkenberg turned to face the limping, petulant figure of Thorne Hagen. Hagen was settling himself painfully on the gray stone of the steps, his face tightening as his legs straightened out. Thorne Hagen at fifty was a handsome man and fond of insisting that he looked no more than thirty. In the bleak December sunlight, sprawled in his unfamiliar riding habit among the dark figures of Falkenberg's retainers, he looked a very exhausted fifty.

Falkenberg reached into the quiver slung under his black cloak and extracted a second arrow. He touched the barbed tip to his forehead in a mock salute. Thorne Hagen was the most unmartial of men, and the idea of the fleshy Deryni lord in his new and uncomfortable riding leathers forcing a horse up from Wenlock Edge in the mountain cold was inherently absurd.

"Good morning," Falkenberg said. "Welcome to Falcon's Hold, Thorne. And how was the ride from Kharthat?" His voice was cheerily mocking.

Hagen slammed his riding gloves down on the stones. "Damn you, Falkenberg, why in God's name aren't there Transfer Portals here? I've been on that bloody horse for four days, and every foot of it's been uphill and into the wind! I haven't ridden this far in twenty years. I couldn't get off the damned thing just now!"

Falkenberg fitted the arrow to the string. "Oh, well,

Thorne—I've any number of Portals here. I just don't like unannounced guests, and not even Rhydon or our sainted Stefan Coram can get past my wards. Which is largely because no one pays any attention to the things I write." He tested the grip of the bow with one gloved hand and pulled back on the string. The bow creaked. It was an angular compound bow from the On-Ogur, the Seven Tribes to the east of Torenth, a steppe horseman's bow. "It's for your own good, Thorne. You can't look High Deryni in a litter. There's no *presence* if you're not on horseback." His smile remained infuriating.

"Bastard." Hagen was digging his fingers into his thighs, trying to unknot the cramped muscles. "Cold, rude, arrogant, paranoid, vicious little bastard!"

"Maybe, only." Falkenberg brought the bow up and drew it taut, averting his eyes from the target and firing with one motion. The arrow stood in the upper left edge of the black, quivering. He reached back for another.

"I'm supposed to be here to raise important issues with you," Hagen said. "You keep creating problems for everyone, and there you stand playing with that damned barbarian's bow. Problems like making people ride up your damned mountain in the cold and the rain."

"Official emissary, then." Falkenberg's eyes shut and he brought the bow up, turning into the target and firing. The arrow drove in next to his first shot, tearing splinters and fletching away from the standing arrow as it buried itself. "And don't whine. They've got you running up here under their seal, so what does the Council want?" He unstrung the bow and turned to face Hagen.

"Denis Arilan came to see Barrett. One of the itinerant bishops down in Gwynedd wrote Denis with a rather odd story—"

"Istelyn," Falkenberg said very softly. "That would be Istelyn."

"—and Denis put the story to the Council." Hagen looked up, tired and irritated. "We all should have known, though, shouldn't we?"

"What was the story, Thorne?" Falkenberg's voice was soft and flat and precise. "What do they want from me?"

Hagen shrugged and looked away. He felt oddly weak. He'd known Christian de Falkenberg for most of Falkenberg's life; Barrett and Vivienne had thought him the perfect choice as emissary. He'd taught Derek de Falkenberg's son his first lessons in the history of the Deryni, and now he was oddly unwilling to meet Christian-Richard's eyes.

"This bishop says that he was in Carthmoor, and out at Point Kintar there's a chapel he'd never seen. Someone endowed a chapel and a priest just to say Mass for the soul of Charissa de Tolan."

"It's mine; what did you think?" Falkenberg's face hardened and his eyes were distant. "She fancied it there, looking out over the Southern Sea. She met me there when I came back from Bremagne the last time. I might even be a believer, in a way. And I've the right to endow a chapel and have candles lit for her. Is it the Church or the Council that objects?"

"It's not that they . . . object, really. It's just that the Council ordered Charissa not to challenge the new King of Gwynedd. She died officially outcast, and Stefan wants to think of her gone to eternal punishment and they all want to know—"

Hagen looked around at the Falcon retainers and the walls of Caer Curyll and felt very alone and afraid. Cold and sore and far from his villa at Kharthat and facing something unpredictable and barely suppressed in Christian de Falkenberg. He tried again.

"They'd forgotten about you. No one sees you, and they'd forgotten. After what you did to them over your books, they wanted to forget. But they're afraid, too. You're like Rhydon used to be; you're too solitary. They all remembered how it was with you and her and they— we—don't know what you'll do. Stefan and Barrett and Denis want to know if you're going south to kill Alaric

Morgan or his king. I'm supposed to tell you that, unof-
ficially, the Council wishes—"

"That I'd go back to the amirates or Alamut or fall off
the edge of the world." Falkenberg restrung the bow and
nocked another arrow. "Somewhere I have a copy of Rhydon's last speech to them all. I'll put my seal to it, and
you take it back to them. Tell Coram it goes for me, too.
I haven't an army to march to Rhemuth with; I'm not
going to wait in an alley with a knife for Morgan. She
went to Rhemuth alone; she forbade me to come. Her
decision. And I'll mourn her any way I want. But the
Council can forget me again—for now. Coram and Barrett
wanted her dead, all along. Ever since the Marluk died,
they wanted Charissa dead. And they wanted to pretend I
didn't exist. I'll come for them, one day—but not today.
Tell them to forget me."

The arrow flew out with a sharp crack and buried itself
halfway up the shaft, dead-center in the target.

THERE WERE MOORISH voices in the courtyard:
Yusuf al-Fayturi marshaling the half-dozen survivors of
Charissa's Moorish bodyguard. They bowed as Falkenberg walked by, expectation beginning to drift into their
faces.

Falkenberg's mouth drew down into a cold smile. You
could taste death on them. *You are the lover of the Lady
of Shadows,* Yusuf had told him. *We come to ride with
you south to the city of the great cathedral. We have spoken with the Amir al-Jabal, and the Lord of the Mountain
has bidden us avenge the lady. We are pledged to be*
feday'in, *and we offer ourselves to the lord of the Falcon
as his death riders.*

Falkenberg put his hand to the poniard at his belt and
bowed back, murmuring to them in his soft, fluid Moorish: "Therefore proclaim to all a woeful doom, save for
those who embrace the True Faith and do good works;
for theirs is an unfailing recompense. . . ."

He watched the thin, approving smile on Yusuf al-Fayturi's face: *Feday'in.*

THORNE HAGEN LIMPED across the room, dragging his chair closer to the fire and the crystal flagons of brandy. He sat down heavily and reached across for the liquor.

"You can't just turn on them," he was saying. "Not even Rhydon and Wencit have defied them directly. No one does. We can't turn on each other, God knows."

"Why not?" Falkenberg was drawn up under his cloak, a dark silhouette turning a great bell-mouthed goblet before its eyes. "You're the gentlest of men, Thorne. How many Deryni have you killed? I know of six: three by poison, two by mortal challenge, and one hand-to-hand with a dagger—which surprised all of us, really. Let's not think about Lewys or MacPherson. Or even Rhydon. The Council always wanted Charissa dead; she reminded them of their failures. Don't say Laran and Vivienne haven't gone out to enforce decrees at dagger's edge. Why shouldn't I turn on them? Being High Deryni's no different from any other kind of lord; no one rules without death on a leash."

"You're heir to one of the half-dozen oldest Deryni families," Thorne said. "Your father—all the Falkenbergs. . . . No one ever sees you, and everybody forgets. But you could have been on the Council. Laran and Kyri wanted you rather than Tiercel."

Falkenberg shook his head. "I don't want a Council seat. God, Rhydon was right: abolish it. I don't share their views about being Deryni. I want them to leave me alone. And I want something for Charissa. Not justice, but maybe satisfaction. But it dishonors her courage and her love if I go around demanding deaths I can't deal out. I want Coram's head on a pike point, though."

"We're supposed to protect our own. The Council

is. . . . We're not supposed to be like the Festils—High Deryni aren't. The Inner Circle—"

Falkenberg stabbed a gloved finger out at Hagen. "They pontificate and mouth all their pious sayings about responsibility, but they can't stop the persecutions and they don't represent even half the known Deryni. Nobody named Stefan Coram God. Barrett may be a great man, but who the hell are the rest of you? You taught me Deryni history, and half of everything you taught me's wrong. They see history in these grand, sweeping, transcendent categories, and they'll never understand anything. They never bothered to *really* look at what we are. I tried to tell them. Only Kyri would listen, and that's only because if you're mostly a radical yourself, you'll listen to other heretics. Only Laran could read a quarter of the sources, and the rest sat there crying blasphemy."

Hagen looked up from the fire. "That's why they wanted to forget about you. You're the only man the Camberian Council and the Gwynedd Curia would have held a joint heresy trial for. You even shocked Rhydon. You said we weren't—that there's no sorcery—that— You sit up here or listen to the Moorish assassin king at Alamut, and you never talk to anyone but Wencit's brother-in-law, and one day everyone knows you're openly Charissa's lover. And the Council—"

"Dislikes Deryni who like being alone. And Deryni who think unorthodox thoughts. And they hated Charissa for a dozen years. She was a Festil, and she stood alone and she wouldn't let them forget that Gwynedd wasn't specially blessed, that their sainted Haldane kings are no different from anyone else. I loved her, and they tried to pretend I wasn't there because she was supposed to be anathema and outcast." He drained off the last of his brandy. "I can't find a way to avenge her; I'm not an important player. She was braver than any of you, braver than me. And I want something for what you did to her, the Council. I'm sitting here at Caer Curyll this season; maybe I'll go back to the amirates in the summer. Tell them to forget me. But I won't let them forget her. That I won't do."

He turned away before the firelight could show the tears forming in his eyes.

"CHRISTIAN."

There was a rider coming in through Dawn Gate, a slight gray figure in black leathers with the golden falcon badge at his breast. Falkenberg brought up his hand in a slow salute. He could feel the Moors stiffening behind him, feel the cold tension in their minds. *All as wrong as wrong could go.* In all the years since a morning in Fathane when Marc-Friedrich Aurelian had joined the Freikorps Falkenberg, no one had ever known him to run to bring good news.

"Christian."

Falkenberg pulled off his right glove and ran his thumb over the crest of his signet. He watched his second-in-command dismount and tried to read his face. He envied Aurelian that face. Aurelian and he were of an age, but even beyond the Deryni defenses, Aurelian's pale face showed only resignation and irony behind the deep blue of his eyes. Falkenberg's face tightened. Whatever it was, there was nothing for it, then.

"How bad?" he asked.

"Bad enough." Aurelian tossed the reins to a black-liveried retainer. "They'll be up soon enough. But you should know now: ten riders up from Cardosa by Tolan, all wearing crescents counterchanged; none of them heralds." He pulled off his gloves and let down the guard around his mind enough to show grief and sympathy. "And not Lionel."

And not Lionel.

Falkenberg nodded. If the Arjenol men were in flight, the story was easy enough. The Haldane king triumphant, the Enterprise of Gwynedd broken into little knots of running men, the captains and kings dead or taken or falling back on Beldour for a final stand.

"And the others?"

"Blue eagles," Aurelian said. "A dozen Marley men; maybe four of them bloodied. They say they're a few hours in front of the hounds."

And handsome Bran, too.

There was a crowd gathering in the court. He looked back at them: gentlemen exiles from R'Kassi and the Forcinn, newer exiles from Tolan, adventurers who had followed him up from Bremagne, the professionals of the Falcon horse. Half of them had been hoping to ride south to savage a defeated Gwynedd, south to the spoils of Culdi and Rhemuth and Valoret. They were all waiting for the months idling in the harsh coastal mountains to end. Colforth looked stricken, the Moors cold and blank, most of the others vaguely disappointed.

Who in? Wencit? Me? He pointed at the Moors.

"Yusuf, Husayn, you'll ride scouts for Brennan. Colforth, get the Tolan horse and go ride the Fells. No one comes hunting onto my lands. Make that *very* clear." He turned back to Aurelian.

"It occurs to me that I'm growing very short of friends—" *No.* He tried again, his voice flat and crisp and military—his free-captain's voice. It was too easy to sound bitter in front of them all. "What else?"

"It gets worse." Aurelian opened one hand, a delicate motion of condolence and resignation both. "But I think that's for you alone."

FALCONS AND WOLVES, Lionel d'Arjenol thought. *Falcons and wolves.* He dropped his black-plumed helmet on the heavy table and looked around the presence chamber at Caer Curyll.

The House of Furstan, legend held, had followed a spectral silver stag west across the Way of Kings, the great ribbon of stars in the spring sky. The hart the Fur-

stans bore on their standards was at least a royal animal.
Only the House of Falkenberg would have chosen such
world's-end creatures for their badge: first the Stalking
Wolf, borne in the great days when the eastern houses had
ridden west and north to found Tolan and Torenth and
Arjenol, and since the Haldane Restoration and the exile
and flight of the house to these mountains, the Falcon
Unfettered.

He crossed to the wall and traced one finger down a
row of spiky steppe script carved beneath the Falkenberg
arms that dominated the chamber. Few enough of the Torenthi and Arjenol nobles learned to read On-Ogur. Who
but Falkenberg would bother, so far west?

When not spurred, no awakening. When not cornered,
no opening through.

Lionel smiled and crossed the room to stand waiting by
the stiff, tattered banners hung down the eastern wall in
commemoration of long-ago campaigns in R'Kassi and
the Hortic lands and the Marchlands and the steppe. Falkenberg's stewards had been busy early, he thought. It
almost looked like someone was in residence at Caer Curyll. In all the years he had been coming to Falcon's Hold,
he had never been able to think of it as really inhabited.
Sixteen dukes had reigned in the great fortress Lionel had
been born in. Nine lords had looked down from Darklair
Edge since the Haldane Restoration. But the Falkenbergs
had made their name as free-captains out in frontier
lands—not least in Arjenol—and Falcon's Hold had an
eerily empty feel to it.

"Your Grace."

The door opened and Marc-Friedrich Aurelian came in,
a slight figure in a high-necked gray tunic. He bowed a
smooth courtier's bow that spoke of eastern ideas of pro-
tocol and deposited a silver serving set on the table. Lionel caught the scent of Moorish coffee. He nodded
acknowledgment.

Aurelian was no man's child, and no one—not Lionel
with his learning nor his brother-in-law with his craft—

had been able to determine where Falkenberg's constant
companion was from. Deryni, yes. Vaguely foreign. Not
Torenthi, surely. But the perfect gray second-in-
command. A Lionel to Christian's Wencit, then.

Aurelian stood to attention, a rigid, parade-ground figure.

"The Lord Falkenberg's compliments. We've Maghreb
coffee for Your Grace, and I can call for brandywine or
darja."

Lionel nodded toward the three tiny silver cups. "Christian's very gracious these days. Very kind and very subtle.
But no map cases today, Aurelian?"

Aurelian passed a cup to Lionel. "Not today, then."
The blue eyes were flat and unreadable. He had Falkenberg's speech pattern, though, Lionel noted. The same flat,
accentless voice, soft and fluid and full of elliptical phras-
ings that might be anything from self-proclaimed clever-
ness to an odd unfamiliarity with the language spoken.

"That's a decision." Lionel turned to look down from
the windows to the secondary court. The next night would
be New Year's, and Falkenberg's people were piling up
great masses of wood and heather for the bonfires. At
Beldour tomorrow night, Wencit would formally proclaim
his Enterprise of Gwynedd to the assembled nobility of
Torenth. Five hundred Arjenoli cavalry were already at
Medras waiting for the last Gwynedd troops to be driven
into winter quarters before cutting the few remaining
paths through the snows to Cardosa. Beldour would blaze
with a thousand arcane lights for the new year; no campaign in a generation had set loose so much excitement.
All the Eleven Kingdoms, the poets were singing. The
Hart once more ran the Way of Kings.

Lionel watched the figures below scurry in the snows,
picking out the black of Falkenberg's men and the bright
plaids of his Gordon cousins.

"Why won't he go, Aurelian?" Lionel asked. "What can
we give him?"

"Besides a kind invitation? What else are you offering?"

The voice was Falkenberg's. He was in the doorway, odd flakes of snow still clinging to the narrow sleeves of his black tunic. He had a scroll carapaced in crimson wax in his hand. He accepted a cup from Aurelian and held up the scroll to Lionel's eyes.

"Wencit's sending out a call to arms to all the free lords. But what's he offering, Lionel?" He tipped the scroll toward Aurelian. "You saw this. Fancy being a duke?"

The two of them grinned at one another, a private joke from Bremagne, long ago.

Lionel put his cup down. "Wencit has an offer for you, if you want. I can give you reasons, though. You might start with high policy: it's time for the Eleven Kingdoms to be unified. You have, after all, been trained to understand building and ruling states. And the lords of Gwynedd seem to have taken something from you, one recalls." He was looking at the black mourning bands Falkenberg and Aurelian both wore.

Falkenberg's mouth tightened. He pulled a high-backed chair away from the table and sat down, pressing his head back against the carven rampant wolves that supported the Falkenberg arms crowning the chair.

"And what would Wencit give me back?"

"A brigade of cavalry, to begin with. Eight hundred horse to harry in Cassan and Eastmarch with. Your grandfather fought under Wencit's father and uncles and came back here with a marshal's baton. You could do that. I couldn't name a better choice for governor-general of Carthmoor or Fallon than you."

Falkenberg tossed the scroll onto the table. "I have a baton. They made me a *marechal* in Bremagne after Shalmyr. We're even lords in Bremagne, somewhere. All that for my services. For all the Falcon horse, all—"

"One hundred eighty-five horsemen," Aurelian sup-

plied. "Another fifty, if you call up Michael Gordon's
men."

"Such an army for Wencit. He has you and Rhydon
and Merritt and half the military talent I can name at his
disposal. Lionel, there's nothing he can buy me with, and
I'm not worth lying to. What does he want me for?"

"You're heir to a Deryni name older than Furstán. Wencit holds your skills as a Deryni in no little regard. The
free lords on this coast would follow your lead if, say,
you chose to interfere in the sea lanes round to Meara."
Lionel's hand came up to finger the end of the black braid
he wore. "And later. . . . After Gwynedd, there will be the
South: the R'Kassan borders and the Hortic lands. You're
a wise investment. Wencit sees that he needs allies for the
while. I know we'll need governors much longer."

"And I have a reason to hate the young king in Rhemuth."

"For you, there would be a matter of honor."

"Oh, well, honor." He held up his left hand. There was
a silver band flecked with tiger's eye on his ring finger.

"This is from her. There's her inscription in it in Old
Deryni. And it says *Outremer* on the outside: *beyond-the-
sea*. She gave it to me the first time I took the Freikorps
south, the year I was eighteen. It's as much a wedding
ring as anything I'll likely get. I'd devastate Gwynedd for
her: plow Rhemuth over and salt the earth and pile skulls
by the thousands on the riverbank. I'd do that anyway—
what's Gwynedd to me? Talk to me about honor. She
loved me and she said she had to do this alone.

"Don't hold up her name to me and cry vengeance. I'm
tired of everyone doing that. I'll fight on the steppe for
you; I'll never fight for Wencit. If the Haldanes come to
Arjenol, I'll fight for you, Lionel—I'm your creation as
a soldier; you were there after my father died. When it's
your war, send for me. I just won't put Wencit on the
throne she should have held. I can't burn Gwynedd to the
bare rock, and I can't cheer for the Hart going up over
Rhemuth Castle. Fight your war. May the sun shine and

all the day be great. You're an agile manipulator and a
general of reconnaissance without peer. I've served with
you, and I admire you, and I hope you leave the Haldane
armies bleeding in the dirt. I'm not going to Rhemuth with
you, though. I can't have any revenge that means anything, and there's nothing you can give me this season."
He looked across at his second-in-command.

"Go get brandy. I'll be polite and drink to Wencit and
Morag and the new year, but I'm not riding anywhere."

LLYNDRUTH MEADOWS.

Falkenberg let the brandy flow back over his throat. He
had been drinking since the afternoon, when Aurelian
brought the news, and even the finest vintages had lost
their taste.

Llyndruth Meadows. He'd been there once, his second
summer back, he and Aurelian taking Charissa from Beldour to Caer Curyll. She rode in men's riding leathers and
thigh boots, her hair trailing behind her in a pale golden
mist. She had put off her hard, Shadowed One aspect for
those days, and the fixed, determined light had left her
eyes for the while. . . .

He drew up one knee and put his boot on the low table.

*More brandy, then. And let us sing of the death of
kings.*

"A morality play, isn't it?" Aurelian said, turning the
crystal of his goblet over one of the candles burning here
in Falkenberg's private study. "It's like some stupid guild
miracle play. The captains and the kings play at the Great
Game, lands and power and high politics, and then, at the
end, all in a moment, there's little theophanies of Light
and Dark and it all has Moral and Meaning. They'll all
think it means something."

Aurelian let his mind drift out toward the dark flare of
Falkenberg's thoughts.

*And you see it as Dark and Light, then, Christian?
Shall I sing for the deeper Meaning?*

Meaning? Falkenberg raised one hand and let dark azure light play around it, traced lines in the air: a twisted, irregular pattern that might have been the Falkenberg borders.

Look at a map. That's the meaning. That's all.

Aurelian's mind formed itself into a query, and he let the flavor of irony flow into it.

And honor, maybe.

The hand clenched tight and the lights vanished. Falkenberg jerked his mind away.

"Not from you. I won't have that from you."

"It's what they're all asking. First the Lady, now your friends. They remember Bran and Lionel. They all cheered for Bran after the Connait campaign and for Lionel after Sömlyö Szillágy. They expect something from you, all of them."

Falkenberg drew his other knee up and pressed his forehead into his knees.

"They'll be singing *Te Deums* for Kelson Haldane and the triumph of Goodness and Light in Rhemuth. Down in the great hall, they all want me to swear personal vengeance for Charissa. Ah, God, it's not evil or being Deryni or having loved Charissa that means anything. It's only in the maps." He reached for more brandy. "Alaric Morgan has more servants underfoot at dinner in Coroth Castle than I have horsemen. . . . We should have ridden with Wencit."

"Could you have stopped Wencit playing the fool?"

"I couldn't save Charissa, could I? Why Wencit de Furstan? A complete fool! Who'd have thought it? Duelsarcane! Bran would have been awed into it, but Lionel should have *known*! God, we're High Deryni, and I'm as good as Wencit ever was at that, but he should have put his faith in cold steel. Even at the end, someone—Merritt, maybe—should have ordered a charge. I could've done that. For Lionel and Bran, I should've done it."

"Reason decideth not at last/It is but the sword decides. . . ." Aurelian pushed his goblet to one side. "Wen-

cit would have had you there with him. You'd only have
been part of Coram's self-immolation."

Falkenberg shut his eyes. "Stefan Coram finally got to
play God. Finally got the crucifixion he'd always
wanted." He smiled, a quick skull's smile. "But ahhh,
don't you think he fancied being Rhydon? All that lovely
guilt!"

"And Saint Camber: *Stefanus Defensor Hominem*," Aurelian replied.

"He was at Kelson Haldane's coronation, you know,"
Falkenberg continued. "*Defender's Seal,* the harpers sing.
He was there to mock her, too. How lovely to taste it all:
being a self-proclaimed saint, or a king, or a king's champion." He frowned. "We could have stayed in Bremagne:
border peerages and the military frontier to command. Or
even in the amirates: under the lemon trees in the cloister
gardens at Qasiya, sherbet and iced milk, chess and meta-
physics at Alamut."

"No," Aurelian sighed. "You could never have stayed.
Even if you'd gone to the Amir al-Jabal and meditated on
Nothing in the blade of a knife. Think about it. You'd
have a holding in Bremagne, and there you are—a great
low villa at Veira. One day a visitor says, 'Ah, have you
heard about the coronation duel up in Gwynedd?' "

"For all the good I did." Falkenberg reached out to
snuff the candles on the table. "Go away. I'm drunk and
I'm starting to pity myself and I'm sounding very weak
and very bitter. Go away."

He pressed his face into his knees and squeezed his
eyes shut.

TWENTY YEARS AGO, Christian de Falkenberg
would have said. On a bleak winter late afternoon, Nasr
ad-Din's Moors had broken the King of Bremagne's
knights at Gate-of-the-Anvil. Half the aristocracy of Bremagne lay among the nine thousand armored corpses
strewn over rock and chilled sand. And the spring after

that, Lewys ap Conall died in his sleep, an old man far
short of realizing his dream of a reborn and unified Connait.

Fifteen years ago, the Marluk had waged his abortive
campaign against Brion Haldane and the young Alaric
Morgan. Philip of Bremagne had never had his longed-
for march through Fallon and Fianna and across the sea
to Coroth. No strong Connait offered Meara or Howicce-
and-Llannedd a counterweight to Gwynedd. The Festillic
revival in Tolan had been crushed. And only the Hart and
the Lion were left on the board.

Too few princes or too many kings; in that much,
Christian de Falkenberg could agree with Wencit Furstán.
One king for the Eleven Kingdoms, or a myriad of free
princes and cities. The Hart and the Lion could not exist
alone in one another's despite. Festil II had not married
a Furstán cousin-german; and in the end was Llyndruth
Meadows. So Christian de Falkenberg would have said.
Any morning after the Marluk's death in the Year of
Grace 1105, one would have seen, looking at the Great
Game, only the two banners flying in Rhemuth and Bel-
dour.

And in Tolan, a single pawn, cast all in blue and silver.
She had been eleven in the season of the Marluk's
death, a tall pale child who smiled and said little. High
Deryni, descended of kings and incest, heiress to the great
empty Duchy of Tolan that filled the north of the Torenthi
plain. Wencit had been younger then, new-settled on his
throne and busy carrying fire and steel to the Seven
Tribes. And so her cousin in Beldour had not contested
Hogan Gwernach's will, and Derek de Falkenberg of Caer
Curyll had, as a temporary measure, joined the Duke of
Arjenol on the Tolan Council of Regency and lodged the
girl at Falcon's Hold.

In the days of Malcolm Haldane, there had been a score
of free lordships on the northern coast, mountain holdings
of lone Deryni or exiled cadets of Riding houses-minor.

On the day in April 1108 when a cerebral hemorrhage
felled Derek de Falkenberg, intermarriage, annexation,
and warfare had reduced the number to under a dozen,
the two largest being the holdings of the House of Falkenberg and its Gordon cousins. Christian-Richard, in-
stalled as Lord of Caer Curyll not many months past his
coming-of-age, inherited the huge, half-empty fortress
atop its mountain, one hundred thirty black-liveried light
cavalry, the friendship and protection of the lords of Marley and Arjenol, the name of an ancient Deryni line, and
between May Eve and Lammas Night, the company of
Charissa Festil de Tolan, newly of age as duchess.

The Falkenberg lords were by no means wealthy. Basalt
cliffs, sere moorland, narrow fjords cut into the coast
made up the lording. Each Lord Falkenberg in his turn
would ride forth with the Freikorps Falkenberg every few
seasons. Falkenbergs had been free-captains by necessity
and tradition since the days of the madness unleashed by
the Council of Ramos. Michael de Falkenberg had broken
the armies of the Hort of Orsal at Amber River, driven
deep into R'Kassan lands under the Furstán Hart, and
come home with crates of silver bullion and a Torenthi
field marshal's baton. Derek de Falkenberg had commanded Marley horse in border raids against East-march
hill clans and ridden next to Lionel's father against the
petty states of the East.

And so Christian-Richard had been born to the breed:
raised not to be a knight, but tutored by his father and
Lionel d'Arjenol to be a military entrepreneur, a free-
captain. Languages, history, politics . . . he had been no
man's page and no man's squire, but at fifteen he spoke
eight languages and knew the intrigues of half the houses
in the Eleven Kingdoms.

And he had been Deryni, and his tastes ran to the history of the Deryni and the theory of what he steadfastly
refused to call sorcery. At forty-five, he might have cut
an impressive figure, but at fifteen . . .

If he had no small skill with the angular compound bow

of the Seven Tribes, still he was no warrior. He fenced
well enough, but with the saber rather than the broadsword of armored heroes. He had been raised alone, he
was neither strong nor particularly handsome, and he was
too darkly cynical and distant to play the gallant. He
spoke to few, laughed apart from the others, envied and
hated the young Gordons who had girls flirting with them.
And so no one had been more surprised than Christian-
Richard when at Christmas court Charissa de Tolan pulled
him out to dance and, later, spurning the young nobles
gathered at Castle Tolan, walked alone with him through
the galleries and—forever beyond his belief—slid one
hand behind his head and kissed him.

Arglwyddes arian niwlen. . . . Lady of the Silver Mists.
He had closed his mind off, drawn all his probes in.
She was almost achingly beautiful at fifteen, pale and elegant and gently vulnerable. She could draw one far into
her aloneness with her eyes. She was a tall girl, and he
looked across eye-to-eye with her, watching the light play
against the high line of her cheekbones. She was very still
and she was biting at her lip. He could feel the touch of
her mind trying to reach his. He kept his defenses up, a
flat, distant image of obsidian cliffs walling him off from
her. Even at fifteen, he knew his own value, and she was
too far beyond him, too much something he'd have bargained away his soul for. Nothing more frightening than
getting exactly what one wants: he knew that as deep
within himself as he could see.

She put her hand to his cheek. "I'm sorry," she whispered. "I'm the Marluk's daughter, and I shouldn't be—
inflicting myself on anyone. I wanted to be something
different for you. I'm sorry."

"Oh, God." He let his face lie against the warmth of
her hand. "I just don't know why you're with me, and I
know enough to be afraid of an answer, if I asked you.
I'm not anything you should want."

She shook her head and tried again to touch his mind.
"All summer I watched you with your books and your

bow and your silences. And. . . ." She held his eyes. "I know what I am. I could have any of them out there—"

"I can't," he said. "There's not a girl there wouldn't laugh at me if I came to her bed. I'm afraid to think about you. I know what I am, too, and I know enough to distrust too great a gift."

She kept her eyes on his. "Don't run from me. I want to show you what I'm thinking. You're what I'm choosing. You keep your solitude and you're there in the dark and they don't frighten you—the great lords or whatever's out there in the dark. Trust me, a little."

Falkenberg reached out to brush her hair. He looked back into the cornflower of her eyes and let her mind begin to touch his.

"I'm so afraid of you," he whispered. "I could fall in love with you so easily. . . ."

Silver and indigo. . . . The colors filled his mind, images of summer skies and the first taste of glacier wine.

She lay one finger against his mouth and traced the line of his lips.

"Christian," she said, *"listen."* Her thoughts interlaced with his, images of affection and vulnerability and caring. "All the things you're afraid of, but you're not afraid of anything I fear. Out there, they'll grow up to be knights and heroes and gallants. I want what you'll be."

"What I'll be. God." He reached to take her hands in his. The long, fine fingers slid through his. He drew in a short breath and his mouth was dry. "That's sad for us both."

He leaned into her and kissed her. Her hair fell across his eyes and the taste of wine chilled in snow played through his thoughts.

Four months later, on the moor near Darklair Edge, they became lovers. *Anwyryfu,* the verb was, in the older languages: *to yield one's virginity.* That she had been his first woman, he could understand. There was little enough to draw any woman to him. But Charissa—he was oddly puzzled. From twelve onward, she had been the loveliest

girl in the North. Women were married and with children
at fifteen. She could have had any of the young men—or
their fathers. That he should be her first lover left him in
some obscure way saddened.

She had been in a set of his riding leathers, perched on
a rise near their tethered horses, turning a wine flask in
her hands. She reached up to unfasten her hair.

Today, her mind called to him. *It's today.*

He looked back from the Edge, startled. He frowned
and she shook her head.

"I'll be sixteen this April; you won't be seventeen 'til
November. It's not Midsummer Eve and it's not New
Year's. Just today. Christian. . . ." She held out one gloved
hand.

He took her hand and knelt at her side, watching the
slender legs in their long boots. He looked up at her. Her
hair fell across her shoulders and the fair skin at the open
throat of her tunic, trailing onto the dark leather of her
vest.

"There's a saying," he said. "The story is that, no matter how much a woman loves the man who has her virginity, she'll hate him a little, too. . . ."

"Oh, well. If I'd slept with half the nobility of Tolan
and Torenth, would you be happier about me? Would I
feel better about lying next to you if I'd been spreading
my legs since I was twelve? Don't be so kind about me."

She squirted the wine flask at him and he dodged backward from the spray and fell into the heather. Charissa
looked down at him and grinned.

"The ladies in Bremagne expect gallantry," she
mocked. "And the Moorish cavalry are quick and deadly.
You shouldn't go falling all over yourself. What will they
think, milord? Get up." She held out her hand again. "You
could get up and make love to me."

He tugged gently at her and she pushed herself away
from the rise and slid down next to him. "I won't hate
you, later. No."

He tangled one hand in her hair and she pressed herself

against him. Her lips parted under his. After a while, she
leaned back against him and pulled off her gloves, smiling
back at him. She touched the line of his cheek, and he
lay his hand atop hers.

"*Caryad,*" he whispered. "*Caryad*-heart-of-my-heart."
He slid one arm around her, under her vest. He laughed,
loving her. "Just don't laugh," he said. "Anything you
want, but don't laugh at me."

She leaned her head back and closed her eyes as he
touched her. She shrugged the vest away and let one leg
glide along his. The leathers creaked as they brushed. She
wore nothing under the dark gray of the tunic, and his
hands brushed at her nipples under the velvet. Charissa
reached down to undo the laces at the throat of his tunic.

"Oh, no," she said. "I won't need to laugh. I won't
mock you, and I won't hate you. That's not what we are."

When it happened, he had been the one to cry out, and
she had only sighed as she settled herself under him.
Later, atop him, she had arched herself against him and
clenched her fingers in his hair.

"Bastard. *Bastard. . . .* " Her eyes opened and she
looked down at him, exhausted. She smiled and brushed
her hair away from her eyes. She reached out to trace a
finger across the dark line of his brows. "Bastard," she
said, smiling. "Christian."

They lay on the moor late into the afternoon, wrapped
in his riding cloak. Her body was long and pale, small-
breasted and small-hipped. He drew a finger down the line
of her thigh and she shivered in the August sunlight.

"*Anwylddyn,*" she said, and she grazed her lips down
his body under the pale canopy of her hair. "I do love
you, *arglwydd curyll. . . .* " She fastened on him and he
closed his eyes, whispering her name.

They sat at dinner that night in Falcon's Hold laughing
at one another down the length of the table, Falkenberg
all in black, Charissa all in clinging dark-amber silk, worn
next to the skin.

"Thou. . . ." he called, raising his cup to her as she sat, silver light playing about her.

That night she left the great hall on his arm and went up to his bedchamber. The ladies-in-waiting of her retinue sat prim-faced and disapproving; the Falkenberg retainers marked the strange, sad lover's face their young lord was wearing. Only Christian's cousin Michael Gordon had the presence to call a toast to them, something light and laughing as they went up the stairway.

HE HAD FOUND his voice that summer, he would recall. The poetry had been all for Charissa, and he had found in her a Lady whose attributes lay outside the measured rhyming formality of the poets and harpers at Tolan and Beldour and in the thin gilded volumes in the library at Caer Curyll. She was something that could not be caught in formal compliments; something that needed a harder, leaner framework, something in a voice of gently dark irony. He tried On-Ogur and Old Deryni and Moorish before he found the austere rhythms that he could conjure her image in:

Wind in your hair, and my lips and fingers move through and through and through./Oh God, Charissa, live forever, young and beautiful./You have driven back the winter for the little I bring: the taste of tears on lips pressed to mine./Stay young, Charissa: even if not for me, stay young.

So they had been together at Caer Curyll, and at Tolan, and at Beldour. He wrote for her in half a dozen languages, and she lay next to him afternoons, her body tawny in the sunlight, reading the spiky On-Ogur or curlicued Moorish script.

He wintered in Arjenol, on Lionel's staff, riding out to maintain the peace of the steppe border. And he sat in his library at Caer Curyll, reading the Varnarite and Gabrilite manuscripts the first lords of Caer Curyll had brought with them from the wreckage of the great persecutions.

First the wards, and only Charissa knew how to use a Transfer Portal at Falcon's Hold. She followed him from the northern coasts to Arjenol and the steppe, flickering into his rooms in pulses of blue light or riding next to him in a military cloak, their secret that she wore nothing beneath her riding leathers.

Lionel d'Arjenol—to Morag's distaste—adored her, had told Christian once that when the day came, he would offer them the great basilica at Arjenol Hold for their wedding. (Much, much later, only Lionel had come to Caer Curyll to stand next to Christian-Richard de Falkenberg at the only requiem Charissa Festil de Tolan would have. . . .)

From the R'Kassan border, he wrote her a softly mocking love poem:

> The sunlight, you would say:
> the white of the afternoon up from the plain,
> the blue tiles of a villa overlooking the sea,
> chilled mist on a wineglass close to hand,
> the weight of the summer upon your body,
> your breath caught between your teeth,
> and two fingers tracing quickening spirals
>   between your thighs.
> The sunlight, you would say.
> I leave you the sunlight, then, and the wine—
> but to the passion add my poems,
> the book lying open at your side.
> The sunlight, you would say.
> But it is my dream, and I am vain.

Caryad, she called him. *Caryad*-heart-of-my-heart. And he began to consider the day when the Freikorps Falkenberg would ride south and east, first to Arjenol and then across the Southern Sea to Bremagne.

Caryad. The Marluk had taught her the arts-Deryni, and she was reaching her maturity as a sorceress. His skills diverged from hers, perhaps something subtler, less requiring of the rhyming spells she mastered. He read over the Marluk's notes and compared them to the ideas he was beginning to assemble, and he sighed for Charissa, for the traps contained in the word *sorceress*.

They had been at Tolan, in her great ornate bed. April it had been, not long after her eighteenth birthday, rain up across the northern plain. She had lain silent half the night, pressing herself against him.

She had grown inward that April, distracted and distant even in her lovemaking. He could do nothing but hold her at night and try to take her away from Tolan and ride each other to exhaustion across the heath. After midnight, she had begun to cry. She sat up, her shoulders pressed against the carven headboard, tears running past her closed eyes.

"Do you know what this room was?" Her voice was strained and near to breaking.

"No. I—Charissa. . . ." She had made him forget self-contempt, the hollow sensations of weakness, and he sat up, ashamed of being unable to help her. She had closed off her mind behind a coldness even he could not breach.

"It used to be a private gallery. My family kept the Festil portraits here, all the portraits back to the tenth century, back to Ariella and Mark." She was twisting at the signet ring she wore.

"Christian, I'm eighteen this season."

"Oh God." He twisted around to look at her, hating himself for knowing what was coming.

"I'm the Marluk's daughter. I'm a Festil of Tolan. I hadn't thought about it in so long." She opened her eyes to look for him in the dark. Tears crawled across her face and she was breathing in short, sharp gasps. "I'm supposed to be something frightening. I'm supposed to be something hard and cold. I'm older than Alaric Morgan was when my father died. I'm a Festil and a duchess and High Deryni—"

"You're my lover. You're Charissa de Tolan, and I love you. You don't have to finish it."

"You know what they did to my father, Morgan and the Haldane king. I'm eighteen, and I should be doing something about it all. I'm a Festil of Tolan, and if I wanted to, I could be Pretender to Gwynedd." She held up her ring finger and made the signet glow a harsh, dark red. "Christian—" She looked at him and opened her mind to him, waves of fear and uncertainty and remembered hatred.

He sat up, reaching for her hand. He nodded and let a silver light envelop them both. She was shivering, her arms wrapped close around herself, her face stained and white and stricken.

"I've never seen you cry. I'm so useless to you, love. I haven't an army. If I had, then, God, I'd burn my way from one end of Gwynedd to the other for you. . . . " He sought her eyes. "If you want them dead. . . . It would have to be done and done well. You can't just decide to kill a king. But just say if you want me to kill them. Whatever you need, I'll try to give you. If you want me, I'll stand at your side. I'm supposed to be something military, and I'm High Deryni, too. I'll fight them for you, if you want."

She shook her head. "I'm the Marluk's daughter. I told you that the first night we were together. They won't help me in Torenth; the Camberian Council all hate me for being my father's daughter. It won't any of it go well, you know. I'm supposed to be something and I have to. . . . But I won't have you destroyed for being with me. I love you and I won't have you hurt. I need you with me, but not to die for what I have to be." She looked away from him. "Do you trust me?"

"With my life. You *are* my life."

She was trying to choose her words. "I don't have a duchy that can raise an army I could march to Rhemuth with. I'm not wealthy. I don't have any natural allies. I'm Deryni, and that something, but I'll have to buy them— allies and spies and generals. Buy them with something. Have something to manipulate them with. Christian—I'm eighteen and I'm tall and blond and I am beautiful and, at least with you, I'm talented in bed. That's the weapon I have. I can buy men with that. You're—it's all I have and I don't want to hurt you; I don't want you to hate me." She tightened her grip on his hand. "Whatever happens, don't learn to hate me. I won't leave you. I won't!"

He twisted away from her, extinguishing the silver light. She caught at him and pulled him round to face her. He sighed and tried to force the sick emptiness out of his mind. He raised a hand to touch the tears on her face.

"I won't hate you. I won't leave you, Charissa. I couldn't do either, not ever. Whatever happens, I'm yours. Whatever happens."

She took to her father's tower at Tolan Castle, locking herself away to work with the Marluk's grimoire. At Falcon's Hold, she listened to Christian explain the theory of the arts-Deryni that was forming in his notes.

Sorcery! he would say, grimacing in contempt at the term. *Power! Only to be reached for.* . . . And he spread out his maps of the Eleven Kingdoms to her, pulling her from bed wrapped in a sable cloak to repeat for him the names of houses-major that had interests opposed to the Haldanes, the names of houses-minor known to be for sale.

He passed on the legerdemain Lionel had taught him— the stiletto flicked casually into the palm, the bowstring whipped backhand around a throat, the short, sharp On-Ogur blows to throat and diaphragm that enabled the small and light to cripple the great.

Flesh is in so many ways a failure, he told her. *In crystal and steel is beauty. Power is death; ruling is about giving and withholding death. Become as steel and thus partake of power and beauty. And death.*

On May Eve she gave him the silver ring. *Outremer,* it said along the outside: *beyond-the-sea.* And inside, in Old Deryni, her name and a fragment from Llewelyn: *Against the Night.*

He lay with her long that night, afraid to make love to

her. She was taking up the role he had thought they might
save each other from playing, and there was so little he
could do for her. Near two, she raised herself over him
and touched his lips. *"Thou...,"* she whispered, drawing
an ankle along his leg. By dawn they had worn one another to ruins. At noon he rode out with his cavalry, bound
for the Arjenol steppe and the fading splendor of Bremagne. She stood watching him, a slender figure in blue
on her balcony above the southern road.

> *You cannot see her from the road.*
> *The balcony lends her distance,*
> *And thus you cannot see the pale fire of her hair*
> *Or mark the fine line of throat and shoulders*
> *Or watch the light against the cornflower of her eyes.*
> *You cannot see her smile across a midnight chessboard*
> *Or feel her waken next to you*
> *And listen to her sighs.*
> *You cannot see her from the road:*
> *And the road leads south.*
> *And ever on.*

It had been twenty-six months before he saw her again.
He had ridden to Sartaq on the steppe to blood his Freikorps with Lionel d'Arjenol in a quick, sharp razzia
against the Qipchak *noyons,* and then to Bremagne, to
harry the R'Kassan frontiers and the Moorish eyries in the
Anvil of the Lord for the peace of the borderline and the
glory of Bremagne. The South was a subtler land than
Gwynedd and the North, its civilization older and more
complex. The South delighted in indirection and intrigues
constructed like intricate clockwork toys, for the pleasure
of the construction. In two years, he began to build a name
for the Falcon horse in the fading kingdom, a reputation
based on finesse, speed of action, and an utter remorse-
lessness that impressed even the Moorish *ghazis* in their
mountain fortresses.

He took his horsemen up the Forcinn littoral to play at

king-making and *coups d'état* in the free cities and petty
princedoms of the Forcinn States. He had been there, enmeshed in the clandestine, bloody, labyrinthine game of
defending the ambitions of Bremagne against the Orsals
and the Haldane Duke of Carthmoor when her messenger
arrived at his camp at Dax. Twenty-six months after he
had parted from her at Tolan, he came to her in the dying
port town of Ravenspur in the west of the Forcinn.

"So Southern, then," she had said. "You're all silks and
Moorish silver." She laughed as he raised her hand to his
lips. "Troubadour. You're like someone's kept minnesan-
ger. . . ."

Charissa de Tolan at twenty had been breathtaking. She
was waiting for him in a low, cloistered town house near
the ruined signory. She was all in pale gray, and he stood
in the narrow garden court, taken with her beauty. She
was like a perfectly balanced blade, beauty and power
fused together in an intricate embrace. Pale hair fell across
bare shoulders, and her eyes were the color of the Southern dawn. For two years he had sent his poetry north to
Tolan, and word of Charissa had filtered back to him: so
lovely, yes, but she had become the Shadowed Lady of
the North, the evil sorceress worrying at the edges of
Brion Haldane's kingship. There was more irony and steel
in her, but her smile had not changed as she clasped her
hands behind his neck.

"Caryad. . . ."

Still, there had been a distance to her lovemaking. She
clung to him, eyes full of apology and loneliness. The
aftertaste of how she had bargained for power and support—that much, he could tell, but he could never ask her
who or *how* or *what*. She was holding on to revenge, but
the dream of revenge did not possess her. That was the
sadness of it. She was the Shadowed One by an act of
will; it was expected of the Marluk's daughter. *The music
plays and all must dance.*

He held her against him, hating the Marluk and Alaric
Morgan and Brion Haldane and his own weakness.

He had played against Nigel Haldane for another year in the Forcinn littoral. The Lord Falkenberg and the Duke of Carthmoor corresponded and offered one another elegant epigrams on history and poetry, the chancellors of Bremagne and Carthmoor denied any foreign interference in the Forcinn, and in alleyways and along the border roads, the dead lay in sodden heaps.

Then the mountains in the Seigneurie of Albret, and the great defense of Shalmyr against Nasr al-Din. After Shalmyr, he had fled the triumphal processions and the court balls and gone to the amirates and, finally, to Alamut on its sheer rock above the rapids of the Kasir in a bleak landscape. At Alamut he retired to the library and a single room and wrote history and sent forth the three volumes of *The Venture of Caeriesse.*

The Amir al-Jabal and his Dais smiled; the young infidel Lord of the Falcon's history of the Deryni was in itself *batiniyyah,* a revelation of the structure of a universe built not on Meaning, but on Chance and Necessity alone. In the North the Gwynedd Curia—and in their secret way, the Camberian Council—were livid. The Amir al-Jabal laughed at the equal discomfiture of the priests and the sorcerers and, knowing the Lord of the Falcon better than his young guest knew himself, sent Falkenberg the gift of a dagger and the scarlet sash of an Assassin *Fidai.*

Her letters came to him full of bitterness and self-mockery: *Charissa of the Shadows to the Lord Falkenberg.* She came to him twice more in the South—once at Étang des Carcans in Bremagne and once at Qasiya in the amirates. Each time he could see more of the tautness within her. She wore glacial cold about herself like episcopal purple about an outcast bishop. She wept in her sleep, and his mind could reach out and taste the black sweat of her dreams.

Evil sorceresses don't cry when they're made love to. He put a finger against her lips.

And captains of mercenary cavalry don't worry about a woman they've taken. She pulled his hand against her

cheek. *I'm sorry. For doing this to you. For being what
I am.*

She kept herself in the far north of Tolan at her father's
ruined tower retreat of Sendal above a glacier grinding
down from the mountains into the sea. He came home
from the South for her, to offer her whatever his presence
might mean. She met him at Point Kintar on the Southern
Sea and returned with him to Caer Curyll. At Caer Curyll
she laughed with him in his solar and read to him the
shrill cries of heresy issuing from the Council. They rode
the moors and she was younger, Charissa and not her
newer mask. At night she was gently passionate and eerily
serene.

Soon, she whispered to him. *Soon, now.*

And in the autumn of 1120, Brion Haldane rode out
for his last hunt at Candor Rhea.

DEUS REGNORUM OMNIUM, *regumque domina-
tor, qui nos et percutiendo sanas, et ignoscendo conser-
vas: praetende nobis misericordiam tuam.* . . .

Falkenberg knelt at the far end of the cathedral and
crossed himself. He looked out into the darkness and tried
to envision the way St. George's would look in the morning as the crowds gathered to celebrate the glory of the
Haldanes. No one else could pray for her, and there was
little enough to say to the God of the Haldanes. The God
of Alamut would have honored her courage, the God in
the chapel at Caer Curyll would have honored her for
standing alone against the Council and the Haldanes. The
God of the cathedral in Rhemuth was a God of kings and
heroes; He had no mercy for the solitary and the exiled.
In some corner deep within himself, Falkenberg was a
believer, but he could not think of how to bargain with
God for the life and soul of Charissa de Tolan.

Those who would let True Love win. . . .

"Tam Lin," then, the words of the old song: *Those who
would let True Love win, at Mile Cross they must hide.*

He grimaced and rose to his feet. He crossed himself again and started up the nave, his boots clicking along the marble.

Eripe me de inimicis meis, Deus meus: et ab insurgentibus in me libera me. Ego autem cantabo fortitudinem tuam: et exsultabo mane misericordiam tuam.

Something. . . .

Falkenberg's head jerked back.

Something tingling and yet only half-sensed.

There was something in the transept of the cathedral: He could taste the faint rush of power across the mosaics on the floor. Something raw and unchanneled out there. . . . He cast about for the source and raised his defenses.

There was nothing of Charissa in it; it was hardly a formed thing at all. It was power, only; a source without its focus, its key.

All as wrong as wrong can go: the sick certainty of that flooded over him. He half raised one hand and began to probe for whatever lurked in the cathedral.

"Turn around!"

The voice was behind him and off to his left. Falkenberg spun and dropped into a half-crouch. His poignard was in his left hand, pale amber fire enclosed in his right. If he could stop the first rush with the knife, he could have time to lock into enough power to burn half of St. George's into black glass. He looked out into the darkness to face Nigel Haldane.

"Falkenberg." There was surprise contesting with grim authority in Nigel Haldane's voice.

Falkenberg brought the poignard up in salute. "Well met, Nigel."

He was concentrating on the gloom around him with all the Deryni senses and all the training from Alamut that he could bring to bear. Nothing moved, nothing breathed, except the Haldane duke.

Falkenberg gestured and a shroud of silver light enfolded him, a small pillar of cold light in the midst of the empty cathedral. Nigel Haldane's hand was fixed on the hilt of his sword.

"I should have expected you, really. What did she send you to do, Falkenberg? The garrote, while I was praying for Kelson? That was always your way—the strangling wire and the stiletto and dead men in the alley. There's been enough death in Rhemuth tonight. Are they all yours?" He slid his sword free.

Falkenberg let his knife hand fall to his side. "Don't, Nigel. You're alone and you won't get halfway here. I'm not here for you. I'm here to see what it'll be like tomorrow. And to pray for her."

"Well, you *are* her lover. I've been half expecting you to be her knife hand." Nigel frowned. In the silver Deryni light, Falkenberg's face was pale and drawn; in another man, he might have called it despair. But it wasn't the clever killer's face he remembered from the Forcinn. He let the sword rasp back into its sheath.

"But it is odd: a Deryni historian condemned as a heretic, standing in the chief cathedral of Gwynedd praying for a Deryni sorceress and murderess."

Falkenberg sagged against one of the pews. "Ah, well. That's a strange enough word for you to be using . . . murder." He sighed and looked back at the altar. "Knifing a man for his wife or his purse, that's *murder*. If you do it for a crown, that's only the way of things. We weren't either of us so gentle, upon a time."

"No. No, we weren't. But Brion was my brother and my king; and Kelson is my nephew and my king. That makes it murder." He walked out into the glow cast by Falkenberg's halo and braced himself against a pew. "There's been too much killing in Rhemuth Castle tonight. All shadow and indirection. You were good at that, once."

"Look to your own people," Falkenberg said. "I'm not her envoy to the Haldanes. She's kept me out of it. They're all praying for your Kelson. I'm the only one praying for Charissa." He thrust his blade back into its belt sheath. "I won't be here tomorrow. No horsemen out of nowhere, no crossbow aimed from a window, no poison in the sacramental wine. It won't be that easy for you and your General Morgan. She'll do it in full ritual. . . ."

"She's the Marluk's daughter," Nigel said. "She's everything the Restoration was against. She murdered Brion, and she's had a dozen others dead, ambushed or knifed, since. Tomorrow she'll try to kill Kelson, and if she wins, she'll destroy Gwynedd. Can you deny any of that?"

Falkenberg's hand flicked out in dismissal. "Don't expect me to weep for Gwynedd. I couldn't care less what happens to Gwynedd or the House of Haldane. Players die at the Great Game, Nigel; that doesn't bother me." He held up his right hand; the Deryni signet glowed a deep crimson. "And don't hold Alaric Morgan and Camber MacRorie up to me and talk about the Restoration. Christ, we were Festillic partisans all the way to the end. Still are. There's something in being Falkenberg loves a lost cause. . . ." He shrugged and looked off. "She won't let me help . . . God. But I love her, Nigel. Charissa's been my lady for most of a decade. I don't give a damn what she does to any of you. She's braver than I am and I'm afraid for her."

"Don't ask me to pray for her." Nigel Haldane straightened and crossed the aisle into the shadows. "She's the most evil thing I know; she's more cruel than Wencit of Torenth. There were days in the Forcinn when I thought you liked killing; the Shadowed One likes suffering. You wrote her poetry, brought her to the South, dedicated your heresies to her. She's very beautiful, everyone says. But if half the legends are true, she's betrayed you, put horns on you, a score of times. I can't think how she holds you, why you can't see her for what she is."

"Nigel, I know what she is. It's just not something a Haldane would understand. And don't provoke me. If you're looking for assassins, don't go looking at me. I didn't come here to kill you and I won't fight you. You can't cry cuckold and have me fight you. I came here to pray for her. To see where it'll all be. That's all. You can pray for your Kelson. I'm all there is, Deryni or not, to wish her anything but a lingering death."

"Like she gave Brion."

"Oh, Christ." Falkenberg's mouth drew down and he twisted away from Nigel. "I haven't your fine moral sense. None of this has anything to do with morality. . . ."

"Is that the historian or the free-captain talking?"

"Both. And the Lord of Caer Curyll. And Charissa's lover. You're brother to kings, Nigel. You can talk about morality; it's part of your birthright. I'm a border lord and a mercenary; we see things in a different light. I'm not a very important man. I'm no one. Not even at Shalmyr. Not even the day we pushed you out of Guisnes Castle and left all your ships burning off the quay. Christ, I hate this place. Your cathedral and your God and everything Haldane and great." He stood up and pulled his gloves from his belt.

"I'm not part of this. Whatever happens tomorrow, I won't be there. I'm outside of this. I'm so afraid for her, and there's nothing I can do. . . . Forget about me, Nigel. Pray for your nephew. I don't want to haunt this bloody cathedral anymore. Spectre at the feast, you know: I'm very good at that. But I'm leaving. Forget about me. I'll spare you an overly Deryni exit."

The silver light vanished and Falkenberg stepped out into the sudden darkness. By the time Nigel Haldane's eyes had adjusted to the dark, there was nothing there.

T HE CUBES OF the Ward Major set around her chamber flared from white to bright red. They gave off a single pale violet pulse and subsided to a dull, somnolent green. A signature, then: ward-breaking and Portals had been the first things he'd taught her. She kept her eyes on the mirror and waited for him to appear. He stood behind her, the last tendrils of blue light from the Portal playing around the black of his cloak. She kept on brushing the pale mist of her hair.

"Christian."

"Lady." His smile was wan and his face was taut.

She looked into the mirror at his face and frowned. "You took a chance, just now. What if I'd not been alone?"

Falkenberg shrugged. "Be more embarrassing to have your guards announce me, no?" He looked around the room. It was an inner, secondary room and not her formal chamber. "I do have a *shiral* at hand. So you were alone. Finally."

She kept looking into the mirror. "How much did you see?" Her voice hovered between anger and resignation.

"Not everything. As long as I don't see it, I don't have to kill anyone for it." He unfastened the cloak and tossed it onto a chest. "I needed to be here—to see you. This night. Tonight."

She dropped the hairbrush onto the dressing table. "I'm sorry," Charissa said. "We didn't have much of a farewell, did we? I always seem to end up hurting you."

"No. . . ." Falkenberg came up behind her and pressed his face against her hair. He looked past her at their reflection in the mirror and saw the tautness in both their faces. "No. I needed to see you. Before tomorrow." He ran his hands down her shoulders across the soft azure of her dressing gown. He closed his eyes and turned away. "I've never seen you sleep in a gown. You never liked to sleep in anything."

She caught at his hand. "Upon a time," she whispered, "there was someone I fancied sleeping flesh to flesh with. Upon a time."

Falkenberg slid his fingers through hers and sat on the dresser. When she looked up at him, there was a twisted coldness in his face. *"My pet!"* Falkenberg spat. "That pretty boy scum calls you *my pet!"*

Charissa shook her head. "Oh, God. . . . You've never

said anything before. You never minded about what I had to do."

"It's just tonight." His voice was a hollow whisper. He could feel the weight of it all on him: emptiness and love and helplessness and all the ruin in the air. "Tomorrow you'll be at the Coronation and you'll face Morgan and the Haldane and you'll be with him. *My pet!* He's a Howell and he'll only—ruin you, betray you. Fail you. In the end he'll turn on you."

"I know. I know all that. I need him. Just a little while longer." She tightened her hand on his. "After tomorrow—"

"*Charissa. . . .*" Falkenberg's voice was full of pleading. "He's in the other bedroom. I can . . . Charissa, let me kill him. Now. Not later. Let me kill him for you. I can be done with it like *that.*" He flicked his hand and the stiletto flashed into his grip. "I'll kill him and I can stand for you tomorrow in Saint George's. Charissa . . . *please!*"

She pressed her forehead against his side. "No," she said. "I can't. Ian's a swordsman. You're not. Alaric Morgan would have you in pieces on the floor."

"It's all going to go wrong. You can feel it in Rhemuth. There's *trap* written all over the cathedral. I always knew in the end I couldn't protect you. I can face Morgan for you, offer you that—and that's all I can offer you. I don't want you to be destroyed tomorrow. Your damned silken Ian will fail you." He tilted her face up to meet his eyes.

"Let me kill him. I can have two hundred men in the cathedral. There are Portals the Haldanes and Morgan don't know about. I have the original plans of Rhemuth and the cathedral and the castle. Camber MacRorie made the Restoration with a few dozen Michaelines. I can put the whole of my people into Saint George's. They'll all be at prayer and we can overrun the major lords, retreat underground into the castle and hold the inner citadel. I've done it in the Forcinn and the amirates. Let me do that. Or let me call out Morgan to the duel-arcane. Let me do it—kill Howell, stand against Morgan. Charissa. . . ."

"No." Charissa reached up to touch the tears running over his face. She squeezed her eyes shut. "It has to be done by the ritual. I want them dead, but it has to be formally. I'm Pretender to Gwynedd. I want them all to see me be a queen. *Formally.* I have to have a Champion, and you can't face Morgan with a sword. I love you and won't have you destroyed. I *have* to do it. I'm who I am. You're the only thing I ever really loved; you're not an instrument and you're not expendable. I won't have you stand there and die for me."

"Damn you," he said. "Damn you, *it's my place!* I'm supposed to be your lover, and for ten years you've given me everything, been everything for me. I'm failing you; I can't protect you. It's the only thing I can give you, to stand for you. Even Imre got to do that much for Ariella. . . ." He looked away from her.

"I don't want you to see me like this. I'm trying to offer you my sword and my life. I don't want you to see how I'm failing you." His face was slick with tears and he turned into the wall.

"You've never failed me. . . . You've never been afraid of what I'm afraid of; I've had you to be with ever since I was fifteen. Half the sorcery I know is from you. You taught me politics and history and the knife. . . . *Caryad,* I have to go to Rhemuth without you. After tomorrow, I can give you something back."

"Oh, Christ." He tried to keep his mind apart from hers, to keep up the fence around the emptiness and exhaustion pouring out of him. "You're not thinking about it, are you? You're not thinking like what you're supposed to be. It all finishes tonight. Tomorrow sunset, you'll be Queen of Gwynedd or you'll be dead. Either way, I lose you. It's all over."

Charissa recoiled and she felt tears springing up. "What are you talking about?"

Falkenberg turned his hands up in his lap. He looked down and tried to find his free-captain's voice. "It's just

conceivable that the Duchess of Tolan might marry a border lord. A queen-regnant of Gwynedd can't. If you win,
you'll have to play the queen, marry someone great to
preserve the Crown. That's the way it is. And I think I
can't stand at your wedding."

"If I win, I'll be queen-regnant. And I can take any
consort I want. I want *you*." She pulled him around to
face her. "I'll be queen or dead. I can make you Lord of
the North: recreate a Duchy of Kheldour for you out of
Claibourne and the Riding. That makes you one of the
great lords. *Prince*—all the North, and then consort. I
need you with me, and a title is all I can give you for
everything I've taken from you. . . ."

"A Falkenberg," he said. "A mercenary. A proclaimed
heretic, if they remember. A Deryni. Don't, Charissa. You
shouldn't even think it. It has to be one of the Gwynedd
aristocracy. Being a queen's more than vengeance and a
pyramid of skulls in front of the castle. You'll be a
usurper; you'll have to be a great queen to make them
forget. Your cousin in Beldour will try to take Gwynedd
from you; you have to hold a kingdom together, make
them fight for you. Lionel would have been perfect for
you. There's the Earl of Kierney; you'd be taking him
from Morgan's sister—that should mean something to
you. If there could be an . . . arrangement . . . about
mercy, and if he were a few years older, then Nigel Haldane's son."

"Not a Haldane. Not *ever*. . . ." She took his hands
again. "I don't want any of them. I've never thought about
really winning, about after tomorrow. I'm supposed to be
the Shadowed One; I'm just . . . doom, and Lady Death
doesn't think about *after*. I wanted to be Lady Falkenberg
and stay with you at Caer Curyll or live looking out on
the Southern Sea. . . . I don't like sleeping alone and I
don't like sleeping in this gown, but I'm not in my own
bedroom because I can't stand Ian's touch all night. I
can't bear any of them all night.

"I don't know if I'll win tomorrow. I have to go and

I'll stand there and face them. I'll be very cold and very sinister and very beautiful. You'll be proud of me. That matters to me. I have to do this on my own, and I want you to be proud of me. I'm Death come out of the North, and I don't know what happens after the Coronation. A pyramid of skulls, maybe. I'll find a way to have you there. You can gut Ian Howell the minute I'm crowned. He's less than nothing, once Morgan's dead. If there's an after, I'll need you. . . . I don't want you to leave, and I don't want to see you destroyed. Close the circle. Don't do anything . . . if I lose. If I win, stay with me. *Caryad*. . . ."

He pulled her hands up to his face. "It's all going to go wrong. There's some ghastly dance going on and I don't know anything about it. I can't save you. But I do love you and I'll be there . . . whatever happens."

"Tomorrow," she said. "It's hours 'til dawn, still." She shook her hair from the shoulders of her gown. "I've come to you before from other men's beds. Not so soon, though. If you can let that not matter, then I want you to stay. You taught me to believe in symbols and gestures and I want you with me tonight. You were always good at the perfect poet's gesture. . . . I want your touch and not Ian's on me when I go to Saint George's tomorrow."

She looked at him and he nodded.

"Caryad," she said, "get me out of this damned gown."

FALKENBERG PULLED HIMSELF out of his chair and groaned. There was a thin band of sunlight slanting in through the window at a low angle. He looked around the room at a row of empty brandy decanters. The far candles had guttered and he could taste wax in the air. Horsemen were milling about in the court and he looked down. The Tolan Horse had come back. They were all still armed and armored, and he could see three of them limping across the forecourt with bright bandages tied on. He made a face.

"Bloody hell."

There was a sharp staccato pounding at the door. He could hear Aurelian's voice from the other side.

"Christian, Colforth's back. You'd better come down."

He could feel his second-in-command's mind reaching for his, but he was too tired to make contact. He shouted back.

"Right."

He pulled his tunic over his head and flung it across the room. His mouth was filled with the dark aftertaste of the brandy. He leaned over a brass basin and poured water across his head and upper body. He shook his head and thin streams of water poured down through his beard and down his chest. He rummaged in a silvered Moorish chest and pulled out a black silk On-Ogur blouse. He jerked it over his head and reached across the room for his wrist sheaths. A thin Arjenoli stiletto lay along one wrist, ready to slide from its velvet nest into his hand; a double bow-string with wooden handles went around a leather band on the other arm. He thrust his thin leather gloves through his belt and started for the door, feeling the soreness in his back and legs from a night in the chair.

"Christian."

They were waiting for him in a knot on the landing: Aurelian, Brennan de Colforth, Yusuf al-Fayturi, his cousin Michael Gordon. Colforth and the Moor were still in armor; Aurelian and Michael Gordon were looking far too pleased—children with a secret.

"What the hell's going on?" He looked at Colforth. "Who did you run into?"

Colforth came to attention and saluted. Falkenberg sighed. Brennan de Colforth had been too well trained as a courtier; it was all out of place in a free company.

"Two score Gwynedd horse were coming up the Fells, lord. They made camp at South Mere last night and started toward Gordon Fell at daybreak. We caught them in the ravine to the south. We counted thirty-four dead; five wounded of our own."

"They took this," Aurelian said. He held up a silver baldric. "General's insignia. They pushed the bodies down into the Mere and left the heads in a stack at the mouth of the ravine."

"Lord." Yusuf was unwrapping an oilcloth bundle. He was wearing the scarlet leather gloves of a consecrated *Feday'in*. "We have brought the Lord of the Falcon this." He held up his trophy, his fingers tangled in the short, bowl-cropped gray hair.

Falkenberg looked back at Aurelian.

"Their general? Do you have the name?"

Aurelian nodded. "This one was a Lord Mortimer, general of the Gwynedd royal armies. Had a holding in the Purple March." He nodded to Michael Gordon. "He was carrying a royal warrant for the arrest of the Marley refugees—and this." He took a stained parchment scroll from Gordon.

Falkenberg took the scroll and looked at it. It was weighted with a huge seal bearing the arms of Gwynedd, and he could see the opening: *We, Kelson, by Grace of God. . . .*

"What's it say?"

"Gwynedd triumphant," Aurelian said. "Tyrants and traitors destroyed. Lists of names under attainder. *Vae victis* all around. You'll like part of it. In view of Bran Coris having been a traitor, Marley's under the administration of the Dowager Countess Richenda and the Duke of Corwyn. In view of Lionel's treachery, Arjenol's annexed to the Haldane crownlands; Alaric Morgan's to be viceroy. Lionel's son is heir to Torenth and Arjenol, and Tolan's part of Torenth now. Alaric Morgan's the viceroy on two of our borders."

"Treachery." Falkenberg felt near to laughing. "*Treachery? Lionel? Lionel stood to the death for his king and his kinsman, and it's treachery. But the Haldanes represent the Truth and the Light, don't they? They can do anything they fucking want." He threw the scroll back to Aurelian. "Michael, go send for your clansmen. Brennan, get everybody into armor. They're going to be all over us."

He could see them standing in the great hall, looking up at him, waiting for him to assume the mask they'd wanted him to wear all winter and spring. In March, they'd painted the Corwyn gryphon on the saber targets he'd been riding at. He could have found out the names, but it hadn't mattered. They all felt it. Fire and glory and vengeance and plunder and apotheosis. He was Deryni, and they expected him to live up to some dark dream of the sorcerer-lord.

Falkenberg. Something in the bloodline that thrives on the romance of darkness and lost causes. That was what Charissa had meant: the music plays and all must dance. He could pick up a *shiral* crystal and call up the image: the Falcon Horse rushing down on the black and green standard of the Gwyphon, the war cry of *Feday'in* rising shrill and alien—*Ya hya chouhada! Long live the fighters!*—into the air, Morgan's young Sean Derry bringing the Corwyn bodyguard around to meet them.

Ah, God, they were mailed knights on their great huge warhorses; they'd grind the Falcon Horse to a bloody paste if they ever got their charge home. It was all passing out of his hands, but there was a certain soft pleasure in ineluctability.

THE GORDON SCOUT pointed at the map. "They're there of a certain, lord, *sa.*"

Aurelian moved the red markers across the great pyrographed deerskin of the map.

"There. Two hundred of them. If they're at the Marley border passes, they'll be all afternoon getting onto the Fells." He looked up at Colforth and the squadron commanders. "These are armored knights now. They'll start to spread out in the passes. If they're going to South Mere to find where Mortimer was cut up, they'll get there in clumps. Yusuf?"

The Moor was pointing at the passes. "They are knights, as you say. Could you get a stallion through there in good order? We should stop them in the mountains. No Bremagni could fight in the rocks against the *ghazis* of the high forts. Why should these be any different?"

"No." Falkenberg was watching from the far end of the table. "We'd be all day trying to ferret them out of the rocks if they dismounted, and if they got up a charge in the passes, they could ride over us. I don't want anybody that close. I want an example to them. Lots and lots of dead. We'll let them onto the moor and let them run. They'll go to South Mere and we'll take them there. Anyone?" He looked around for questions.

FALKENBERG HELD OUT his arms and Husayn dropped the black Moorish cloak over his head. He clenched his fists and worked the brass-studded riding gloves tight over his fingers. He turned his wrists inside the sleeves of the cloak, feeling for the stiletto and the garrote. Husayn fretted at his shoulders, tightening the laces of the black-enameled steel back-and-breast. The metal pulled tight against the dark leather of his buffcoat and Falkenberg waved the Moor away.

"Falcon Lord." Yusuf was there, holding the scarlet *Fidai*'s sash across outstretched gloved hands. "You are a lord in the *Dar al-Harb,* but we come from the Lord of the Mountain as your death commandos, and you are a *Fidai* of the Amir al-Jabal at Alamut. Here in the *Dar al-Harb,* the land of the Unbelievers, there can be no *jihad.* But loyalty is the way of God, and the Lady of Shadows was our liege." He stepped forward and wound the sash around Falkenberg's waist.

Aurelian pushed his horse next to Falkenberg. "Falcon *Bahadur,*" he said, "I should have a song written for this. We're riding out with an Assassin lord to avenge Charissa."

Falkenberg swung up into his saddle. "No. It's not that.

They're coming to us. Morgan and the Haldanes are on *my* frontiers and they're hunting across *my* lands. Don't make it some romantic thing; it's about the maps."

Aurelian snorted. "Sing me new songs, why don't you?" He brushed crisp graying chestnut hair from his forehead and pulled on his helmet. "You're an easy *shiral* to conjure in. Tell me you don't like the idea of it all. I was half in love with her, too. . . . There should be something in life worth losing everything for, no?"

Falkenberg looked over. "Caer Curyll or Charissa de Tolan?"

"Ah, well," Aurelian said. "If you'd paid attention at Alamut, they're the same." He grinned and rode over to the clump of Michael Gordon's men waiting by Dawn Gate.

Falkenberg signaled to his squadron commanders and his standard bearer. "*Sa, sa,* loves. Let's go find them."

Twenty fugitives, including Bran Coris's second-in-command, Gwyllim. He wasn't going to have the Haldanes hunting on his lands. He was no man's vassal; sanctuary offered at Falcon's Hold meant something. He'd wanted to go to the amirates in the autumn. Alaric Morgan's head on a pike was less important than showing the Camberian Council—something. He couldn't have Gwynedd and its kings destroyed, but the Council. . . . The Council had hated her, plotted against her, decreed her outcast and outlaw, perhaps had a hand in her death.

He had a sudden vision of a rush of *Feday'in* into the Council's great chamber. There would be mercy for perhaps only Thorne and Kyri. Today. . . . He would kill them out there; there would be no little pleasure in that. Caer Curyll was his to defend; he wanted them to leave him alone. But there should be a way to make them remember her, let Morgan and Kelson know who he was. *Bloody hell.* He spurred through Dawn Gate, Aurelian and his standardbearer close behind.

*   *   *

ᗰICHAEL GORDON BROUGHT his horse up behind the top of the rise and pointed down the ravine that led away from South Mere. *"Sa,"* he said. "Ravens and eagles, all. It must be quite the feast."

"Thirty-odd heads," Aurelian said. "The birds aren't used to it; it's a poor country."

Michael Gordon was fidgeting at the silver wolf's-head brooch fastened at the shoulder of the Gordon plaid he wore over his mail shirt. He looked around at Aurelian and grinned. He was a fair-haired man, but he had the dark eyes and thin smile of his Falkenberg mother. "Oh, well. They'll have enough to keep them 'til first snow soon."

Two hundred Gwynedd knights milled about below in the mouth of the ravine. They had come up to the Mere in clumps of ten and twelve, the afternoon sun bright on their mail. Armored knights on their great warhorses, they weren't suited to ride the mountains; their order was as good as could be expected. If they'd come through the passes from Marley that morning, they would be hot and exhausted under their armor, and there was precious little water to be found except in the corpse-laden Mere.

Aurelian's mouth drew down. He knew what Lionel d'Arjenol or a Moorish amir or a steppe *noyon* would have done with the bodies of the first party. Knights were odd about that. He wondered what they were thinking about the pyramid of heads and the flights of scavengers that marked the end of Lord Mortimer's party.

A rider moved across the bracken to where a knot of horsemen were bunched under the red and gold Gwynedd standard. Michael Gordon leaned across to Aurelian and Falkenberg. "That one's in McLain plaid," he said. "I think you've Cassan men down there."

Aurelian rose in his stirrups and looked out to one clump of knights. "Lions *dormant* and roses," he said. "Cassan men. The rest are all Gwynedd royal knights." He nodded to Falkenberg. "The commander's flying a Lindestark banner: very old house, Haldane loyalists, always officers of Haldane household troops."

"Ah, well." Falkenberg smiled. "We're all old nobility here, then. . . . And knights do so well in mixed commands." He motioned to his standardbearer. "Donal. Let's go up."

They trotted up over the crest and halted. Twenty of the Falcon Horse and ten of Michael Gordon's men waited in a motionless line across the top of the rise. Donal unfurled the standard and the Falcon unfettered drifted black and gold in the last of the wind. Down in the ravine, the knights looked up and began pointing and shouting. The nearer ones began to form into ranks.

Falkenberg pointed at his standardbearer and the banner dipped twice to the left. The knights pointed down the ravine and shouted. Forty Falcon horsemen rode in to the other end of the ravine and halted. They were light cavalry, and next to the knights they looked like children. The Gwynedd destriers loomed above the steppe horses the Freikorps Falkenberg favored. They were all cloaked in black, but the knights could tell that they weren't facing armored opponents. The Falcon riders wore leather coats and steel breastplates; a few wore light mail shirts. Only Brennan de Colforth's Tolan horsemen, left back at Caer Curyll, wore hauberks among the Falcon men. They were steppe and desert horsemen, *razzia* riders and Southern coup-makers. The Gwynedd knights were like small fortresses in their hauberks and great, high lancers' saddles. The knights looked down the ravine and sat taller; their confidence was apparent.

A single rider moved out from the Falcon line and rode into the ravine. He jammed a lance into the bracken and rode back, leaving it standing at a sharp angle. Atop the rise, Michael Gordon brought up a trumpet and blew the *View Hallo*. The hunting call drifted down to the knights and they stared grimly at Mortimer's head atop the lance point. Lances clicked into rests and the Gwynedd knights started off down the ravine in a tight, yelling mass.

The Falcon Horse hovered for an instant, then whipped

their horses around and fled out of the ravine onto Gordon
Fell. The knights cheered and followed at full gallop.
They poured out onto the Fell and gave chase. Great
chunks of the earth flew away from their path. Falkenberg
watched, drawing in breath through his teeth. He'd seen
nothing to give him any respect for Lindestark as a commander, but the mass of knights touched a deep fear. Until   •
their line spread out on the flat, their bunched weight was
irresistible; they could ride over anything in front of them.
Knights were, almost by definition, brave, ill-disciplined,
easily outmaneuvered, and none too bright, but they could
grind up any light cavalry they could carry a charge
home to.

Arrows were coming back from the fleeing Falcon men.
Shields swung up to meet them. The arrows whined away
for the most part, more infuriating than deadly. One of
the Gwynedd horses took an arrow through its neck and
pitched forward; its rider flew headlong across the bracken
and lay in a broken heap. The charge swept on, trying to
close the thousand feet between their lances and the men
who had left the heads piled in the ravine. More arrows
came back and two knights fell from their saddles, long
steppe arrows driven through their mail. The Lindestark
banner moved up toward the head of the line and the royal
knights tried to shoulder aside the McLain men for the
honor of the kill.

They were passing under Falkenberg's rise. The Falcon
Horse were still firing thin volleys, pulling the knights
after them. The knights had lost cohesion on the flat; two
hundred individual horsemen were at full gallop, vying
with each other for position and speed. Falkenberg motioned to his standardbearer.

"Full dip."

The Falcon Unfettered swung down and vanished from
the skyline. The fleeing riders drew their bows and swung
around to halt. At eight hundred feet they began firing
massed volleys. Forty arrows skipped out into the knights
and a handful of saddles emptied. A horse dropped to its

knees and three others rushed over it. The knights steadied
themselves and rushed onward.

The charge closed on air as the black riders spun away
at the last moment, still taunting Lord Lindestark's men
with their arrows. The knights swept by the rise. Only
Falkenberg and Aurelian and Donal were left, and the
knights, even if they could have got their horses up the
rise, were locked into the chase. They curved across
the fell, a loose crescent now, turning after their quarry.
They'd lost a dozen men now, their horses were lathered,
and their tormentors wouldn't stand and fight; blood rage
had taken them.

Like Bremagni, Falkenberg thought. *Knights.* Terms of
contempt. His father and Lionel had taught him that. *Sans
peur et sans reproche,* perhaps. But nothing else. Lindestark was a fool, and so were his knights: great, blond,
broad-shouldered men bashing at each other with
greatswords. They'd never have lasted a season in the
amirates or on the steppe. He turned to Donal: "Full banner." He pulled his bow from its case and nocked an arrow.

Falkenberg sighted into the end of the crescent and
fired. The arrow arced away, the sun catching at the triple
barbs of its head. The last knight but two flung up his
hands and fell across his horse's neck with the arrow
sticking up in his back. The two behind him looked back
and pointed desperately. From the rise, Falkenberg could
see their mouths opening in surprise.

The knights began to turn at the sudden noise from
behind. The rest of the Falcon Horse and Michael Gordon's men were racing out in two wings from behind the
rise. There were forty black riders in front of them and
perhaps four times that number behind. The lead riders
around Lindestark and the standards reined in to turn and
the rest began to run into them. The charge faltered and
the knights bunched up or turned in confusion. The sky
behind them filled with arrows. The rear range was only
a few hundred feet and the trajectory was flat enough to

allow for maximum impact. A dozen men and four horses were swept away in the first flight.

Knights were trying to regroup and charge the rearward enemy. A third of the mass broke off and charged back, their shields held up, their lances clutched grimly at their sides. The Falcon riders melted off to the sides and kept firing. Men and horses screamed and fell. The steppe bows pulled at one hundred fifty pounds, and at that range the arrows drove through the hauberks without problem. A knot of men in the McLain plaid threw down their lances and charged out to the side with their broadswords. Four out of eighteen managed to close the distance. One of the steppe horses was lifted bodily and flung away at the impact of the destrier, and one of the black riders lurched from his saddle with a broadsword driven through his leather buffcoat.

Then the Falcon men closed about the four and sabers flashed at close range. The McLain men were hauled from their saddles and left bleeding for the horsemen to ride over. The rest of the knights passed between the rows of Falcon Horse, dead and wounded dropping away. They bunched together to make a stand; a fair number leaped clear of their wounded horses and stood or knelt behind their shields, clutching their swords. Arrows poured down on them.

Lindestark and his vanguard had given up the chase when the rear group attacked, and now the first forty had come back, firing measured volleys into the knights. Horses crashed into one another and fell over. Lindestark's banner moved forward with sixty of the knights with him. The forty skipped around the Gwynedd van, firing at low trajectory. The horses were exhausted now, and there was no energy to build up a charge that might have carried them through. The van fell back under the pressure of the arrows. The Gwynedd standardbearer fell and one of the others snatched up the Lion. Forty of the rear group darted around the main body the van had left, keeping them from the dismounted knights to the rear.

The Gwynedd command had been cut in three; only the van was still moving. The knights had been trained from boyhood to fight with lance and broadsword; no one had taught them to face mounted archers at long range. They were visibly losing heart and other cries were going up across the field: *Mercy!* and *For the love of Christ!* and the few surviving *Gwynedd! Saint George!* calls being drowned out by a harsh *Falken-berg! Falken-berg!*

Falkenberg drew the edge of his scarf up and fastened it across his nose. Between the helmet and the veil, only the polished burnt-sienna of his eyes showed. He laid an arrow into his bowstring and kneed the horse over the rise. He jerked at Aurelian's arm. "Let's get the hell down there."

Aurelian uncased his bow. "Oh, well, then. Personal courage. I'm not all that used to it in you." He laughed and moved to keep pace at Falkenberg's left. Behind the latticework of his burganet, his eyes were a glacial gray-blue and his knee pressed at the hilt of his saber in its saddle scabbard.

They galloped down the rise, Donal close behind with the Falcon standard. The banner dropped right three times and Michael Gordon led a dozen of his clansmen away from the rearmost fight to fall in behind Falkenberg. Half a squadron of the black cavalry followed. They were shouting across the field: *À Faucon! À Faucon!* The easterners among them were howling in On-Ogur. Across the fell the arrows still flew, slaughtering the knights.

Lindestark was trying to lead the van out from the carnage, and he had run his knights at an angle across the fell, riding hard for the mouth of the ravine. Bits and pieces of the main body had streamed away to try to follow him, and the first forty Falcon men were in close pursuit. Falkenberg and his men ran up parallel at thirty yards and began firing. The knights flinched away. Many of them had broken shafts jutting from their mail and they were all white with fear. Only a few had lances now, and some had dropped their broadswords. The Gwynedd stan-

dardbearer had a full arrow protruding from his elbow.
Their horses were breathing in sharp, sick gasps and the
clanking of their mail had a jerky, desperate quality.

Aurelian raised his bow and fired deep into the mass.
The arrow drilled into the face of one of Lindestark's
aides. He fired again and the Lindestark bannerman
sagged, an arrow driven through his knee and into his
horse's flank.

Beside him, Falkenberg was firing in fluid, paced mo-
tions. He saw one of Falkenberg's arrows dart out into a
blood-slick helmet coif and bury itself in the knight's
skull. Pieces of bone flew up and away. He looked back,
fitting an arrow blind. One of the Gordons darted in toward the knights with his saber and a knight swept out
blindly with his lance. The shaft struck the Gordon rider
in the chest and he fell away and vanished under the rushing Gwynedd horses. He could see Michael Gordon yelling at his men; his voice bright and liquid among the
harsh war cries. He fired again and a horse reared, blood
spurting from its throat.

Falkenberg pressed his horse alongside Aurelian. He
shot, trying for Lindestark on his great R'Kassan dun, and
the arrow skipped off someone's helmet and plunged into
the shoulder of another of Lindestark's aides. He hit at
Aurelian's arm and pointed ahead with his bow. The
knights were coming up onto the mouth of the ravine. If
they got in the rocks and scattered, a few would get away;
he wanted no survivors. The last two dozen knights could
see the ravine now. Close together they could throw back
their pursuers; the narrow gap looked like a measure of
safety.

Falkenberg raised an arm and motioned his line inward.
He reached for his saddle scabbard and pulled at his long
Moorish cavalry saber. The blade had been gold-washed,
and it glinted tawny and firelike in the late afternoon.
Verses from the Qur'an ran its length: *Praise be to Allah,
Lord of the Creation, the Compassionate, the Merciful,
Lord of the Judgment.*

The knights looked up as they approached and tried to beat them back with their broadswords. Falkenberg leaned down under a great wide swing and galloped alongside a lathered chestnut stallion. He shifted the saber to his right hand and swung at the knight. The man turned to look at him and opened a mouth in a red-bearded face. The blade slashed across his eyes and mouth. He shrieked and raised his hands before his face; the next slash bit into his wrist and Falkenberg felt the bone shear through.

He spurred ahead, conscious of the heavy mass of knights behind him. He aimed a heavy down-hand cut at a man's thigh and blood fountained up from a severed femoral artery. They were all in among the knights, forcing them together in a jumble, hacking at their edges. He saw Aurelian hammering at a wounded knight, smashing him from his saddle. Michael Gordon thrust two-handed with his sword and impaled a young blond knight in Lindestark livery. Two steppe horses ran by, riderless.

A horse collided with the Gwynedd standardbearer and he went down, shrieking, clutching at his shattered elbow as his horse fell atop him. A knot formed around the fallen banner and the knights' speed slackened. Half a dozen tried to close around Lord Lindestark and the banner in a mailed bulwark. The Gordon clansmen cried and flourished the Lindestark banner. The black riders surged around the few survivors defending the Lion and their general. Falkenberg and Aurelian plowed in among them. A great mailed fist struck Falkenberg in the chest and he flinched away, striking downward. The knight grunted as the blade bit into his side and he fell from his saddle. Aurelian was hacking at the ground, cutting at the Lion. Blood and scarlet silk dribbled across his blade. The R'Kassan dun stood with its saddle empty. The Falcon cavalry drifted across the field, hacking at the wounded and dying. Falkenberg rode up to Aurelian and unfastened his veil. It was over, here.

They trotted back across the fell as the last of the knights were giving up. The knights were all dismounted now, crouching under their shields in a press amid a field of dead men and riderless horses. They threw down their swords and stood, pulling off their helmets and crying, "Yield! Yield!"

The black cavalry drew up and spread out around them. Arrows poured into the knights from three sides and they screamed in rage and fear as they were cut down. The last handful staggered to their knees, arrows tearing through their hauberks. They pitched forward into the bloodied bracken and the black riders swept in, hacking at the bodies. Falkenberg rode back into the line with the sword lying fire-gold across his saddle. Aurelian was beside him with the fallen Gwynedd Lion on a broken staff. They looked at them and cheered. Cries of *Falkenberg!* and the Moors' *Ya hya chouhada!* came up to meet him.

Falkenberg passed the goatskin bag on to his standard-bearer and looked down at the shredded Gwynedd Lion and the Lindestark banner on their broken staffs lying atop a growing pile of arms and armor. He swirled the wine around his mouth and swallowed.

"Two hundred of them at a throw. Aurelian, what's the final cost?"

His second-in-command looked back from the assembled squadron commanders. "Eight dead; half of those are Gordon men. We only closed with them the once. They were running to form. All frontal charge and the melee."

Out on the fell, parties were moving among the knights, slashing the throats of the wounded and stripping the bodies. Aurelian nodded at the pile of captured armor.

"That and the horses we can sell around the coast or in the Connait. But if the Haldanes have Torenth and Arjenol, I don't know how we're going to recruit or get steppe horses."

Michael Gordon came up. "Two hundred of them. Two hundred thirty-odd of them and two royal generals. It's that you're bloody good at this, but what happens now? Are we having the Haldanes back?"

"It's my land," Falkenberg said. "I won't have them

here. Christ, I don't know what they'll do. It doesn't take being Deryni to have it occur to them that they've misplaced two hundred royal knights."

"It could be a while," Aurelian said. "Wencit and Lionel had their eastern wars, and Morgan and the Haldane king inherit those. Morgan has to rebuild his duchy, play the viceroy, and still keep the R'Kassans out of his sea lanes. Attainders and executions in Marley and Torenth and Arjenol. Occupation garrisons. They'll never be able to afford to maintain a full field army past the end of summer, and they won't be getting Cassan and Kierney men after Rengarth. I think we have a while."

"A while," Michael Gordon echoed. "And then we're at war with the Haldanes. All of Gwynedd."

Falkenberg frowned at him. "Bran Coris was your friend, too. Did you want to just go out and ask them to turn back? You're a free lord, too, cousin. Do you want the kings coming up here to hunt? Michael, you're family. You should fancy this sort of thing."

Aurelian kneed his horse closer to Falkenberg. "They'll have a name, you know. It's not that they won't find out that Caer Curyll exists. You wrote Bran and Lionel; they'll have written offers of sanctuary to Kelson Haldane's enemies. That will give them reason enough."

"A border problem, then." He looked out at the bodies lying in the twilight. "This was all for the maps, for my sovereign rights. Do you believe that?"

"No," Aurelian said. "I don't believe a word of it. And nobody else does, either."

"Good. I let Yusuf and Brennan go out yesterday, I knew they'd find an excuse to kill. And today. . . . There's nothing quite like this, love: planning an ambush and walking past the dead. Nothing. Morgan and Kelson Haldane will go look at their maps and this will be just a border problem. A year, and they won't even remember Charissa; she'll be just a small adventure on the way to Llyndruth Meadows and Gwynedd the Great. Their stewards will go through Sendal and clear it out, and they'll never think about her. . . ." He shook his head. "I'm losing any idea of what it's supposed to be about."

"Morgan's never heard your name," Aurelian said. "Neither has Kelson Haldane. The Council wants to pretend you're only a heretic they can forget about. The Haldanes will be back here for one reason or another. The others want to pretend you never existed. I'm eastern; there's a certain poetry in it—riding out to make them know *who* and *why*. Think about it: even after the Fall, how well could God sleep, remembering? Once upon a time, Lucifer stood there, knowing what would happen, and said *Non serviam.*"

Falkenberg laughed. He looked up at his standard: *Or,* on a pale *Sable* a falcon in flight voided *Or,* bearing in its dexter talon a chain of four links, the first and fourth open, *Or.* World's-edge heraldry, Lionel had said. The Falcon Unfettered.

"For the exiled, then?" he asked. "For the solitary?"

"Do you want them to think it was all a morality play, a set piece about being Deryni and the soul of kingship?" Aurelian returned.

Falkenberg shut his eyes. "She died to be a queen. She wasn't an adventure on the way to God in His Heaven, Kelson on his throne, human and Deryni reconciled. God, I'm sick of morality!" He looked at both Aurelian and Michael Gordon.

"Pile their heads up in the ravine. We're going to the amirates before autumn. To Alamut. And then—*for the exiled!* Let's play at being spectres at the feast." He caught Aurelian's eyes. "It's not like I have anything else to do, is it?"

Aurelian shook his head. "Not and be what I always thought you were."

Caryad. Falkenberg spun his horse and trotted off across the fell. Next spring, the bracken would grow up through the skeletons of Gwynedd warhorses.

Charissa. He was High Deryni and it meant—what? That there was power lying there in the air, a way to force them to see that it was Chance and Necessity, that the world wasn't Morality and Meaning. There wasn't a way to exact the vengeance he wanted. Coroth and Rhemuth couldn't be burnt to pools of black glass this season.

But he wouldn't let them make her into part of their myths. That was the one thing he could save her from. She had been twenty-six and tall and blond and gentle and an exquisite lover. She had been the only thing he'd ever loved and she'd been the only lady he'd ever written his poetry for. *The Venture of Caeriesse* was dedicated to her; her tiger's-eye was as close to a wedding ring as he'd get. She had been brave and had had the strength to make herself into the Lady of Shadows and stand against them all. She might have been Lady Falkenberg or Queen-Regnant of Gwynedd.

Caryad. The Haldanes and Alaric Morgan lived in a world of little theophanies; he wouldn't let them have her for their grand categories.

He trotted the horse among the dead. They'd learn. Charissa and then Lionel. Revenge, yes. But something else: a rejection of reification. *The Venture of Caeriesse* had been that; so had everything he'd learned at Alamut and Arjenol Hold. The God of Rhemuth against the God of Alamut and Caer Curyll; the neo-Gabrilite piety of Stefan Coram against the irony and historicism of the three volumes of *Caeriesse*; the chivalry of Morgan against what he'd learned from Lionel. The dialectic of it all was what had sent the House of Falkenberg to its mountains long before. But they'd learn. First the amirates, and then perhaps to the east: the steppe come once more to the West. He would never be Alaric Morgan's banesman, but Morgan and the Haldane boy and Denis Arilan and the Council could watch their carefully built plans be so coldly put in disarray. . . .

He reined in and looked back across the fell. The last of the sunlight was fading, and the Falcon retainers were small black shapes moving over the field. The dead knights were no more than shapeless, colorless lumps.

There wasn't anything to cry in defiance, not *Ya hya chou-hada!* or the Falkenberg war cry. It would be for Charissa, and it would be for something about those who lived outside Meaning.

She was dead, and perhaps Alaric Morgan and his king would never understand *why* or even really *who*. There was a poetry to it, something austere and perhaps even elegant in its fascination with exile and fate. He was Christian-Richard de Falkenberg, and he had loved Charissa Festil de Tolan. He was a border lord and a poet and an historian and a sometime commander of mercenary cavalry, and he had loved the Lady of Shadows. *Chance and necessity, then.* But if the Haldanes and Alaric Morgan and the Camberian Council needed to see a point to it, then there was one to give them.

He pulled his hood up in the evening chill and spurred back across to rejoin his second-in-command.

※

A MATTER OF PRIDE
1118

While we can place an approximate date on this next story because of its mention of Archbishop Corrigan (who was elected to the See of Valoret in 1117), it actually could have taken place at nearly any time in the previous two centuries. For unlike our other stories, this one deals with a concept rather than any of the particular characters who inhabit the Eleven Kingdoms. In specific, the author has chosen to explore the nature of artistry and the artistic gift. The Deryni element is almost incidental to the story, which proves to be, indeed, "A Matter of Pride."

A MATTER OF PRIDE

✳

Leslie Williams

TORCHLIGHT SWUNG DIMLY around pillars and sent shadows crawling across stone walls. Shivering uneasily and avoiding the dark, the abbot puffed up to a hewn door and stopped, clutching a sweat-moistened roll of parchment. Blotting paunchy cheeks against a rough sleeve, he tried the door and then pounded on it, his plump fist beating a musty echo up the corridor. For the thousandth time, he wondered why he had ever let a novice monk have private quarters in the cellar.

Sure, Brother Vajen might be his best script illuminator; indeed, he was a star on its way to holy glory among Saint Foillan's Abbey's manuscript artists. But that didn't mean that the promising youth had to choose the most secluded, inaccessible reaches of the monastery for his studio, then have the nerve to lock the door.

Pounding harder, the abbot leaned against the wood, heard sandaled steps approaching, and stood away. As the lock uncaught and candlelight blinded the corridor, he braced hands on hips and belligerently addressed the artist.

"Brother Vajen, will you kindly tell me the reason for locking this door?"

A hesitant voice somewhere in the lightened doorway stammered, "I—well, I—"

"Never mind." Scuffing pompously into the tiny, well-lit room, the abbot approached the only table and peered closely at a parchment spread across it. A castle loomed at the upper left margin, its hedges of thorn and berry vine winding delicately along the immaculate letters, tiny birds, and lizards playing through stippled leaves. To one side of the keep's moat, a tiny knight in gilt armor rode a prancing leisure horse to meet his lady who, no doubt, was in the curtained window on the lowest parapet.

Good. Damned good!

The abbot looked away, swallowed irritably, then spied the monk still standing by the closed door.

"Come here, Brother Vajen."

With a tentative smile, the monk swung awkwardly forward, robes flapping vagrantly against his thin frame, bony hands chafing nervously. Nearing the table and catching sight of his work, the sparkling black eyes glowed affectionately as ascetic features softened. He ran a hand through dusty black locks and smiled at his superior.

"It's for Saint Piran's Priory. I wanted to do a good job." He looked away uncomfortably, tracing the rough edge of the inkwell with one cramped finger.

Warmth coursed through the abbot. Saint Piran's—ah, that was a good place. Several pretty maids there. . . .

Clearing his throat, he remembered the moist parchment in his fist.

"Here's your next job. This page of Saint Matthew has been so stained that it's unreadable. You're to copy it over, illustrations and all. And mind you, do it well. It's for His Excellency, Archbishop Corrigan."

Extending the sheet, he was astounded as Vajen stared at it for a moment, then slowly turned away, withdrew.

For a long, silent moment, Vajen faced the door and the hands chafed themselves again.

"Father, I don't think I can do it," he said hesitantly.

What? But Vajen was the best. Why would he possibly refuse? Oh, no—did he want a servant, someone to fetch and carry candles and ink? Well, if that was so . . .

As the abbot drew a deep breath and pulled himself together, Vajen spoke up again.

"Father, I want to make a confession."

Confession? Now? Couldn't it wait?

"It's a terrible sin, and I—mmm—" The monk's voice cracked, he swallowed loudly, and continued. "I feel unable to continue my work."

Oh, damn. He must have smuggled a girl down into the cellar. No wonder he wanted such a secluded spot, and why the door was locked. In fact, she was probably stowed away through the adjoining door and in his bedroom. These young monks—what was to be done with them?

"I am vain, Father." The words tumbling, it all spilled out. "All the time I drew, people praised me and I tried harder, thinking it was for the good of Saint Foillan's; and the better I did, the more people praised me, and I got the idea of experimenting and painting and drawing things not dealing with scripture—and now I can't look at anything I've done without feeling the shame of pride, and I can't help myself, and I've begun to hate even being an artist."

Whirling and striding to the abbot, the monk dropped to his knees and clutched the pudgy hand, kissing its ring frantically. "Help me, Father. Take me away from this temptation before I condemn myself and those who admire my work."

A long minute of silence held as the abbot gathered his thoughts.

Damn! So much for Archbishop Corrigan's manuscript! And for what? Brother Vajen's sin was not so great: all artists had a measure of vanity; it was a trait of the profession. But Vajen was naive enough to be disturbed. Perhaps he could be dissuaded of the enormity of his sin.

"*Brother.*"

Bloodshot eyes peered bleakly up.

"Show me your experiments."

In one self-condemnative sweep, the monk swirled to the bedroom door and threw it wide. As the abbot entered, a gasp involuntarily escaped his lips. For Vajen indeed had a problem.

He was talented. The canvassed landscapes almost captured the essence of life, the sparkle of sunset on castle windows, the purple distance of mountains. After a minute more, the abbot withdrew and closed the door, then started pacing heavily up and down the room. Waiting miserably beside the table and its manuscript, the monk reached unconsciously for the pen beside it, then started and pulled back his hand as if it had been burnt.

Now what? Vajen should be kept near art, but in a way that precluded this pride. Something functional that would keep the monk's hands busy and his ego idle. Something slightly messy to provide the discomfort necessary for repentance. Perhaps . . . pot making?

Halting triumphantly and eyeing the downcast monk, the abbot smiled. Of course! The ceramic master was an old friend, and resentful of the understaffed condition of his department; he'd love an extra pair of hands. Especially if those hands came from a rival department better staffed than his. That should prove humbling enough for one young monk.

Donning a benign smile, he motioned Vajen to approach. As the monk knelt, he laid a hand on the bowed heed.

"Your penance will be to leave this art and help with pot making for three months. If, by then, you feel your vanity expelled, then you may return to your work." Perhaps Archbishop Corrigan's manuscript could wait until then.

Scuffing to the door and jerking it open, the abbot stopped as a bony hand caught his and Vajen smiled up gratefully.

"Thank you, Father."

Shaking the hand loose irritably, the abbot grumbled, "Don't thank me. Thank God." A small, blustering storm, he shuffled from the room.

DESPITE THE UNDONE manuscript, Archbishop Corrigan did invest in the abbot's favorite gelding, and the winnings from that race were tallied by the ceramic master. The abbot peeked in the shop and glanced about muddied wheels and shelf after shelf of chamber pot and water pitcher, then snuck cautiously in and tried to disappear as a door slammed and someone approached. Ducking around a stack of plates, he watched a vaguely familiar black-clad figure pass into an adjoining room. Groping through his memory, the abbot recalled the monk Vajen, their talk two months ago, and abruptly decided to check up on him.

Looking guiltily about and creeping to the door the other had entered, the abbot paused, his suspicions stirring. Another cracked door gleamed invitingly past a drying rack stacked with bowls. The abbot laid one hand on the doorjamb, brought his face to the crack, then threw back the door and entered.

Bent over a lump of clay, one hand clutching a tool firmly, Vajen stared guiltily at his discoverer. As the abbot neared, the tool fell to the table and he backed away, conscience blushing redly into his face.

It was a statue—a dove. Porcelain wings spread, the delicate beak probed for a mite among feathers as the tail spread for balance. Each plume was exquisitely drawn, and the abbot's hard stare left the statue and fastened on the cringing monk.

"I thought I had gotten you away from this."

Vajen wouldn't meet his eyes.

"I thought it might—"

"Might what? I see no use for this"—a fat finger brushed the bird—"except as an ornament."

Scrutinizing the floor, the dusty black head nodded. "Yes, Father."

Leaning closer, the abbot stared at the feathers. Good. Very good. Even the ridges and rings on the feet. Clearing his throat and wiping sweaty palms on thighs, he snapped, "And what exactly was it supposed to be? The dove Noah threw from the ark? I see no olive branch in its beak."

"It was just a pigeon from outside." Vajen's voice broke and a shaking hand rubbed his nose.

Drawing himself erect and moving toward the door, the abbot glanced back once more. "This experimentation is what got you in trouble in the first place. So once and for all, I'm getting you out of it. Tomorrow, report to the blacksmith. You'll start shoeing horses. Perhaps that will keep you out of mischief."

Pausing, he turned and saw the thin, slumped figure near the table lay a finger on a curved wing, then seize the bird with both hands and hurl it to the floor. As the unfired porcelain smashed dully, the abbot turned and swept from the shop.

IN THE PAST, the abbot noted, that damned monk had done as much organizing as arting, and with him gone, it seemed that nothing was getting finished in the manuscript archives. Laying aside that department's latest petition for extended time, and noticing the red sunset streaming through his study window, the abbot sat back and closed his eyes for a quick nap before dinner.

It had been a bad day—too much ill luck for mere coincidence. He must be doing something wrong. First the collection had come up empty. Not that none attended the services from the surrounding villages, just that none could afford to pay. Certainly, they were loyal—but that wouldn't keep up his table or reputation among the other abbots and the bishops.

And then his prize filly had thrown a shoe and lost the race she had been a certain bet to win. And then those backlogged files, because that illustrator was now with the blacksmith when he should be—

Blinking, the abbot sat up, then ordered that same monk brought before him. He could not help wondering who had shod his mare this morning.

A knock, and Brother Vajen entered—or at least the abbot thought it was the same man. Gone was the glitter-eyed, pale cleric of five months before. He slumped dully in the sunlight, his muscles knotted through the stained, soot-scarred folds of his robe. Standing and circling his desk, the abbot noticed small pocked scars along those long fingered hands. Hair hung in trailers down the bent neck, and both arms draped slackly at his sides.

Halting at some distance away and folding his arms, the abbot recalled his question. "Brother Vajen, who shod my horse this morning?"

Not looking up, Vajen replied, "Which horse?"

The abbot stomped angrily. "*My* horse, the filly. Did you or the blacksmith shoe her?"

The monk seemed to be having trouble thinking. Finally he droned, "The blacksmith shoed your horse. I shoed the mare."

"But my horse was a mare!" This was infuriating. Seizing the bent shoulders, he rattled Vajen until the monk looked up. An empty black stare met his and the abbot let go, stepping back. Finally an answer floated to those dim eyes, and Vajen said, "There were two horses, both mares. I shoed the bay."

"You shod the—" Biting off his reply, the abbot circled the man slowly, then exploded. "*My* horse was the bay!"

"Oh." Vajen seemed unconcerned.

Anger drained. Oh, well. There would be other races. There would have to be.

Turning away, the abbot started to his desk, then froze

and stared. Hanging at the monk's waist was a hand-cast bronze crucifix. To the bowed head on the cross and the puncture marks in the palms and feet, it was perfect, washed red in the sunlight shrouding Vajen from the window.

The cross fit in the abbot's pudgy hand. Speaking past a hot coal in his chest, he managed to ask, "What is this?"

Vajen shrugged. "It's a crucifix, Father."

Riled anger boiled out, deadly quiet. "Did you make this?"

"Yes, Father."

"And why?"

Another shrug. "I carelessly lost mine and was afraid to ask for another."

The abbot's soft fist closed around the object and he gave a jerk. The tattered leather thong snapped. Ignoring the figure's tarnishing and green stains, he carried it to his desk and set it soundly upon the wood.

So, this was why Vajen's penance of pride was taking so long, why the bay mare had thrown a shoe. Instead of the duties of a blacksmith, this monk was arting again. After all the care the abbot had taken to help ease the man's conscience, Vajen was still toying around behind his back. Eyeing the still figure before him, he sighed.

"Brother Vajen, what am I going to do with you? You have not repented of your proud attempts at experimentation, even through various trials of labor. I, therefore, place you in confinement for devout prayer and fasting until next spring or your repentance, whichever comes first.

"You may go."

As he left, Vajen stumbled and scuffed as if even walking was too great an effort. As the door shut, the abbot glanced down at the crucifix. A single last ray of bloody sunlight impaled the right hand of the figure, its tiny nailed palm and miniature rivulets of shed gore. The nail almost resembled a pen stylus.

With one swift motion, the abbot swept the figure off his desk, where it rang loudly against the stone floor.

SPRING CAME, BETTER than the abbot had expected. The black mare foaled, and her long-legged colt showed promise. Several acquaintances from Saint Piran's Priory idled over to visit and gossip, and exchange quite unchristian rumors. It seemed a serving maid had lost her virginity, then claimed the child was kin to someone in Saint Foillan's Abbey. Luckily, it wasn't the abbot's—by accident, not design.

Donations poured in with baptisms of the human spring crop, and vegetable contributions kept tables well covered, especially the abbot's. Brisk green breezes promised high wagers and spirits for ensuing fall races.

Waddling awkwardly down shadowed, pillared corridors, the abbot glanced curiously into gaping cellar doors and considered his next task. Spring had gone well, except for those damned manuscript files. That cursed monk had finally gotten out of confinement and cloistered himself in his old quarters where his best work had once emerged; yet nothing, not one blessed parchment, had left the pocked door that now loomed before his superior.

Setting his jaw and suppressing a wad of anticipated outrage, the abbot raised one bloated fist and pounded the door.

Damp stone echoed, but there was no answer. Temper rising, the abbot grasped the handle and turned—it was open. Swinging the door wide, he stepped into the tiny room, its muted candlelight—

And mountain air. Pushing gently through his robes, chilled, thin wind whispered past and out into the open corridor. Hesitantly the abbot followed the breeze toward its source and found himself before a painting hung upon rough stone. A slow sunrise spread across purple crags, and stacked cliffs jutted stiffly to the picture frame; spattered ochre foliage held where it could. Wind whistled over abutments, blasted past the frame, and it seemed bushes moved, swayed with the wind—

Breaking into a cold sweat, the abbot retreated and looked away, found another painting. Black, occult jungle panted moistly in warm greenhouse sweat.

Eyes narrowed, the abbot turned and took in the walls; paintings lined them all. Curiosity was lost in fury as, swiveling toward the room's center, he spied a table littered with unfinished parchments. A soft sign of movement indicated activity. Stalking that noise, the abbot approached, then paused and examined the source of the illumination. Peculiar and dim, a golden-pink shine came from the wicks of a sconce of strangely bright tapers. Breathing warmly on their slim surface, the abbot went pale as the "wax" misted—the candles were hammered bronze.

And their flame? Checking closer, he extended a trembling finger and felt. The light danced; the flames were polished slag.

He could stand no more. Turning sharply about, he faced the table.

"Brother Vajen!"

From behind piled manuscripts, a figure straightened. Sable lanced beneath dark brows, gleaming black hair shone brightly down the collar of clean monk's robes. Lean and muscular, the shoulders were unbent, hips and pose arrogant. Balanced in one long-fingered hand was a narrow ceramic needle. The abbot's eyes fastened on that sharp instrument as the man answered.

"Yes, Father?"

Slowly the abbot's gaze left the tool, fastened on the pile of parchments. Suddenly he remembered the cause of his visit and swung an arm in their direction.

"Brother Vajen, are you aware of the state of these files? They are months behind!"

"I am aware."

Flabbergasted irritation. "Then, why haven't you done anything about it?"

Deliberately setting the tool down, Vajen slouched
slightly and smiled. "I found something more important."
Wrought silver flashed at his waist: a new crucifix dangled
from one hip.

The abbot's mouth popped open. Reluctantly he found
his stare sweeping the room and its furnishings again.
Amused sable eyes watched as he finally looked back.

"Brother Vajen, this work—what is the meaning of it?"

A grin. "You tell me."

"This is experimentation." The grin widened and the
abbot continued accusingly. "This is exactly what I've
been trying to cure you of. I thought I'd succeeded. Did
you learn nothing in all your penance?"

"I did learn."

Aghast, the abbot propped plump hands on his hips.
"And what? You piddle around here and let the files get
behind—I think you need more abasement. I think I
should assign you some more."

Vajen's hand dipped to the ceramic tool and idled it
about. "If you do, I'll abandon my vows."

The abbot's eyes bulged. "But your soul—your salva-
tion! What will you do when you stand convicted for this
vain work—this foul exploration beyond the proper art
for the glorification of the Church! Whatever happened to
humility?"

The needle *klunked* firmly into the table top as sable
eyes smoldered softly. "Art is not a humble gift."

Frozen in shock, the abbot met that black stare and
silence stretched thin. Then Vajen smiled wryly.

"Don't you want to see what I've made you?" He gestured toward the pile of parchment. Drawn against his
will, the abbot circled the table and found that the pile of
scrolls had obscured his view of a tiny lump of clay. He
looked closer and its gray tones resolved themselves.

It was a horse. A tiny, thin-limbed, small-headed stallion with shod hooves. Delicate needlework frothed the
mane and smartly lifted tail into curls. Bending absorb-
edly over the work and lifting one tentative hand, the ab-

bot hardly heard Vajen move closer beside him.

"What did I learn? To humble the gift is to cripple the talent."

The abbot's fat finger touched the horse. The warm clay moved, lifted its head, and surveyed him with tiny eyes. . . .

✳

THE GREEN TOWER
1052

Our last story is my own, and no doubt will only frustrate many readers who already have been wondering about the incident that is its subject. "The Green Tower" is back-story for the novel I have just begun, the first book of the Childe Morgan Trilogy, and refers to the incident wherein the Deryni master Lewys ap Norfal disappeared while working a mysterious magical ritual at Castle Coroth that went seriously awry. Three years previously, he had defied the authority of the Camberian Council in a way I've not yet specified, though I've alluded to the incident in *High Deryni, The Bishop's Heir,* and *The King's Justice.*

Needless to say, these passing references to what clearly was a fascinating episode in Deryni secret history have continued to pique the curiosity of true Deryni fans. Over the years, they've begged to know more about Lewys, and what he did to defy the Council, and what kind of experiment went awry, and how, but I've kept resolutely silent until now.

It still isn't time to tell you *all* about that episode; but in working out the beginning of the first Childe Morgan book, I realized that it *is* time to tell you a bit about it, if only from the point of view of Lewys's daughter Jessamy and young Stevana de Corwyn, who is Alaric Morgan's grandmother. The grown Jessamy will be a major player in the first Childe Morgan book, along with Stevana's daughter Alyce, who will be Alaric's mother.

Of course, Jessamy and Stevana are only eleven and ten respectively in this story, poised on the brink between childhood and young womanhood, so they aren't being told what's really going on in the Green Tower; but the events of the story will have very real repercussions nearly four decades later, when we pick up Childe Morgan. Yes, it's a blatant teaser for the next book, though I prefer to regard it as a tasty tidbit or appetizer; but I think it stands on its own as a further fleshing out of what has become the ongoing saga of the Deryni.

Finally, a special thanks to the readers who were in the Deryni Destination chat room at www.deryni.com that night in February when I asked for research help on a subject that isn't often written about in fiction. You know who you are. I didn't end up using most of the specific information you helped me dredge up, but it helped a lot to have a clearer picture in my own mind as I wrote the ending of the story. For the vast majority of you who weren't there, you'll probably have figured it out by the end of the story.

THE GREEN TOWER

❈

Katherine Kurtz

STEVANA DE CORWYN was ten on that afternoon of an early spring, watching from the battlements with her mother as the newcomers rode into Castle Coroth. In the courtyard below, mounted on a pretty dappled pony with green plumes nodding in its headstall, she could see another girl-child of about her age, pretty and well dressed, as dark as Stevana herself was fair. A mass of glossy black ringlets cascaded down the other girl's back, caught by a ribbon of fresh green silk; her riding dress was of a rich, tawny velvet that almost seemed to glow in the sunlight, lavished at hem and sleeves with bands of glittering embroidery.

Stevana allowed herself a wistful sigh, suddenly less pleased with her own simple gown of good, serviceable green wool, but she knew that her mother would never allow *her* to wear velvet anywhere near a horse. Grania de Corwyn would make clucking sounds and say that both the fabric and the very style of the newcomer's gown were unsuitable for a child that age, especially for riding. An upward glance at her mother confirmed that Stevana had best not even comment on the subject.

It was because the girl had no mother, Stevana decided.
Lady Ilde had died the previous summer, leaving her two
children to the somewhat distracted care of their father.
The boy was already squired to the court of King Malcolm
of Gwynedd, living at court in Rhemuth. The rather plain
and stoop-shouldered man riding a big roan beside the
girl's pony could only be Master Lewys ap Norfal himself—hardly as impressive-looking as she had expected,
after all the talk of the past week. At supper the night
before, the grown-ups had talked of little else. Stevana
had nearly fallen asleep over her trencher.

"Well, he *is* bringing his daughter, *Beau-Père*," Grania
de Corwyn had said to Stevana's grandfather. "He can't
have in mind anything *too* dangerous."

Stiofan de Corwyn, the Deryni Duke of Corwyn, shook
his head and twisted off another chunk of the fresh man-
chet bread heaped on a pewter platter between him and
the mother of his only grandchild.

"I wish I could be sure of that. You know very well
what he did three years ago—or at least tried to do. I'm
almost surprised they let him live. God knows I've tried
to talk him out of it. But he's thought of another approach,
and he's convinced that he's the man who can make it
work. That said, I figured it was better to have him work
here, where responsible souls can make sure things don't
get totally out of hand—or pick up the pieces if they do."

Stevana wondered what it was that Master Lewys was
supposed to have done—and what might happen if he did
try to do it here! She knew, though no one had said as
much, that the trickle of important visitors arriving daily
for the past week had been Deryni. In and of itself, that
marked the occasion as unusual, for even here in Corwyn,
those of their race had been looked upon with uneasiness,
if not hostility, for more than a hundred years.

But it was better here than in the neighboring heartland
of Gwynedd. There, except for a very few who enjoyed
powerful patronage and protection—and even they were

always wary—Deryni mostly kept very quiet about what
they were.

Of course, Corwyn was on the fringes of the kingdom,
and had once enjoyed sovereignty of its own, always under Deryni rulers. The Dukes of Corwyn were still virtual
princes within their own borders, sufficiently respected
that the most draconian of the old anti-Deryni laws had
rarely been enforced in Corwyn, other than the prohibition
against Deryni clergy. Stiofan Duke of Corwyn had
fought for the Haldane king at the bloody Battle of Kill-
ingford, as had his father, and had been duke for more
than a quarter century. He was regarded as a fair and
evenhanded ruler, even if he *was* Deryni, accepted and
even admired by his people, so there had never been any
serious attempt to oust him from the lands held by many
generations of his ancestors.

Still, for most Deryni west of the border with Torenth,
even in Corwyn, it was wise to be circumspect—a difficult thing for Stevana herself, she thought, as she set an
elbow on the balustrade and leaned her chin against her
hand, for as the granddaughter and heiress of the Deryni
Duke of Corwyn, she could hardly expect not to be recognized for what she was, once anyone knew her name.

That meant that she had been taught from the earliest
age to guard her tongue and, even more, to curb any display of her powers as they began to develop. Yet this
circumspection about demonstrating one's powers seemed
not to apply to grown-ups; or at least not to those now
gathering at Castle Coroth. It seemed clear that the man
now riding into the castle yard—by all accounts, a very
powerful and clever Deryni—was intending no small
demonstration of his power, and apparently with the approval or at least the tolerance of some of the most accomplished Deryni mages living. Several of them had sat
in her grandfather's hall the night before, or were watching in the yard below.

"Her name is Jessamy," Stevana's mother said beside

her. "She's but a year older than you are. Shall we go downstairs and meet them?"

Stevana craned her neck somewhat dubiously, watching a man-at-arms lift the other girl down from her pony.

"She's pretty," Stevana decided, "but she doesn't look very friendly."

Her mother's arched eyebrow made it clear that she did not regard her daughter's comment worthy of Corwyn's heiress.

"Well, she doesn't, *Maman*."

"Aye, and if you approach her with that kind of attitude, I very much expect you'll be proved right."

Stevana only rolled her eyes as she put her hand in her mother's and dutifully followed down the turnpike stair to the hall.

SHE FOUND THAT more of her grandfather's Deryni friends had arrived during the day, while she was at her lessons. Not far from the foot of the stair, she spied her cousin Michon, who sometimes tutored her. He was young and handsome, and flirted with her outrageously, and she wanted to run and fling her arms around his neck for a hug; but he was deep in conversation with another young man somewhat older than himself, with curly red hair and piercing brown eyes.

"Who's that with Cousin Michon?" she whispered to her mother, as they made their way toward the door to the castle yard.

Grania smiled, answering softly. "Don't worry yourself about *him*, my darling. That's Sir Sief MacAthan. If there's trouble over the next few days, other than from Master Lewys, it's apt to be from him. But don't worry; Michon will keep him in line."

Stevana only nodded, wide-eyed and blithely unaware, as they came down the steps into the yard, that such candid observations were not usually shared with ten-year-olds. She had never known her father, who had died

before she reached her first birthday, so she thought it
normal that her mother should have come to regard her
as a confidante.

Her grandfather was talking to Master Lewys, whose
daughter was doing her best to look poised and grown-up
in the presence of their noble host. Duke Stiofan glanced
in the direction of his daughter-in-law and granddaughter
as they approached, smiling as he extended a hand to draw
them closer for introductions.

"Ah, here they are now," Stiofan said. "Grania my dear,
I should like to present Master Lewys and his daughter
Jessamy. Lewys, this is my son's widow, the Countess
Grania, and my granddaughter, Stevana de Corwyn."

As courtesies were exchanged among the grown-ups,
Stevana eyed the other girl from closer on, vaguely envious of her dark curls. Jessamy, for her part, lifted her
chin and returned Stevana's scrutiny unflinchingly—her
eyes were a deep, almost violet-blue—but she looked
more nervous than prideful, Stevana decided.

"*Maman*, may I show Jessamy the garden?" she asked,
when a lull in the adults' conversation permitted.

"Of course you may, darling. But do try to stay out of
the mud. Jessamy won't want to spoil her pretty gown."

Making a moue at her mother, Stevana darted out her
hand to take Jessamy's and tugged her toward the gate
that led into the castle's walled garden, off beyond the
stables. After her initial surprise, the other girl let herself
be drawn along with good humor, thought she looked
faintly puzzled as Stevana swung back the barred iron
gate and glanced at her hopefully.

"It's—very nice," Jessamy said politely, though her expression was less than enthusiastic. Her voice was lower-
pitched than the younger girl's, with a faint accent Stevana did not recognize.

"I know it's still mostly dead, from the winter," Stevana
allowed, "but it *is* only just spring. Lots of the bulbs are
poking their heads out of the ground. *Maman* says that
it's warmer here at Coroth, because we live by the sea.

After Easter, there will be all kinds of flowers. Do you want to see the bulbs?"

"I guess."

Following where Stevana led, the newcomer let herself be guided deeper into the garden, where closer inspection did, indeed, reveal the wonder of spring's first tender shoots. In one shady corner, Jessamy crouched down to admire the beginning of a variegated carpet of crocuses.

"Look at all the colors!" Jessamy exclaimed. "I thought crocuses only came in purple."

"You don't have yellow ones where you come from?" Stevana asked. "Or white ones?"

Jessamy shook her dark curls, rising to run to another bed whose flora had caught her eye.

"And look—are those jonquils . . . or narcissi—or is it narcissuses?"

"I think it's either way," Stevana said good-naturedly as she bent to pull one of the tiny yellow flowers and sniff its powerful aroma. "This one's a jonquil. Here: smell it."

"Mmmm, I love those," Jessamy murmured, closing her eyes to inhale its perfume. "Just a few can fill a room with their smell. I like the way they look with purple-y flowers."

"Me, too," Stevana agreed. "Hyacinth is good. Or rose-mary. . . ."

It quickly became clear that the two girls had a love of gardening in common, and soon the pair of them were scurrying energetically along the garden's muddy paths, chattering and laughing as Stevana explained the layout and identified what beds would blossom into what. By the time they had worked their way to the farthest corner of the walled garden, hair now untidy and hems mud-bedraggled, she was ready to share one of her favorite treasures with her newfound friend.

"This is one of my special places," she said as they came before a barred iron gate set into a rocky facade.

As she shook out her skirts and slicked back errant wisps of fair hair from her face, trying to make herself more presentable, her companion tipped her head back to look for the source of water rippling merrily down the rock to one side of the entrance. The rocky outcropping jutted upward nearly to the height of the castle rampart beyond the garden wall, and was studded with silver-gray lichens and patches of velvety pale green moss along the joins.

"What is it?" Jessamy asked.

"The Grotto of the Hours."

"Why do they call it that?"

"I dunno. It's a grotto—and sometimes people spend hours here, I guess. I know I do." An unlit torch was thrust into an iron bracket to the right of the doorway, sheltered under a slight overhang, and Stevana stood on her tiptoes to reach up and take it down.

"My ancestor, the first Duke of Corwyn, built this," she went on, dusting dead leaves and cobwebs off the head of the torch. "No one's been in here all winter, so it'll be pretty dank and full of dead leaves, but it's still beautiful. And in the summer, it's a grand place to come and cool off—and to keep anyone from finding you to do lessons."

"I *like* to do lessons," Jessamy said somewhat huffily, though she started back slightly and cast a nervous glance behind them as the torch whooshed to light in the younger girl's hands. "Oh! You shouldn't do that where other people might see!"

"It's all right to do it here," Stevana replied, somewhat taken aback. "I wouldn't do it outside the castle," she added.

"It's still dangerous," Jessamy murmured, though she craned her neck to peer past Stevana as the younger girl pulled the gate open on squeaky hinges.

"Anyway, I like to do lessons, too," Stevana went on. "Just not *all* the time—and not on fine, balmy summer afternoons. Sometimes I just like to be by myself, where no one can find me. Come on."

So saying, she led the way inside, the torch preceding them into the damp, musty smell of mildew and stagnant

water. The ceiling was low and uneven, made to resemble
the natural cavern it pretended to be. The wall opposite
the entrance was pierced high by a small arched window
guarded by a metal grille—glaring enough against the
shadowed interior that Jessamy all but fell over the low
chair of carved black stone set in the center of the chamber.

"Careful—" Stevana started say, but too late, though
she kept her companion from actually falling down.
"That's where you sit to visit Duke Dominic. His tomb is
there under the window, against the wall. It's black, so
it's hard to see. He was the first Duke of Corwyn. My
grandfather is his direct descendant."

"I think I've heard of him," Jessamy said. "Wasn't he
some kind of royal?"

"I suppose he was," Stevana said, nodding. "But that
was a long time ago. He and his father came with Festil
the First in 822. His father was a Buyenne, a younger son
of the Duc du Joux—"

"A Buyenne?" Jessamy interrupted. "Then, we're cousins of some sort! My father doesn't use the name, but he's
also a Buyenne of Joux; *his* father is Duc Regnier. But—
how did your Buyenne ancestor get to be royal?"

"I think his mother was one of King Festil's cousins,
so he and his children became Buyenne-Furstán—and
everybody knows the Furstáns are royal."

"I've met some Furstáns," Jessamy said. "They're—"
She broke off to look over her shoulder, then back at
Stevana, obviously still nervous at speaking openly about
such things. "They're powerful Deryni. No wonder Papa
wanted to consult with your grandfather."

Stevana shrugged. "I guess. But the Furstán blood must
be pretty diluted by now. Still, I think the Corwyn men
have almost always married Deryni. I know that Dominic's son married a MacRorie—so I guess that makes him
related to Saint Camber." She paused a beat. "Would you
like to see a picture of him?"

"Who? Dominic's son?"

"No, Saint Camber."

She had already started to turn toward the left, lifting her torch toward the mosaics set into the plastered wall there, so she only heard Jessamy's gasp.

"You have a *picture* of *Saint Camber*?"

"Well, it's safe enough, in here," Stevana said, though she did not follow through with illuminating the wall by torchlight. "You're Deryni, or I wouldn't have mentioned it. Believe me, no one else comes in here except family— and you *are* a cousin. Do you want to see it or not?"

"Oh, I do!"

Without further ado, Stevana turned back toward the wall and again lifted her torch, this time moving farther into the room. Along the side walls, life-sized mosaic figures processed toward the looming hulk of Dominic's tomb. The torchlight glinted from the golden tesserae set amid the other tiles to highlight haloes and crowns and, on this side, the golden trumpet of Saint Gabriel, the archangel of the Annunciation. Paired with holy Gabriel was the Archangel Uriel, who sometimes served as the Angel of Death.

Beyond them, however, between Uriel and the representation of the Holy Trinity that adorned the east wall below the little window, above Dominic's tomb, a grayrobed figure knelt in adoration of that Blessed Trinity, but with one hand gesturing toward the tomb, as if in entreaty for its occupant. The face that peered from within the monkish cowl was turned to look directly at the beholder, the light eyes seeming to follow wherever the viewer went—eyes that caught and held and could almost plumb a person's soul, even if only made of fired tiles.

Beside her, Stevana sensed Jessamy sinking to her knees, face buried in her hands as her shoulders began to shake in silent weeping. Touched with compassion, Stevana knelt beside her and held her while she wept. After a few minutes, Jessamy raised her head, snuffling as she wiped her eyes on an edge of the fine linen petticoat under her velvet gown.

"That's what I've always thought he would look like," she said softly. "I didn't know that anyone in Gwynedd would dare to have a likeness of him."

Stevana shrugged. "Grandpapa says we aren't really in Gwynedd; we're in Corwyn. Besides, like I said, only family come in here—and even then, it's hard to see him unless you know where to look."

Snuffling again, Jessamy let Stevana help her get to her feet, again dabbing at her eyes as she slipped her arm through the younger girl's.

"I hate it when I cry in front of other people," she said, with a final snuffle. "Tante Ellen says I'll be a woman soon, and that sometimes I'll cry before my monthly courses." She swallowed with an audible gulp. "I hope that doesn't happen soon, because they—they'll marry me off at once."

"Well—but you'll be a woman then," Stevana said reasonably.

"No, you don't understand," Jessamy whispered. "It's because of what Papa did—and I don't even know what it was. But they're afraid of him. And they're afraid of what I might become. That's why they want me married quickly. My future husband is already chosen."

Stevana's eyes had gotten wide as the words tumbled from the older girl's lips.

"Who are *they*?" she breathed.

Jessamy shook her dark curls. "I'm not supposed to talk about it," she said. She sounded so forlorn that Stevana hugged her again and changed the subject as they turned to leave the Grotto of the Hours, for the hints she had gleaned from her own kin also suggested something so terrible as to be beyond discussion.

THAT NIGHT, THOUGH Stevana knew of no particular feast day that should have occasioned celebration, her grandfather hosted more formal dining in the great hall. Lewys ap Norfal had not traveled with a large retinue, but nonetheless the hall seemed markedly more crowded than it had the night before. The servants had set up a second trencher table at right angles to the usual one, arranged like the stem of a T, so that Stiofan presided from his usual place at the top, with Lewys at his right hand and Stevana's mother on Lewys's right. The venerable Master Norfal, Lewys's teacher, was at Stiofan's left hand—nearly a hundred years old, Stevana had heard—accompanied by Taillifer Earl of Lendour. Michon de Courcy and Sief MacAthan sat directly opposite, where the stem of the T began. Even to Stevana's unsophisticated eye, the arrangement had every appearance of trying to ensure that Lewys ap Norfal was well surrounded by very competent Deryni.

Jessamy apparently noticed this too, seated with Stevana a few places down from the Countess Grania, for she went very quiet as she surveyed the other guests at table.

"What's wrong?" Stevana whispered when dining had begun and musicians were playing from the gallery at the end of the hall.

Jessamy looked at her sharply, then back toward the diners seated near Stevana's grandfather.

"They're all here," she murmured, averting her eyes to her trencher. "Even my future husband."

Stevana's mind whirled, but she managed not to react, and to keep her voice a whisper. "Which one is he?" she breathed. "And *they*—you mean the *they* who are afraid of you and your father?"

Jessamy closed her eyes briefly, then picked up her goblet and drank, keeping it close to her mouth as she glanced sidelong at Stevana.

"Please don't react, whatever you do," she pleaded. "Yes, it's the same *they*—some of them, at any rate. And I'm to marry Sir Sief MacAthan. He's sitting there, across from your grandfather."

Stevana made herself pick up a joint of chicken and bite some off, holding it in her two hands as she chewed and finally allowed herself to glance casually at Sief.

He was older than she had thought when she first saw
him with Cousin Michon earlier that day. Probably close
to thirty. There was gray in the stubby red tail of hair now
queued at the nape of his neck, and there was gray speck-
led in his neatly trimmed beard and mustache. But his
dark eyes were bright and looked kind. His hands, as he
gesticulated in conversation, were small and graceful. His
attire was simple but of good quality.

"Why do you think he's here?" Stevana whispered, before taking another bite of chicken.

Jessamy shook her head. "Same as the rest. They're
worried about what my father will do. He's come here to
work, you know. That's why they've all come."

Further discussion was curtailed by the arrival of the
next course.

LATER THAT NIGHT, as Stevana settled into bed
with Jessamy beside her, she was still trying to figure out
what was going on. As soon as the nurse had blown out
the last candle and withdrawn, she turned toward her bedmate.

"You said they'd all come to work," she whispered as
she kindled faint handfire between them, just above their
heads. "Do you think they're working tonight?"

Jessamy's dark-haired head turned on the pillow to regard her.

"No. It will be tomorrow night."

"How do you know?"

"Because they ate. When you work high magic, you're
not supposed to eat beforehand. You're supposed to fast."

"But you think they *are* going to do something."

Jessamy slowly nodded. "That's why we came. Papa
trusts your grandfather. He said that Duke Stiofan would
monitor for him."

"Monitor for *what*?" Stevana whispered.

Again Jessamy shook her head. "I don't know. I just know that it's dangerous."

"Then, why is he going to do it?"

"Because that's the only way to learn," came Jessamy's reply. "But he'll be careful. He promised me." .

That answer caused Stevana to fall silent, for it confirmed the danger in whatever Lewys had done a few years before—and apparently intended to do again. But she could think of nothing to say that would not also give her new friend even more reason to be anxious. So instead, she merely let herself snuggle a little closer for warmth and drift into sleep. She did not dream, but she sensed that Jessamy did. The older girl tossed and turned all the night long, waking her bedmate several times. But when daylight finally came, she claimed to remember nothing of what had disturbed her sleep—and Stevana's.

HER MOTHER SENT them on a ride-out the next morning, with Stevana's nurse and the constable and several of the castle's squires for escort and company. They had a splendid outing—the squires were hardly older than their charges, and gently teased and flirted with them—but it seemed likely to both girls that the excursion was a ruse to get them out of the castle for most of the day.

That evening, their surmise of the night before seemed to be confirmed, for instead of supping in the great hall, they were sent to Stevana's chamber, where a table had been laid for them.

"His Grace feared he might be taking a chill, so he's asked Lord Hamilton to preside at table tonight," Stevana's nurse told them as she poured ale for both girls and then helped them spread big napkins over their skirts. "And your lady mother knew you'd both be tired after riding all day. I know *I* am. I'll come to clear up after you've eaten. Now let us give thanks for this food."

The woman left them after hearing them say grace.

When the door had closed behind her, Stevana glanced at her companion.

"D'you think the real reason we're having supper here is because the adults are fasting?" she murmured as she tore off a chunk of bread.

Jessamy had been about to sip at her cup of ale, but abruptly froze with the rim of the cup just at her lips, her eyes going slightly unfocused.

"What is it?" Stevana whispered, suddenly a little afraid.

The older girl blinked, then carefully set the untasted cup back on the table.

"Don't drink the ale," she whispered, glancing at the door before slowly passing her hand over several other items on the table. "No, it's only the ale. But they counted on the fact that we'd be hungry and thirsty after riding all day—especially thirsty."

"Well, I *am*," Stevana began.

"So am I," Jessamy replied. "But if we drink, we'll fall asleep in minutes and sleep until morning."

Stevana's eyes widened.

"There's something in the ale?"

Jessamy nodded gravely. "They don't want us awake for whatever they're going to do."

Chills running up her spine, Stevana carefully set her chunk of bread back on her trencher, no longer hungry or thirsty.

"You're serious, aren't you."

"Never more so."

Dry-mouthed, Stevana wadded at the napkin spread across her skirts, unconsciously wiping her hands on it. Jessamy had her head bowed over tightly clasped hands, though Stevana didn't think she was praying.

"Do you want to try to find out what they're doing?" she asked very softly.

Jessamy's head lifted in question.

"How?" she breathed.

Surreptitiously Stevana looked at the door. If they were

drinking the ale as expected, her mother or the nurse would come in soon to check on them, and would expect them to be asleep.

"Can you put yourself to sleep for a set amount of time?" she whispered, adding as the other nodded, "I mean, really deep asleep."

Cautiously, Jessamy nodded again.

"Go listen at the door," Stevana whispered, taking up the two cups of ale and getting to her feet. As Jessamy complied, watching her curiously, Stevana padded quickly to the garderobe set into the wall near the window and dumped most of the contents of both cups down the privy hole. As she brought the cups back and sat down again, she jutted her chin for the older girl to rejoin her.

"Now, you've got to properly put yourself to sleep for—let's say, two hours. They probably won't start until they think the rest of the castle is asleep. Can you do that? If we're not really asleep, they'll know."

Wide-eyed, Jessamy nodded wordless agreement and took her place across from Stevana, who sloshed a little ale on the table, then set the cup down in the spill and stretched one arm along the edge of the table, lowering her head to rest against her forearm. With her other hand she picked up the chunk of bread from her trencher and let that hand fall heavily to her side, fingers opening to drop the bread. As Jessamy did something similar, Stevana drew a deep breath and let it out, silently mouthing the syllables of a sleep spell. She slipped into oblivion before she could finish it.

SHE WOKE SOMETIME later in her bed. Someone had removed her riding clothes and dressed her in her nightgown, and even brushed and braided her blond hair—probably the nurse, but it could have been her mother. Curled beside her, still asleep, Jessamy had been similarly dealt with. Judging by the small night sounds of the castle sleeping, and the moonlight streaming through the win-

dow, it must be nearing midnight. From far away, Stevana
dimly heard an officer of the watch cry the hour, but she
could not quite make out what hour it was.

Resolute, she slipped out of bed and padded to the window that overlooked the castle yard, craning to gaze toward the tower where her grandfather always retired to
carry out his magical workings. The moonlight was glaring against the tower's pale stone, but she could just make
out the glow of candlelight behind the narrow, green-
glassed window slits along the top floor.

"Is that where they work?" Jessamy whispered close
beside her.

Stevana had sensed her approaching, and only nodded.

"Is there any way we can get up there?"

"If we're careful, I think we can cross the yard without
being seen," Stevana replied, keeping her voice to a whisper. "But from there, it's a single turnpike stair going
up—though there are three or four landings on the way,
if we have to hide. I've heard that there are secret pas-
sages within the walls, but that may be just servants' gossip."

"A pity we don't know for sure," Jessamy murmured.
"But we'll make do with the landings, since we must."

A QUARTER HOUR later, with cloaks wrapped
around their nightdresses and soft slippers on their feet,
the two girls were huddling on the ground floor of the
green tower, poised at the foot of the spiral stair. Now
that they were nearing their goal, they spoke only by gestures and mind to mind. Neither was very accomplished
in this latter skill, for the maturation of the powers peculiar to their race tended toward physical manipulations
before the development of more cerebral abilities. But the
physical contact of their joined hands eased the effort of
communicating mind-to-mind—necessary, lest their whis-
pers be detected, if not by those working within the

tower's topmost chamber, then by some warder set to guard the outer door.

They made their stealthy way up the spiral stair, pausing at each landing to listen with minds as well as ears, hearts pounding so that they were sure the sound must be reverberating on the level above. They had more floors to go—Stevana had lost count of exactly how many—when Jessamy suddenly doubled over with a gasp, cradling her head in her hands and crumpling to her knees. At the same time, a flash that was more felt than seen seemed to light up the stairwell, and a high-pitched, keening sound briefly pierced the silence.

Then from somewhere higher up the stairwell, perhaps the very topmost floor, came the hollow bang of a door crashing back on its hinges, accompanied by muffled exclamations and the sound of coughing.

Stevana kept her head down, pulling Jessamy back into the shadows of the nearest landing, clamping a hand over the older girl's mouth to stifle her whimper as footsteps and voices came nearer.

Not a sound! she sent. *They're coming this way.*

At the same time, she was feeling for the door to the room that opened off this landing—fortunately, unoccupied. Half sick with fear, she drew Jessamy in after her and all but closed the door, crouching then to peer through the keyhole as she began to make out words.

"But what could have happened?" she heard a male voice say. "Where did he go? It wasn't supposed to happen like that!"

"We did everything that could be done," her grandfather said. "I have no answers for you."

"The Council will have to be told," a third voice said. She thought it was her cousin Michon.

"Is that really necessary?" *That* was her mother's voice.

"You know it is," yet another male voice said. "If we could be sure he was simply dead, it might be different—but even then, they'd need to be told."

"I really thought he might succeed," her grandfather said as footsteps trooped past the doorway.

There seemed to be more footsteps than could be attributed to the voices Stevana had heard, and they kept passing up and down the stair outside the door for most of an hour. It soon became clear that something had gone disastrously wrong, but the fate of Jessamy's father remained unclear. From what Stevana could gather, it seemed that Lewys ap Norfal had simply disappeared. Whether or not he still lived, no one seemed to have any idea. Behind Stevana, Jessamy herself sat on the floor in a corner of the darkened room with head ducked and arms clasped around her knees, rocking back and forth, silently weeping and whimpering. Once the footsteps finally seemed to have died away for good, Stevana summoned handfire and went back to her friend, who now was merely resting her head on her knees, all her tears spent.

"Are you all right?" she whispered, crouching to lay an arm around the older girl's shoulders.

Jessamy snuffled and lifted her head, face haggard in the greenish yellow light of the handfire.

"He's dead, isn't he?" she whispered, in a voice devoid of emotion.

"We don't know that," Stevana replied. "*They* don't know that."

Jessamy snuffled again and dried her eyes with an edge of her nightgown, but said nothing.

"Do *you* think he's dead?" Stevana said, after a beat.

"If he doesn't come back, it hardly matters," Jessamy said bleakly. "Either way, I'll become Sief MacAthan's ward until I'm of an age to marry—and then, his wife."

"Is that so bad?" Stevana asked. "He looks kind. And he's handsome enough."

Jessamy shrugged. "He answers to other, more powerful Deryni. I don't know who," she added sharply, when Stevana opened her mouth as if to speak. "They're horrified by what my father could do—and wanted to do. Now that he's done . . . whatever he's done . . . they'll be afraid I might try to do the same thing. So they have to marry me to someone who's safe, who can prevent that. God, I feel sick!"

Her expression was so bleak, her tone so forlorn, that Stevana could only hold her closer for a long moment, helpless to offer any better comfort to her friend. When they eventually drew apart, Stevana took the other girl's hands and started helping her to her feet.

"We'd better get back to my room," she said quietly. "They may have missed us already, as it is. In any case, they're going to come eventually to tell us what's happened—or as much as they know, at any rate."

"I can't imagine what went wrong," Jessamy whispered, automatically dusting at the back of her cloak as she straightened. Her hand came away sticky and wet—and red, in the light of Stevana's handfire, as she thrust it into the faintly greenish glow.

A stifled, inarticulate little whimper escaped her lips as she and Stevana both whirled to look where she had been sitting. There was no mistaking the smear of bright blood on the bare wood.

"Oh, no!" Jessamy whispered, her face draining of color. "Not yet. Not *now*. . . ."

Stevana knew what the blood meant—and what it meant to Jessamy.

"We'd better get you back to my room," she whispered sensibly, taking Jessamy's arm.

"But we'll never be able to hide it," the stricken girl replied. "Sief is *here*, and my father is *gone*. They'll have me married before—dear God, what's to become of me? What am I going to *do* . . . ?"

Her lament trailed off into a low wail, muffled against Stevana's shoulder, and indeed, Stevana had no better idea what they were going to do. In the end, she waited until Jessamy's sobbing had subsided to hiccups and sniffles, then led her back down the stairs. By dint of sheer luck, they managed to make it back across the castle yard and back up the stairs without mishap, and even back to Stevana's room.

But Stevana's mother was waiting for them there, gazing out the window. They did not see her as they first entered, quietly closing the door behind them, but they froze at the rustling sound of her skirts as she came out of the window embrasure.

"I watched you cross the yard," she said quietly, looking very sad. "I thought you might have tried to come."

The two girls exchanged guilty glances and huddled closer together, eyes wide and frightened.

"Dear child, I'm not going to scold you—either of you," Grania de Corwyn said, opening her arms to them. "It—didn't go the way anyone planned. I am *so* sorry."

Her words loosed a floodgate of new tears from both of them this time. Weeping, they flew to her arms and sobbed. Grania merely held them, enfolding them in the motherly embrace of arms and mind and making comforting shushing noises until the sobs finally ceased.

"I see what has happened," she said softly as Jessamy shifted slightly in the circle of her arm. "It means that you are a woman now."

Jessamy sniffled and lifted her head, but would not meet Grania's eyes.

"It means that I shall be married, and *soon*. I don't *want* to be married yet."

"I know, my dear," Grania replied. "But Sief is a good man. I think he will be a gentle husband."

"They're afraid of me," Jessamy sniffled. "Because of my father."

"Yes, they are. But your lot could be far worse."

"Could it?" the girl murmured dully.

"Come, child. Let's get you cleaned up," Grania said. "Now that it's begun, there's no way it could be long hidden. Let us make the best we can of a very sad circumstance. I am so very sorry about your father."

That very afternoon, in the chapel at Castle Coroth, Stevana watched with her mother in numb disbelief as her grandfather set Jessamy's hand in that of Sir Sief MacAthan. Old Father Wenceslaus led the couple in the vows that made them husband and wife, though Sief had promised earlier that the marriage would not be consummated until the following year, when Jessamy reached the age of twelve, and had added that amendment to the marriage contract. He had also promised that tutors would be found to teach her proper control and discretion in the use of her formidable potential. He did seem kind enough.

Watching Father Wenceslaus lay the end of his stole over the couple's joined hands, symbolizing the vows that now bound them, Stevana de Corwyn, Heiress of Corwyn, bit at her lips and wondered what her own fate must be. She had always accepted that her marriage would be arranged, both to political advantage and to further her potential as a Deryni, but she did not know whether she dared to hope that she might also come to love the man she one day married. Certainly, her mother and her grandfather would do their best to choose her a husband who at least would be kind to her; but things could change, as had been amply proved when Lewys ap Norfal disappeared to wherever he had gone.

As for Jessamy, the sad image of that white-faced child-bride fulfilling her duty as the daughter of a noble house would stay with Stevana de Corwyn until the day she died.

❀

THE CAMBER EMBROIDERY
1982

Our last piece is a second offering by Laura Jefferson wearing her archaeologist hat. It was so delightful that I had to share it. The article is based on an actual piece of embroidery that Laura stitched for me, exactly as described in proper archaeological terminology, which occupies an honored spot in my office—above a Gothic reliquary cabinet, as it happens, now converted to a display case for some of my angel collection. The Camber tapestry is one of a number of delightful and generous bits and pieces that my readers have bestowed on me over the years. The article that follows, along with a sketch of the tapestry also done by the author, is a wonderful example of how the Deryni universe impinges on the real lives of many readers—and vice versa!

THE CAMBER EMBROIDERY

Report of the Royal Gwynedd Archaeological Society

❊

Laura Jefferson

(This report is being published in advance of the full excavation report on Dun Cymbr, in the Rheljan highlands. The site of this Camberian oratory, one of the least disturbed known to us, is in the process of consolidation by the Ministry of Works. The excavator, Rhiannon Evans, assures us that she has begun to write up her discoveries at Dun Cymbr, and that she hopes to be able to devote more time to it after the conclusion of her rescue dig at Nyford.)

ALTHOUGH WE HAVE a few examples of older, Festillic needlework, the so-called "Camber embroidery" is unique in the entire pre-Persecution textile corpus. We can tell from internal evidence that the work was not begun before 906; and from coins and certain pottery fragments in the destruction layer of the oratory, we can state with certainty that it was completed before 921. The style of the illustration is identical to that of certain manuscript illuminations of roughly the same period; thus its value extends beyond the realm of merely textile arts. More important, perhaps, is the hanging's comments on political alignment of the Servants of St. Camber toward the Haldane monarchy.

The embroidery as we now have it is a fragment, some 62 cm by 33 cm (approximately 25 × 3"). It must have been part of a much longer piece; the scene depicted comes well into the middle of the story. The survival of this fragment is due to its proximity to a hoard of silver altar plate, found buried to one side of the cemetery and well below the general rubble layer ending the site's use. It is possible that rumors of the suppression of the order reached the community in time for them to conceal some of their treasures; but it is equally likely that one of the plunderers hid an extra share of loot from his fellows. In either case, the hoard was never reclaimed. Both ends of the embroidery rotted; despite painstaking excavation, only the inmost layer remains, because of its association with and contamination by the silver.

The background of the hanging is an evenly woven linen of fine quality; the actual embroidery, of one-, two-, and three-strand wool, was originally of eight colors. There were two dark blues, now aged to a very similar shade, a blue-green, a sage green, a forest green, and red, brown, and golden yellow. The stitches are very simple: outline stitch, backstitch, and laid work. Neither the workmanship nor the design is as sophisticated as we might expect. It seems likely that the design was derived from a cartoon made by an illuminator. It is, very likely, a votive gift. In their short life, the Servants of St. Camber were well able to afford the best, so it is not unreasonable to posit a noblewoman, perhaps tutored or chaplained by one of the monks and enthusiastic about their saintly founder, working her daily stint on something more inspiring than yet another set of table or bed linens for her hope chest.

The panel is divided into three areas: two narrow (5.5

cm) borders defining and commenting on the main body
of the work. Though dubbed the "Camber" embroidery,
the fragment's subject has more to do with Cinhil. Were
its provenance otherwise, we might very well conjecture
that it is a piece of Haldane propaganda. From the left,
the main area shows an architecturally detailed view of
Cinhil's abbey, carefully if uninhibitedly labeled St. Foillan's. The artist's perspective was not up to portraying the
steps in an entirely convincing manner, but the foundation
planting at the east end of the monastery adds a friendly
contemporary note.

The building is separated from the next scene by a
stylized tree. It grows from the hill on which stand an
obviously pleased and friendly Cinhil and Camber. They,
too, are labeled, both in letters and by their very different
attire. Cinhil is tonsured; he wears the habit of his order,
strikingly similar to that of the later Continental Cister-
cians whom the Verbi Deists so much resembled (cf.
Citeau, Cluny, and Gwynedd: *St. Stephen Harding and
the Vision of Reform,* by D. Knowles, London, 1952).
Camber is richly dressed in doublet, cloak, and hose.

As any student of the period has surely realized, the
designer of the embroidery has drawn not from the more
historical and complete Michaeline version of Camber's
hagiography, but the more popular and devotional *Acta
Sancti Camber.* This was an anonymous work appearing
almost immediately after the Battle of Iomaire. It was simpler and more telescoped than the Michaeline account,
and the subtle and unstated bias of the Servants against
the Michaelines (probably due in part to Joram Mac-
Rorie's continued resistance to his father's canonization)
provides an additional reason to adopt that text of the
legend. The *Acta,* more complimentary to the Crown, rep-
resents Cinhil as eager to leave his cloister for the sake
of Gwynedd. Camber is informed of the true King's
whereabouts by an angel, and goes at once by magic to
find Cinhil, who is praying alone in the abbey gardens.

Portents of divine favor remove the stigma of Cinhil's dispensed vows, and we are shown this clearly by the Hand of Blessing within the frame over the King's head. The labels read (I am much indebted to Michael Aquaviva for help here): AND URGED [him] To TAKE THE THRONE (ET HORTATU [R] UT [NUM] CAPIA [T].

The margins contribute to the legitimacy of Cinhil's kingship. Along the lower one, we find an apparently irrelevant dragon; a shepherd tending his flock (an obvious regnal allusion); and the Red Lion of Gwynedd menacing a fawning jackal. Behind the first, another, female, jackal sits looking upward, as if baying the moon. It is difficult to see these two dangerous and ignoble beasts as anything other than Imre and Ariella. Along the upper margin, two peacocks salute the cross and dome of St. Foillan's. They are symbols of immortality, but royal birds as well. Next, a phoenix rises from its nest of flames and ashes as the Haldanes did from the massacre. Over Cinhil's head, a figure in Biblical attire pours oil from his horn over the head of the young man kneeling in front of him. This is almost certainly David's anointing by the prophet Samuel: another case of Heavenly election of one man to take over the kingship from one unworthy of it. It raises a curiously twisted parallel: Samuel, the man of God, calling a secular man to power, while Camber the layman sought out a cleric.

Thus far, the marginal comments have seemed purely royalist; once again, we recognize the folly of the bigoted human nobles in their eradication of staunch allies of the throne. But this hanging belonged to a Camberian foundation; it behooves us to look closer before we announce a single-minded royal bias. The last, mutilated frame along the top shows us two angels. The first is carrying a crown. We are tempted to dismiss it as a reference to Camber's vision. But the second holds a stylized palm frond.

The art historian is forced to pause: the crown is not just a symbol of mundane power, but also of martyrdom, like the palm. The angel is over Camber's head, not Cinhil's. Its halo is larger than that of the angel following, and has four vanes; the angel's wing has seven carefully delineated pinions, and its gown is green. Is it possible that this is one of the Angels of the Four Quarters, one of the Seven who stand before God's throne, whose heraldic color is green? Surely this is Uriel himself, foreshadowing the death Camber would die for his King. Camber stands slightly higher on the hill than his Prince; and as we look again, one last detail becomes apparent. The hand and arm reaching down from the cloud in blessing wear the same green doublet, with yellow cuff, as Camber himself. Although the artist supports the Haldane monarchy, we feel instinctively that Camber and his true Lord wear the same livery. Perhaps the phoenix, after all, refers to another revenant than the Haldanes.

The Camber Embroidery

AUTHOR BIOGRAPHIES

�֎

LAURA E. JEFFERSON was born in Chicago in 1956. Since then she has moved to Boston, acquired a B.A. in Classics (Brandeis, 1977), and after some years of consideration, an M.Div. (Weston Jesuit School of Theology, 1997). In between degrees she worked, mostly outside, for the Canterbury (England) Archaeological Trust, where she met and traveled with a pen pal who was researching *Lammas Night.* Laura used to be married, has two actually wonderful children, and includes fandom, Wiccans, SCA-dians, Jesuits, New Hampshire archaeologists, and the Order of St. Michael among the influences that have kept her sane. Whether they would say the same of her is dubious.

DANIEL KOHANSKI was working in New York City as a computer programmer when he and Jay Barry Azneer wrote "Arilan, the Talmud Student." He still does programming for a living, but now lives in San Francisco with Jean, his life partner, and their cats, Archie, Tristan, and Cyrano. He has published one nonfiction book, *Moths*

in the Machine: The Power and Perils of Programming,
and is working on another one, *The Tree of Knowledge
and the Information Age,* as well as a fantasy novel, *Old
Dreams Bought and Sold.*

JAY BARRY AZNEER was born in Philadelphia in 1946.
In 1976 he moved to New York to begin his medical
practice as well as to complete his vocal studies, which
he had begun during his internship. [Jay is a *helden-
tenor*—which, for the operatically uninitiated, means that
he has a robust tenor voice particularly well suited for
singing the heroic roles associated with Wagnerian
opera—and he's good!] After twenty-five years of study
and over twenty years of performing in smaller opera
companies, he says he is finally content to practice med-
icine.

Jay lives in Kew Gardens, New York, with his life partner of eighteen years and a maroon-bellied conure named
Poopers. Besides this short story, he and Dan have also
collaborated on a translation of the Friday Evening Liturgy, which is currently used in a number of synagogues
throughout the United States.

SHARON HENDERSON is an Independent Catholic priest
and technogeek currently residing in Fairfax, Virginia.
Born several miles north of Boston, Massachusetts, she
had the original Kelson series dropped into her lap by a
friend she still thanks profusely—even though the books
were literally life-changing for her. Sharon met Katherine
because of this very story, "Deo Volente." Like many others, she says her spiritual life has been opened to wider
and more wondrous pathways by interaction with this
walking blond catalyst. (Katherine cheerfully bullied her
into returning to school and completing her B.A. in history [with honors!], which she received from George Ma-
son University in 1992.) All this while, she has been
married to James (since 1978) and mothering son Brian
(since 1982).

When not wandering over the playing fields of Gwynedd, Sharon leads a small, peripatetic congregation of Celtic Catholics in the Northern Virginia area, and functions as verger for the ecumenical Order of St. Michael. She is owned currently by five cats, and has a horse named Jasper. Sharon enjoys embroidery, theological and liturgical debate, writing, and spending far too much time online. She knows far too much about WWI aviation, Germany, Medieval and Renaissance history, and is painfully fond of writing about herself in the third person.

MELISSA HOULE, an avid cat person and artist, earned a B.A. in general music from Linfield College in 1986, and went on to obtain a library technical assistant's certification. For the past decade she has worked for the Santa Clara County Library, currently in the Cupertino Branch. She is a member of a writers' group that meets twice a month and is one of the three sterling individuals who run the www.deryni.com website. When not at work or online, or writing or painting for the website, she also enjoys cooking, baking, and needlepoint (although the needlepoint doesn't get a lot of attention these days), and she listens to classical music on the radio or on CDs throughout the day.

When ANN W. JONES wrote "The Fortune Teller," she was working at the University of Liverpool, running the Admissions Office in the Department of Education, and living with her parents and her twenty-year-old son, a student at the University of Sheffield. She spent most weekends and holidays traveling around the United Kingdom and visiting castles, abbeys, churches, and stately homes, indulging her interest in church architecture and monuments, particularly from the Saxon and Norman periods. She also took classes in local history and traveled extensively.

Now officially retired, she has crossed the River Mersey to live on the Wirral Peninsula with her collection of seventy-two teddy bears, some from foreign parts. Son Simon, himself now a published author, is married and has presented Ann with two granddaughters: Morgan, who is five, and Rhianna, who is two. She has had to curtail her travels, because of rheumatoid arthritis, but still enjoys antique fairs and craft fairs and visiting friends in Wales. At present, she is editing the first novel of a science fiction trilogy she has written; the subsequent two books are already in draft form.

LOHR MILLER writes of himself: "I wrote 'Lover to Shadows' long ago, when I was at Yale. Christian-Richard is, of course, very like me at that age—and he's still like me, I expect. Since then, I wrote another Deryni story, 'Season of the Sword,' which was also published in *Deryni Archives.*

"I finished Yale, did a Ph.D. (history) at Louisianna State University, and I've taught at several southern universities. I've lived in Vienna and Budapest and Venice; I've taught military history for the U.S. Army both here and in the Balkans. I even taught—oh yes!—international relations and human rights to the Turkish security police. At the moment, I'm completing a law degree (LSU teaches in the civil law tradition) and hope to get back to Europe. I haven't married as of 2001, but then it *is* hard to find a girl like Charissa de Tolan."

LESLIE WILLIAMS wrote "A Matter of Pride" while working on her art teaching degree at Baylor. Up until then she had regarded herself as one of the better artists in her high school, but found that at Baylor's college of art, everyone was at least as gifted as she, most better, and to succeed in her studies required that she accept feedback and critique from her peers. Her ego took some deserved blows in the process, and the idea of art and pride presented itself.

Currently the librarian of a small high school, Leslie is called upon by her students to fill many different roles—

that of researcher, writer, editor, artist, costumer, special effects artist, reviewer, and music editor—as any educator can testify. Her chief satisfaction has been to be there when a gifted student comes to her for help.

[I might add that it was another librarian, Melissa, who helped track Leslie down when this anthology was being assembled. Never underestimate the power of a librarian! If it weren't for such dedicated individuals, none of us would probably be where we are today!]